Sweethearts of Ilford Lane

Farzana Hakim

New Generation Publishing

This book has been produced with assistance from
The London Borough of Barking and Dagenham Library Service
Pen to Print Creative Writing Project 2017/8
with funding from
The Arts Council, England Grants for the Arts.

Supported using public funding by
**ARTS COUNCIL
ENGLAND**

LOTTERY FUNDED

London Borough of
Barking & Dagenham

lbbd.gov.uk

To my sweethearts Iqbal,
Najam, Sameer and Saniya
Ammi and Daddy
Love you all
Always
X

Chapter One

'Ten, nine, eight,' cheered the crowd, eager for the remaining seconds to move on as they danced and laughed the way into the New Year.

I observed with a cup of frothy chocolate and my feet clad cosily in fluffy socks. The BBC guy on the telly screamed, 'Three, two, one,' and the flat screen became a canvas of colourful glitter and noise.

'Happy New Year…'

Switching the television off, I tuned the sounds of celebration out. It was best I got some sleep.

Unfortunately once settled in my queen sized bed, sleep had plans to stay away. And I was fully aware of the reason why. The little organ, the one which pumped blood and promised my body the kick to function was playing up.

It often did, on this particular night.

And despite having studied it with an obsession, no science book, journal or Professor could explain this malfunctioning. I mean eight years and it still did it. It still made me queasy and needy for a certain somebody.

Why?

This night, this day, the first of January, it didn't mean anything. Okay I had signed the thing binding myself to him but it didn't mean I actually was his and it no way justified my heart's silly actions over him.

Throwing the duvet on the carpeted floor I sat up on my bed, rattled.

For a few minutes I busied myself by combing my fingers through my dark hair. It had reached beyond my waistline and sometimes, only sometimes, did I risk braiding it.

'Ding Dong. Ding Dong…'

Now why was this happening? Why was I knotting my hair and imagining myself an eleven year old geeky girl in class and him pulling it and troubling me? Why did my heart do this to me every time? Why these constant reminders? Why these feelings he was near?

Why was he tormenting me despite the fact I hadn't seen him in years?

Apart from the annual greeting card, I knew nothing of him anymore. And I was sure the one due to arrive on the coming morning would express the same message the rest had.

'My dear Samina,
Forgive me. Please come back.
Love H.'

Leaving my braid sitting over my shoulder, I opened the box which I kept hidden under my bed. In it I kept the said cards. They were simple but elegant enough with images of pastel coloured roses. Behind the fold of each one his writing hadn't changed much, still scruffy and a little too slanted to the right. Exactly how it had been when I'd first seen him write.

However it wasn't his writing but the blank bits between his words which disturbed me. Because they reminded me of how much I had missed of him.

In this time I had done all the things I'd set out to do. I completed my Medical degree and juggled my way through the vigorous years of training. Successfully I had obtained the right to use Dr in front of my name.

Currently I was in the second year of further training to obtain my General Practitioner's licence. After all it was what I'd always wanted. My own surgery, like Doctor Patel's back home.

Home?

There went my heart again. Why wouldn't it accept this place, this city, Oxford, as home?

Knowing I shouldn't have dwelled on things for too long like this, I hastily put the cards into the box and pushed them back under my bed.

Fireworks. They were still crackling outside. Another year I thought as I pulled up my duvet, feeling a chill hitting me. I shivered knowing full well this year was different from the others. This year I was returning.

Returning to Ilford Lane.

*****

'Just open your eyes and look at the scenery.'

'Get off,' I whined moving his hands away.

'Tower of London,' said Sebastian as he pointed out of the window of his moving car.

I rolled my eyes and sunk back into the seat. Seb would be excited. Anything excited him. He was like a little child in a grown up's body. My best friend he was. Both of us had been paired on our first assignment at University and believe me we'd been super-glued together since.

He was coming as well. We were required to work at a busy London hospital as part of our GP training. It was essential in order to secure a banded rate of pay. Seb had spent three rounds in Greater London already, adding Great Ormond Street, Guys and Royal London hospitals to his impressive CV. Whereas I had my reasons for not wanting anything to do with this city. But now it had become unavoidable. I had less than two years of training remaining and I needed to experience the hustle and bustle of the Capital's emergency wards. It was for my career.

Trust my luck though, out of all the hospitals I'd applied to my last choice was the one accepted. King George's Hospital. The same hospital where I was born.

'For someone coming back here after eight years, you don't look half as excited,' said Seb with a mouth full of crisps.

'What's there to be excited about? It's freezing. The roads are covered in ice. And the traffic is mad,' I said gazing outside.

The car slowly rolled into Aldgate. Home wasn't far.

Seb had managed to find us two self-contained flats within one huge house on Goodmayes Lane. Although this was good as we'd be saving money on rent by sharing and on occasion travelling to work together, I wasn't too sure. Because after Seb had gone and paid the deposits, I'd realised these flats were only a five minute drive from Ilford Lane. And Ilford Lane was the last place I wanted to be anywhere near.

'You are such a boring woman sometimes,' said Seb throwing a bag of crisps at me. 'Tomorrow is the last day of our holidays before we get bombarded with all our hospital stuff, so my treat okay, we're going out. I'll show you how to enjoy this place.'

'Whatever you say,' I said as I bit into a chilli tortilla. And the rest of the journey, on my part at least was spent in complete silence.

I couldn't help but stare out of the window at the wet and grey roads as he took me closer to my childhood, and everything I was and knew.

Chapter Two

The flats were nice. Typically I got the one with the larger kitchen and Seb took the one below it. Knowing he was close was good. Truth be told, I'd been on edge since arriving the previous day. I hadn't liked the way the neighbours had gawped as we unloaded the car. The woman, the Indian looking one, she didn't think it was necessary to even smile back. Was it because Seb was White? Were we being judged?

There was also the other neighbour, the one on our left side. An elderly White male. The way he snorted as I threw a bag at Seb didn't fare well in my mind either. What was his problem? Was a hunk like my Seb not allowed to have a laugh with a 'Paki,' like me? However even though we both heard him using the word 'Paki' loud and clear, in respect of the man's age, I'd pleaded with Seb to simply ignore it.

Wow we were back in East London.

Oh I know I shouldn't have been totally cynical. But my past experiences here made me feel this way. Maybe I was ratty and escalating my negativity because the craving in my heart to see a certain someone, was the actual problem.

I could sense him everywhere. I swear I could.

Seb knew how to cheer me up though. He took me to Oxford Street for the treat he'd promised. And without complaint he waited patiently whilst I shopped in the millions of stores there. He even carried my bags. We walked on to admire the Christmas lights which were still up, and giggled like idiots whilst taking heaps of goofy photos on our phones. We ate ice cream on a cone and laughed at each other's expressions when having a brain freeze.

The best part of the trip was when he pulled out two tickets to the evening show of 'The Lion King,' something I'd been dying to experience since I was little. And if that wasn't enough, later on we went to a great Turkish restaurant he knew, and ordered heaps of food.

It was the best time I'd had in a long time.

On the way back home though, we were on the tube discussing a recent case one of our colleagues was involved in, whereby a patient with Downs Syndrome was violated and as a result had fallen pregnant, when a group of Asian youngsters got on at Whitechapel station. They must have been around sixteen to nineteen years of age, and I stopped talking when overhearing what they were saying about me in a language I understood too well.

'Damn how our girls are being brainwashed by the White guys these days...'

I stared at him flabbergasted.

'I wouldn't mind a piece of her either.'

And another one of them said, 'Nah she's disgusting. Not decent to be going about with a White guy like that in the open.'

'What is it Hun?' said Seb poking me with his phone. Curling my fists I tried hard to ignore the judgements these youngsters were making about me. How about I told them this White guy was the only person who had helped me pick up the pieces, when a guy much like themselves had destroyed me.

What difference did race make anyway? Working as a doctor had opened my eyes to how diverse a place England was. And if Seb and I had no prejudice about each other's backgrounds or skin colour, what was anybody else's problem?

'Samina you okay?'

Seb saying my name caused a few gasps.

'She's Muslim,' one said and I couldn't sit down and take it any longer. I got up and pointed a finger at the one who'd spoken.

'Haan toh?'

Me saying, 'Yes and what?' in Urdu, caused six open beaks and a protective Seb to come in between us.

'What is going on?' he said in his all too protective manner.

'Nothing. It's nothing,' I replied with a sigh as I shook my head actually feeling sorry for the boys. They were ignorant.

'Sorry,' said one who perhaps held an ounce of empathy. But before I could say anything back, the train stopped and the lot of them got off at Stepney Green.

They left me fuming though. What bothered me was the fact these were young men, teenagers, the new generation of our country's future, and if they held such hostile thoughts there was no chance of peaceful coexistence and tolerance. Ever.

Idiots.

*****

The first couple of weeks flew by. I was busy and overworked. Typical of any hospital staff. Working was good for me. It kept my mind off how my past was lurking around the corner. And it wasn't like I hadn't been tempted to take the bus or cab to Ilford Lane either. Although in the end I couldn't get myself to do it.

What use would it have been?

I blew into my gloved hands wondering where the cab had got to. I desperately needed to get my car sorted. It loved being unfaithful. So here I was, waiting for a ride home, while my car gathered dust in the garage. It was almost four in the morning and I needed to lie down and relax my aching muscles. Working in the paediatric emergency ward was a tough one. Rewarding too, I suppose. Bringing ease to a sick child, there was definitely something in that.

'212 Goodmayes Lane...' called a man from inside a huge black car earning my attention.

7

'That's me,' I said hurrying towards it. Once inside the car and having confirmed my address to the driver, I took my gloves off, glad the heating was on full. I grinned as I began reading the messages on my phone. Too consumed in Seb's quirky and hilarious sentiments towards his new friend Anthony the radiologist, I failed to pay any attention to the driver until I heard him clearing his throat.

'Samina?' he asked looking at me through the rear view mirror. When he turned and I got a full view of his face, I held a hand over my mouth and my eyes widened.

'Uncle Ilyas?'

'I thought as much,' said Uncle Ilyas turning his attention back to the road.

Delighted, I shifted closer. 'How are you? Oh my God, I can't believe it. How is Aunty? And the kids must be all grown up…'

'What are you doing here?' The indifference in his tone caused my smile to falter. 'Jawed didn't mention anything about you being back.'

My silence and dropped shoulders, gave him the right to press further.

'He doesn't know does he?'

I shook my head and Uncle Ilyas grumbled something under his breath as he too shook his head. In disgust.

A few minutes of cheerless quiet passed and I was glad my flat was quickly nearing.

'Why were you at the hospital?' he said with a cluck of his tongue breaking the uncomfortable silence. 'You better not be in trouble again. Your previous antics haven't been forgotten.'

I looked down at my hands as a cold sensation seeped into my fingertips.

'The shame you brought on us all,' he continued. 'Jawed till this day hasn't recovered from the trauma you inflicted on his family. And after everything he did for you. Bushra Bhabhi was spot on about you. No respect,' he said bringing the car to a stop outside my flat. 'And to think I adored you as a little girl.'

I had adored him too. However it was in the past and I wasn't willing to open up wounds I had long sealed. Pulling out my purse from my handbag, with shaky fingers I held out a twenty pound note to pay for the fare.

'I have daughters. I take home an honest living and I'm not sure your money is clean money…'

'What do you mean?' I said pretending to be oblivious to his insinuation.

'I dropped two men to this same address the other night. Two White men. And now you are…' he said looking at me up and down whilst shaking his head. 'I don't even want to think what you have become. It pains me massively. No wonder both Jawed and Bushra Bhabhi are suffering from heart problems.'

Throwing the note at his face as a result of the fury which came over me with the mention of those two names, I surprised myself by raising my voice, 'I'm a doctor at the hospital. My money is as legitimate and clean as any righteous person's. And perhaps you can tell your good friends to come and see me some day. I may be able to take a look at their hearts and tell them a cure.'

'Insolent girl, get lost.'

Slamming the door after I got out of the car, I didn't offer him a goodbye. How could he say those words to me? I wasn't her anymore. I was a doctor. A woman who held ranking in society. And a woman who had accomplished a hell of a lot in such a short time. I shouldn't have felt little and pitiful and regressed into the state I was in eight years before.

But I did.

As soon as I was inside the comfort of my own dwelling, I slid against my front door, banged the back of my head on its cold surface and cried into my shaking hands.

And as the outburst continued, I felt angry. I felt weak and I felt regret for coming back here. This place was cursed. There was no peace here. It was the most rotten place on earth with the most spiteful people. People who made hurting others their favourite pastime. No, actually it wasn't even a pastime it was a trait of their character. Everybody here was fucking deluded.

Believe me I hadn't uttered a swear word in years, and here I was, sitting in my new flat crying fuck at every person who graced the streets of this bitter portion of London.

Chapter Three

Seb was a worry pot. I disturbed his sleep when he had heard my cries and now he wouldn't leave me alone. Not until I told him all.

'What's wrong?' he asked as he ushered me towards the sofa. His voice was gentle.

'Same old,' I said taking a deep breath. Seb crossed his arms over his chest and raised a brow. 'Seriously I'm all good.'

'I haven't seen you cry in all the time I've known you, so don't tell me you're all good when obviously you're not all good.'

I relaxed my shoulders and Seb sat down beside me.

'It's nothing important.' He wasn't convinced and his expression irked me. 'I met someone I know okay. A cab driver. One of my Uncle's friends. Let's just say he wasn't impressed to see this face again. He might even have nightmares, as of tonight.'

Seb's features softened and pulling a face he said, 'I have nightmares as well when I have to stare at this.' He poked a finger to my forehead.

'Get off,' I said frowning and moving away from his touch. 'Seriously why did I ever come back and decide to live with you here?'

'It's alright living with you Seb,' said Seb wiggling his brows, bringing a slight smile to my lips. And for the next few moments both of us sat on the sofa doing nothing but giving the space we had become experts in providing one other.

'Ant and I are getting on real good,' Seb said breaking our rest. 'He said, 'hello,' to you by the way.'

'I'm happy for you,' I replied finally getting up to get some food. I was starved.

'Hey Hun.'

'Yes,' I said turning back to look at him.

'If you ever see this Uncle's friend and I'm with you, tell me. I'm going to break his bones, alright.'

The seriousness on his face humbled me. 'You're a doctor,' I said nonetheless. 'You're meant to fix bones not break them.'

'Where it concerns you I'm willing to forget this. You're the only family I have and I am not letting anybody hurt you.'

'I know,' I whispered as he continued to stare. 'I know.'

*****

Friday night arrived and as expected I found myself on the children's emergency ward and my feet were killing me. I wanted the night to end so I could go home and sleep before coming back for my next shift the following evening.

I had only discharged a drunken teenager and her distraught parents when the triage nurse sent me the report card for my next patient. Taking a sip of my cold coffee, I skimmed through the vitals. A child of five. Bad cough. Breathing difficulties. Slight fever. Wheezy chest.

I placed the card in the red box. He needed to be seen urgently. I instructed Geraldine the duty nurse to set the child up in a cubicle and I'd be there after logging the required information in the record sheets. This was procedure. We had to do it to save our own backsides in case of litigation.

Minutes later whilst making my way to the child, I clumsily dropped his file and my pen rolled into a curtained cubicle. After picking up the file and quickly sorting its papers, I chased to pick up my pen.

'You're Batman. Batman doesn't cry. Madge tell my champ Batman never cries when he's ill...'

That voice?

I knew that voice and because my heart knew that voice even better, it decided to race out of my chest. I had to grab onto a fair amount of curtain to steady myself.

'Please don't cry. Where's this damn doctor?'

'Relax Madge.'

Madge?

It couldn't be. No. He wouldn't.

'Dr Iqmal, are you ready?' said Geraldine making me drop the curtain and suck in a sharp breath.

Applying pressure on the file against my chest to keep my heart where it should be, I stood and regardless of my nerves, I managed to say, 'Yes.'

But Madge's attempt to talk in a hush voice failed and her words, 'Doctor Iqmal. It might be your Dad,' reached me clearly.

I heard him laugh. A hearty laugh. A fulfilled laugh.

He was happy. He deserved it.

I was the one who went away and had spent eight years without any contact with him. It was on my terms after all. So why had I expected him to stay single for me?

Because I had for him...

'Dr Iqmal?'

'Yes,' I said. And like a robot devoid of emotion, I pulled back the curtain and dashed straight to the child.

Ignoring the sharp intake of breath behind me, I kneeled down coming level to the child, urging myself to smile, at least a little.

'Is that you Samina?' said Madge equally alarmed as she gasped. I ignored her query and began lifting the child's vest up. 'Samina. My God, it's you right?'

Finding her questions irrelevant, I concentrated hard on the child's breathing instead. I kept focused. I was on my job. I had to make sure the child was okay. Madge and the person breathing behind my back were insignificant.

'Take a deep breath for me darling,' I pronounced without a hint of anxiety in my tone, making sure to be extra polite and younger for the patient's sake. 'Deeper,' I said trying harder to listen to his lungs over the harshening breaths close behind me. 'What a brave boy you are?'

The boy smiled weakly and I looked at his mother's hand, avoiding making eye contact with her. 'Does he have a cough at all? Like a bark.'

'What?' she said as her forehead creased.

My heart banged against the temporary layer of iron over my chest.

'He isn't a dog.'

Of course my sudden appearance out of the blue wouldn't sit too well for her.

'Dr Iqmal didn't mean it like that,' said Geraldine clearly amused.

'I need to recognise what his cough sounds like,' I responded calmly. 'Has he been like this before?'

'No,' said Madge as she frowned looking over at the person behind me.

'Hmm, we'll need some x-rays of his chest.' Reading the name on his file to fill out the x-ray request, I pondered over why the boy's name was Omar Khan and not Iqmal. 'Geraldine will tell you where to go to have it done,' I said peering down at Omar's eyes. There wasn't a trace of sapphire in them anywhere. But genetics weren't always as simple as this. Because his father had the oddest blue eyes didn't mean he would inherit them.

'Daddy...' cried the boy. My heart snapped out of its defences and not being able to keep myself composed any longer I turned towards where I'd come in from, hoping the earth would expand for me to slip in and hide forever.

But his shadow was standing right in front of me blocking my way. I could see his jumper covered chest. I could hear his breaths. Fast but unsteady. His pulse. I could hear that too. His fists by his sides were curled tightly and his feet were apart, shoulder wide.

He was anxious.

Not meeting his eye, I nudged past him and accidently bumped my shoulder on his arm. My own hand automatically went up to where his touch had burnt

14

through my clothes and into my skin but I carried myself onwards regardless.

When I heard him say, 'Samina,' I walked even faster.

I didn't stop until I had exited the ward and began searching desperately for a vacant corner to cower away. The x-ray form was still in my hand and I stomped my feet cursing myself for being unprofessional. The child was suffering from a chest infection and was most likely about to be diagnosed with asthma and I had walked out delaying his treatment.

'Sweetheart…'

'Huh?'

The next few seconds were sudden and unexpected, him coming near and embracing me with open arms and at the same time pressing his lips to the sweaty skin above my brow. His hands came first on my head then moved downwards towards my back and up again. His face nuzzled against mine, his breaths were ragged and his pulse coarse.

My own heart lurched as my hands tightened around his neck begging me to keep connected with him like this. My heart had been deprived of its other half for far too long and thus when he loosened his grip on me, it forced me to lean into him again.

'Hass…' I whispered as his breath on my skin blew life back into my reclusive body.

'It really is you, isn't it?' he asked narrowing me against his chest and looking into my eyes.

'Yes,' I said releasing a choky breath.

'It's you.'

The joy in his voice brought tears to my eyes which he wiped away. The pads of his thumbs traced the curve of my cheekbones, leaving behind a warm trail of longing. His touch froze on the top corner of my upper lip and as he leaned closer a loud exhausted buzzing shifted his attention to the device stuck to my blouse. His gaze lingered and my clumsy fingers moved from his familiar

15

face to the pager attached to the cotton over the swell of my breast.

Coyly I took a step away from his warmth. 'I have to go.'

'No…'

I touched his outstretched hand with the tip of my fingers as I stepped away. And tapping my pager, with difficulty I said, 'It's urgent.'

The look on his face told me to drop the emergency and let him carry me somewhere where it would be only him and me. But I had a duty. I had to go. And I did what I'd become expert at. I ran.

I ran ignoring him calling me back.

Chapter Four

It would've been unfair if I'd left him there and sneaked home from another exit. Geraldine had relayed his message four times already. He was waiting in the children's reception area for me.

His son had been discharged. Why was he here and not with him? He didn't have to stay and wait on my account. I mean his child was far more important, right?

However forgetting about his son and his Madge for the moment, feeling a little conscious after having worked a ten hour shift, I popped into a toilet on my way. I redid some makeup and sprayed a little body mist. I also untied my high pony tail and brushed out the tangles in my hair.

Taking a step back, I stared at my reflection in the mirror. Older, fatter and my boobs were already sagging. Okay that was an exaggeration. They weren't but it didn't stop me from tightening the straps on my bra, giving them a slight lift.

My cheeks tinted red. The memory of the intimate moment we'd shared earlier was still tickling me. And unable to hide the school girl grin from my face, I thought, 'Sod all,' and hurried to him.

As soon as I saw him bent over a small table playing with the beads on the giant abacus, my smile changed into an uncertain emotion thinking again he had a son and a Madge.

'Doctor Iqmal,' he said before I could change my mind and scarper. His smile was huge as he came over and held out a hand.

I rolled my eyes but shook his hand anyway, something I regretted because my face warmed and I could bet I was also blushing. Certainly I was when like a gentleman he pressed his lips to it.

'I should go,' I said struggling with the turmoil he was causing my heart all over. I tried to pull my hand free. 'I'm really tired and need my bed.'

For a second his grin reminded me of the mischievous boy he once was. The little smarty pants from our childhood. He was such a pain. Always bothering me. Always causing me grief. But as I stared into his blue depths, I witnessed his eyes darkening and his smirk disappeared.

'I'll drive you,' he said releasing my hand.

'No I have my own car,' I replied looking at the waiting parents and their kids in the room. Consciously I began to fiddle with the straps of my handbag with the fingers he'd kissed, trying to rid them of the sensations he'd left lingering inside them.

'When did you come back and how come I'm always the last person to know anything about you?'

'What difference would my coming back make to you anyway?' I whispered moving towards the doors.

'Do I need to answer that?' he said. 'And stop doing that?'

'Doing what?'

'This…' he pulled my fingers loose from my bag.

'Unbelievable,' I frowned before exiting the room. And just to make a show of it, I fiddled with the straps some more.

His response was to snatch the offending bag from my grip.

'Give that back,' I said halting in the corridor and holding my hands on my hips.

He instantly looked away.

'My bag...'

When he looked at me again his lips were tilted upwards, and with a nice little laugh he came closer, growled my name, cupped my face in his hands, and kissed me on my head.

I swear I could have cried for the second time that night as he cuddled me against him and said, 'I'm glad your back.'

*****

We were about to enter my flat despite his persistence to take me to his place, where he could have a heart to heart with me. Obviously I had declined. With Madge living with him there was no way I was entering his house.

'You've been here for over a month living two minutes away and you don't think there's anything wrong in that,' he said as I unlocked my door coming into the landing. I also unlocked the second door which led up to my flat.

'Get over yourself.' He was bugging me. He'd said the same thing twenty times already. 'Just sit down okay,' I said, giving the living room a once over as we entered it. It was clean and tidy. Good. 'I'll get some tea or do you prefer coffee now?'

'Nothing, I want to talk.'

Sighing and thinking it best to get this over and done with, I gestured to the sofa. But he was about to sit down when his eyes narrowed behind me. 'Who the…'

'Hun you took your time tonight.'

With my mouth opened to its fullest, I watched a shameless Seb walk out of the bathroom in his superman bathrobe. His flat was being fitted with a new suite and he had been using mine for the last couple of days. His timing was awful.

'Long shift was it?' he asked, busy shuffling through his dirty laundry and throwing it into a plastic bag. 'I'm about to make French toast in a sec. Freshen up and join me before you hit the bed.'

'Seb,' I said, annoyed he hadn't looked up yet. When he finally did, I shot an imaginary bullet to his head.

'I know, I know my girlfriend is starving,' he sang like the idiot he was. Ignoring him, I turned to my unexpected guest. He had his back to me and both his hands were on his head. He was also muttering something under his breath.

'Oh my manners, who do we have here?' said Seb finally realising I had company.

19

'Please Seb,' I pleaded hoping he would quickly run to his own flat. 'I'll see you in a bit okay…'

'Introduce me first.' The fury in his voice made me jump and when he turned to face both Seb and I, his expression was one I had hoped I would never see again.

But Seb being Seb didn't wait for me to introduce him. Oh no, with his hand held out, he reached forward to do the honours himself. 'I'm Sebastian. And you are?'

Before replying he gave me a look. A look which had me taking a step back as I shook my head. No one knew who he was to me. He was my past. A past I'd kept hidden from everyone in my new life. Even from someone as dear as Seb. My life had moved on and it was wrong on so many levels for me to have brought him home in the first place. What had I been thinking? Had I not learnt anything from my mistakes?

'Are you alright?' Seb was fast to recognise my unease. I was pressed against the wall with my past staring back at me with a million threats.

'Seb please can I have some privacy?' I choked as a sweat broke out and my heart thumped.

'Let me introduce myself,' said my visitor taking the few steps to reach me. Pulling me by the waist and eliciting a sharp breath from me, he glared at Seb. 'I'm Hassan, Samina's husband.'

A tear escaped my eye and this time Hassan didn't caress it away like he did before. He let it roll until Seb's initial shock turned to confusion.

'Husband?' Seb asked looking from me to my husband of nine years. 'What is he saying Hun?'

Releasing me, Hassan charged towards Seb. In a quick motion he had grabbed the back of his head yelling, 'Call her Hun again and I'll set fire to your tongue.'

'Stop it,' I cried trying to pull him away. But Seb was also strong and after managing to push Hassan off, he pulled me to his side, further infuriating him.

'Samina what have you done?' shouted Hassan. 'How can you stand here after eight fucking years forgetting everything we went through together? Why are you with him? Who is he and why does he not know you're already married?'

'I don't appreciate the way you're yelling at her,' said Seb. With his face burning red he pressed on my forearms despite knowing I didn't like being touched forcefully.

'My wife is sharing a house with a guy. He calls her Hun and girlfriend and makes her fucking French toast wearing nothing but a bathrobe, and I'm the bad guy here for yelling my frustrations at her.'

'Loser,' said Seb. 'You really married this lowlife?'

Seb's words weren't appreciated and pulling myself free I flew myself at Hassan. Cupping his face between my trembling palms, I said, 'Listen to me. It's not what you think okay. Seb lives in the downstairs flat, he's…'

My words were cut short when Hassan removed my hands from his face and took a step away from me. 'How dare you do this to us?' His voice was shaky and his eyes told the extent of his regret.

I tilted my face and my heart wept at how broken he looked.

'How fucking dare you?' he said pointing a finger at me, making Seb pull me back.

'Don't swear,' warned Seb. 'Give her some respect.'

'I can't deal with this,' said Hassan waving his accusatory finger from me to Seb before marching towards the front door.

'Seb let me go.'

Hassan rushed down the stairs. I gave chase. Grabbing his arm I said, 'Where are you going?'

'Home. I'm going home and when you're ready to honour the promise you made, you know where to find me.'

'Hassan wait…'

He didn't. He slammed the door and left.

Chapter Five

'Get your hands off me.' If this man knew what was good for him, he needed to release me right away.

'For crying out loud what's wrong with you?' said Seb dragging me up the staircase and back into my flat. 'Calm down. The moron left, you know that, so stop whatever this is. This look doesn't suit you. Seriously stop it.'

'You're not helping Seb,' I hissed as he held me down on the sofa, easily breaking the boundary which I'd firmly set in our relationship from the onset. 'Will you just unhand me?'

'Look I know I crossed my line here with you but Samina he was insulting and sorry to say this, you too are insulting the woman you are by behaving like a bloody damsel in distress.'

Letting me go Seb tried to appease me by surrendering his hands above his head.

'Don't touch me like that again.'

Jutting his chin he said, 'Sorry I got worried that's all.'

'Oh go away. Take your big brother costume and go save another, '*damsel in distress.*''

'Now that's unfair.'

'What's unfair Mister Sebastian Angus Jones is the extent of my agitation right now.' I got up to stand face to face with him. ''Promise,' Hassan said before storming away. He spoke of my promise, the one I'd given him. How convenient for him to put it all on my conscience, when he's the one with a kid and perhaps a wife in that Madge.'

Seb raised a brow in confusion but witnessing the drops of anguish rolling down my cheeks, his face hardened leaving no trace of the soft spoken and gentle man I'd come to know and love.

'He said, 'honour,'' I said trying my best not to cry more. 'Can you believe it, the word honour? The mere sound of it makes me sick. In every waking moment of a woman's life she's reminded of honour. The weight of this word forced on her and she alone burdened to carry it until her last breaths. Why will this word not leave me alone?'

'Samina Iqmal please calm down.'

'Iqmal, the surname Iqmal reminds me of the man I had honoured by adding his name to mine. When I left home, I had felt it was an apt decision to start afresh with only his name supporting me. How pathetic was I then and how pathetic am I now?'

'Hun…'

'But I wasn't pathetic. I mean I was his wife. I still am for God's sake. Don't I have every right to his name? And the promise, I swear Seb I have kept it.'

'You would never break a promise, I know that much at least,' said Seb with a yielding voice. I wiped at my tears. God why had I brought Hassan here only to make myself vulnerable again? In fact why had I ever returned?

'What I don't understand is how you could delete this piece of information when I thought we knew everything about each other.'

'Seb…?' I questioned as he began walking towards the front door making me realise I didn't want him to leave me alone at all. Not now, not ever.

'I guess I was wrong.'

'Seb…'

'Its best I leave. I've told you the worst of me. Damn I let you in and exposed my weaknesses thinking you had done the same with me. I can't help but feel kind of let down right now.'

'No not you too,' I said rushing to him. The expression on his face wasn't one I'd seen before. I grabbed his arm. 'You're not allowed to think this of me. Not you as well. I've let down many people in my lifetime and you're not going to be one of them.'

'You have a husband,' he snapped nudging my hand away. 'A fucking husband who spoke to you like you were the dirt under his soles.'

'He's always been like that,' I screamed whilst running my hands over my head. 'He torments me Seb. That's his job. He's tormented me since the first time I saw him. He used to pull my plaits when I was little. He'd steal my homework and plant worms in my pencil case at every chance he got. He was never good. Never could be and look, just look how he's still tormenting me by taking you away from me too.'

Putting my arms around him I held onto him tight. I was desperate. He was my brother in every sense aside from the blood running in our veins and I was stupid to have ever drawn this no touch boundary between us in the first place.

'Whoa…' he said and this time when Seb's comforting hands relaxed around my shoulders, I didn't flinch or struggle or push him away, as I'd always done before. I let him direct me to the sofa and as I babbled my apologies into his shoulder, I began my narration of the details I had deliberately erased from my story to him.

As hard as this was, I had to do it.

Sixteen years earlier

Chapter Six

Hate at first sight…

The object of my displeasure sat next to me, tapping away with my pencil's freshly sharpened tip. He wasn't sitting, he was half lying and half sprawled, hardly even touching the plastic of the dirty red chair.

How was this possible? Who even cared because what was bothering me was the fact he'd taken my brand new, Blackpool Pleasure Beach, eraser. The expensive, souvenir, rainbow coloured, glitter sprinkled, glow in the dark one. The one I'd bought whilst holidaying at my Aunty Asma's during the summer.

My nightmare had officially begun.

It would have been okay, my first day at secondary school, had it not been for his presence next to me. In fact I should've been sitting with the only friends I knew from primary school, Parveen and Ranjita. For this I had my brother Habib to blame. If he hadn't dropped me off twenty minutes late, I may have had a better destiny altogether.

I was on the verge of crying because the boy continued rubbing away, completely demolishing the top of the Blackpool Tower. And all I could do was stare at him, kind of afraid.

Was this what a bully looked like?

I'd heard stories from my previous neighbour Jessica Walker about bullies in secondary school. She had come to this school too but within two years her parents had pulled her out and home schooled her instead. She was bullied, that's why. By a boy named Piss-Taker Pete.

Was the same going to happen to me?

'Thank you very much,' he said placing the eraser in my pencil case whilst flashing a crooked grin.

I gulped feeling the taste of the awful breakfast Habib had given me and this was the moment I decided I hated stale bread with butter and jam, and I hated the boy sitting next to me. I hated him more than the fact my two best friends were laughing and enjoying a joke with a brand new friend on their table at the front of the classroom. And to top that, this new friend had a bigger and brighter pencil case than mine.

Feeling a sense of betrayal, I swallowed the imaginary gob stopper down my throat and made a silent prayer by opening my palms under the table.

'Please Allah make it possible for me to sit with Parveen and Ranjita…'

My prayer was hardly a small request. It was a major deal. Seriously I knew all their secrets and I could do anything to be with them on their table.

'Don't worry I don't usually bite girls.'

'What?'

'I said I don't bite girls.'

I looked at him thinking, *'Why?'*

'Well I don't want rabies do I?'

I looked back at the sparkling table with the invisible halo illuminating it and sighed. My friends Ranjita and Parveen were still giggling.

'Do you know them cows?' said the bully boy.

Nodding I said, 'Yes from primary school and they're not cows.'

'I agree they aren't cows because they're fucking ugly bitches.'

My head shot up and if my neck was a twig, it would have snapped from the force of my reaction.

'You swore.' My voice came out like a shocked elephant's would after spotting a mouse because I was in the same situation. I was going to be in trouble on my first day. This boy had said the worst swear word. I probably couldn't even spell it and he said it like it was his alphabet.

26

What if Mr Philpot, our new teacher had heard him? Even worse what if Parveen or Ranjita had heard? They'd think I was talking bad about them with a boy with the unusual dark blue eyes...

'Is there a problem back there?' said Mr Philpot standing up from behind his wooden desk, making the class of thirty odd curious pupils turn their faces towards us.

My eyes widened and my body froze unable to respond. I was getting told off by Mr Philpot who minutes ago had kindly written my timetable for me because I was the only one late.

'No problem here,' said bully boy swinging on the legs of his chair. I managed a quick glance at him and couldn't believe how he was so relaxed and severely annoying at the same time.

'It's Hassan isn't it?'

'Hassan Iqmal.'

'Okay Hassan Iqmal, do I need to keep an eye on you?' said Mr Philpott.

'If you want,' replied Hassan with a huge grin. 'Good things are to be looked at.'

I closed my eyes knowing my day had got a hundred times worse. Sitting next to this boy was going to ruin all my plans of becoming a doctor when I was older.

'You wouldn't want a detention on your first day would you, Hassan Iqmal?'

'No.'

'Then drop the attitude and get on with your work.' Mr Philpot's spectacled eyes looked my way, 'Is he troubling you young lady?'

'No,' I said when what I wanted to shout was, 'He is troubling me, and I want to sit on Parveen and Ranjita's table...'

'Then stop talking and complete copying the timetable out in your diary.'

Immediately I wrote 'Room s7' under Maths on a Tuesday afternoon shaking like a fish which had been thrown out of its water.

Hassan snickered. In fact he was unaffected altogether. I was affected. My cheeks were burning and I was trying my hardest not to cry. Instead I remained concentrated on my timetable, managing to ignore Hassan as he shamelessly continued to help himself to my new stationery. I didn't look up until the buzzer signalling lunch time made me jump.

'After lunch I want you back here for registration, then I'll escort you to your first lesson,' said Mr Philpot as an excited classroom of eleven year olds began packing their things and scurried out in search of the lunch halls.

I rushed towards Parveen and Ranjita glad the boy next to me was already leaving the room.

'Sorry I was late this morning and couldn't sit with you two. Maybe this afternoon I can…'

'Oh don't worry, Saira is way cooler than you,' said Ranjita rather rudely.

'I'm not cool at all,' said Saira the new girl, with a big smile. 'I can't believe you're sitting with Hassan Iqmal, like the Hassan Iqmal. Now that is what I call cool.'

'You can swap seats if you want,' I offered praying she would say yes.

'No way, I'd rather watch him from afar.'

'Gross,' said Parveen, and I was glad she shared my sentiments. Was Saira oblivious to how majorly annoying the *Hassan Iqmal* was? Who would want to look at him?

'Come let's grab some lunch,' said Ranjita rushing forward.

Reeling in the utter regret for coming in late, I tagged along whilst fiddling with the straps of my ruck sack. A cold shiver travelled up my body. And I knew this was because of my first encounter with Hassan Iqmal.

Unfortunately this encounter was to be the first of many.

Chapter Seven

Oh brother...

'Habib,' I called running to where he was standing.

'How was your day?' he said giving me a high five which I reached up to clap.

'This is the best part of it.'

Habib raised a brow before gesturing to the girl sitting in his car.

'This is my sister Samina,' he said as she poked her head out of the window and waved her hands crazily.

'Aw she's so cute.'

I wanted to gag at how excited she looked but faked a smile releasing a strained, 'Hi,' instead. I guessed she was my brother's latest girlfriend.

'Good first day Baby?' said Habib.

'I'm not a baby,' I groaned jumping into the back seats. 'And my first day was crap, all thanks to you.'

Habib chuckled, got behind the wheel and began manoeuvring the car between the heavy crowds of children leaving the school. For the time being I decided to keep quiet. Once home though, I would turn into a lioness and Habib would have to make up for every minute of my horrid day. I was planning on the full works, pizza, and a pineapple deluxe from Cake Cabin, as pay back. And if by any chance he refused, Uncle Jawed would have to find out about whoever her face was in the car.

'My brother also comes to this school you know,' said the girl looking back at me.

I must admit she was beautiful with those stunning eyes and perfectly straight hair. Her creamy complexion was dabbed with pink blush and her smile made me think I'd seen her before. She looked rather familiar.

'My name's Yasmin by the way. I can't wait to get to know you better. I have a feeling you and I are going to be great friends.'

'Me too,' I replied awkwardly, kind of touched by her warmth. But going by the way my brother shifted in his seat, I knew this was unlikely.

Habib would have a new girlfriend by the end of the week.

*****

'What's wrong?' asked Habib as soon as *giggle is my second name Yasmin* had bade us goodbye, anticipating another meeting with him as early as the next day. The girl was already swimming in the deepest ends of one sided love with my brother.

Nevertheless getting out of the car and rushing towards our front door, I ignored his question.

'I know I made you late this morning. You didn't get in trouble did you?' he said grabbing my hand which I pulled back stubbornly.

'If you would let me walk to school in the first place I'd be there on time,' I snapped.

Habib unlocked the front door and I followed his hastened steps inside our house.

'Everyone walked to school today. It's only five minutes away.'

He dropped my school bag in the landing and shoved his jacket off.

'I'm going to walk tomorrow,' I said.

Stopping halfway in the landing, Habib turned to face me, 'I can take care of you.'

'I know you can,' I yelled and Habib sat down on a step on the staircase and sighed into his hands.

'Why are you doing that?' I asked stopping my tantrum. He looked tired and it was confirmed, I'd upset him. This realisation made me sad and now that I was home, in the safest place known to me, I could unleash those tears which had been threatening me all day.

Somehow before my first tear rolled down my face, my brother had already cuddled me. 'I'm sorry,' he said.

'Why are you sorry? You're the best brother.'

'Then stop crying.'

And it didn't take long for me to stop the waterworks. My brother was magical like that. He always had been.

'What brought this on?' he said once we were sitting in our living room.

I wiped my nose not truly understanding why I had freaked out. My day wasn't too bad. Although Hassan had been a pain, I did make a new friend. Saira was amazing.

'Listen,' said Habib. 'You're my responsibility. Not only will I take you to school, I'll be taking you everywhere for as long as I live. Once I'm dead you can…'

'Don't say that,' I said trembling at even the thought of him being taken away from me.

'Just don't cry again. You look scary when you scrunch your eyes and wiggle your lips like that…'

'Stop it,' I said slapping his chest.

'I'm serious,' he said moving away from my assault. 'Baby sisters look pretty when they laugh not when they cry.'

Offering him a scowl, I began walking towards the kitchen.

'I had to sit with this horrid boy today. He kept using my stuff without asking. It's not your fault I had bad luck. And it's not your fault you work nights and have to take me to school as well.'

'I'm a lousy brother if I can't take you to school on time. Truth is, it gives me an excuse to spend a little time with you,' said Habib as he squeezed my cheeks.

I quickly moved away from him to inspect the contents of our fridge, only to hear him tease me further by singing a silly Bollywood song about sisters. But in reality it made me break into giggles.

31

When his song ended, with a mouthful of chocolate mousse I said, 'That was kind of weird.'

'*Kind of weird...*' he mimicked reaching to pull my braid out of its knot, something he loved to irritate me by.

'Don't you dare,' I warned because after loosening my hair, out of habit he always flicked the band at me. 'No...' I shrieked when the elastic stung like crazy as he got me on my arm and began running up the stairs.

'I'll get you for that,' I said running after him but he was too fast and had locked his bedroom door before I had reached up. 'That's two slices of cake for this,' I demanded banging on his door.

'I never agreed on getting you anything. It was your first day at school not your first day as a queen.'

'I'll have to tell Uncle about the pack of cigarettes I found whilst cleaning under your bed the other day then. And what's her name who was in the car? Wasn't she the butcher's daughter?' I teased knowing full well she wasn't. Habib had dumped the butcher's daughter months back.

'You wouldn't dare...'

'What wouldn't you dare?'

With a jump I turned to find Uncle Jawed standing outside his bedroom. He was combing his bed ruffled hair with a dingy plastic comb.

'Aslaam Alaikum Uncle, how was your day today?' I said hoping he hadn't heard anything. After my long day I was in no mood for one of his lectures.

'Walaikum Asalaam. It was good until you started screaming the whole house down. Beti you know I work all night, still you fail to appreciate I need my sleep during the day,' said Uncle as the comb moved down his forehead to tame his bushy eyebrows.

Withholding my desire to laugh, I sucked in my lips instead.

'You were saying something about a butcher?'

Habib's door flew open.

'Err, yeah, she was asking for that steak from the butcher's. The one she liked the other day,' said Habib fibbing like a pro whilst widening his eyes at me to play along.

Uncle raised his brow looking from Habib to me. 'I'll pick some up tomorrow when I make the grocery rounds.'

'Great,' said Habib poking his tongue at me before slamming his door shut again, a little too carelessly.

Uncle shook his head at my brother's action and gestured for me to come downstairs with him.

'How was school?'

'It was good. We made a time table.'

'Ahan, what subjects will you be studying?'

As I spoke about my new school, Uncle listened attentively. And when I finished explaining why we had two different teachers for Science, he patted my head.

'Your brother didn't manage one decent grade but I want the whole family to know what a fine child I raised by making you a doctor,' he stressed. 'My brother will be proud I raised his children in his absence as mine.'

Uncle Jawed flashed a wide smile of extremely white teeth and I couldn't help smile back. Uncle had wanted me to be a doctor since I could remember and truth be told, I couldn't wait to be one either. I wanted to please him so bad.

'Come your hair is loose.'

I crossed my legs in front of him on the floor and allowed Uncle to use his tiny comb to straighten my hair out and tie it in a neat braid again. He hated my hair loose because detangling it later could be a mission for the both of us.

'There, better.'

I got up to turn the television on.

'Has your brother given you anything to eat yet?'

I shook my head forgetting I'd scoffed a small pot of mousse moments earlier.

'As expected,' said Uncle. 'I'll make parathay. You can give the useless boy a couple too. I doubt he has eaten. Smoking fills not only his lungs with poison but his stomach too. And after what your mother died from, he should know better.'

My shoulders dropped and the design on the flocked curtains behind the television cabinet appeared more interesting than 'Blue Peter,' on the screen.

'She wasn't a smoker but the cancer still killed her within months of it being found. But why would he understand? Beti…' Uncle tapped my back, moving my gaze from the curtain. 'Come eat. Watch telly in peace later. He thinks I'm his enemy when I speak sense in him. I have high expectations from you though because you are my sensible beti.'

Following him into the kitchen, I sat by the dining table and stared into our back garden whilst Uncle got busy with the food preparation. Another few minutes passed before I was jerked away from my thoughts again, and Uncle handed me a plate with a steaming keema paratha on it. My favourite.

'Why do you seem lost?'

'I don't,' I answered taking the plate. 'Can I take Habib's upstairs to him?'

Uncle regarded me for a second before his face broke into a smile, 'Yes, you can eat in his room too. Let me heat up some chicken for him first. Oh my Allah how your world works in wonders,' sighed Uncle, turning the flame on the hob higher. 'My brother's children after all… Oh how easily I gave up my own life to take care of these orphans. Whether they thank me or not, only you know…'

I stared down at my paratha as Uncle muttered his own praises over and over, something he did often, never letting me forget my parents were dead.

Chapter Eight

Registration rocks…

My Tuesday morning began as bright as the pleasant September sun. Thankfully Habib had managed to drop me at the school gates way before the buzzer went off, and he also gave me two pounds to spend at the tuck shop.

The day before, Ranjita and I had discovered the lower school tuck shop, which a Mrs Balls ran from a closet in her classroom. She had a humongous closet. Mars, Snickers, Kit Kat and Malteasers, she had them all. She had stacks of crisps, and believe it or not she also stocked the Worcester sauce ones. And drinks, she had strawberry Ribena, and even those protruding bottom fizzy pop bottles, at only twenty pence each. At primary school twenty pence only bought us a bruised banana, or a crinkled skin apple. Our head teacher there had been overly health obsessed. We weren't even allowed juice for our breaks. Only water.

Mrs Balls wasn't only selling high in sugar foods and brewages. Oh no, she had other stuff too, great stuff like pencils, pens, rulers and rubbers. Things a stationery loving geek like me could die for. I had already set eyes on a lovely set of luminous pens. During break I was going to buy them for sure. I was super excited.

'Yo Samina…'

My happy thoughts were hacked and the bright smile I was wearing was ripped from the map of my face as soon as I heard his voice. He was swinging on the legs of his chair. And he was chewing bubble gum. Cola flavoured. Brown and sickly.

'Hello Samina,' he said.

'Hello,' I replied because Uncle Jawed always said, 'Replying to someone's greeting was as vital as breathing.' One of his many lessons in etiquette.

'Come sit down,' grinned Hassan gesturing to my chair as the largest balloon of disgusting gum burst over his lips. 'Sit sit.'

He was acting weird but I ignored the shiver of curiosity ringing alarm bells, and reached for my chair. My rear was about to plop down when I spotted his ruck sack was on it. I stood up straight, not failing to notice how he had cupped his mouth with his hands and was quietly chuckling into it.

'Ha ha very funny…' I waited for him to move it and when he didn't, I decided to take matters into my own hands. I would simply remove his dirty bag from my chair myself. Only it didn't budge. I gripped the straps more forcefully but it weighed a ton.

I looked at him frowning. The tormentor frowned back and I pointed at his bag. He shrugged and popped his gruesome gum.

I stared at him. His antics had been depressing the day before but now they had upped a level of my patience. His eyes, those blue balls of his were bouncing with delight. He was enjoying himself and here I was trying to analyse why he was the way he was.

I suppose there was a time and place for such critical examination of the bully species because a mixture of laughter broke me out of my trance. Everybody including Parveen and Ranjita were laughing. Darren was laughing the loudest.

Darren Wilkins wore red braces and had matching scruffy red hair. He spoke a little funny, a bit like my cousins from Blackpool did, and he was a trouble maker because he hadn't wasted a second in becoming Hassan's friend.

'Samina didn't have her breakfast today,' he guffawed and everyone in the classroom erupted into more laughter.

Hassan was banging his head on the table overcome with hilarity.

And I was embarrassed. Totally upset and totally hating him. He had spoilt my morning.

'Sir's coming,' said Darren as he ran back inside the classroom from where he was stood at the door, and immediately Hassan with his help removed the bag from my chair and hid it under the table.

'Settle down back there.'

I sat down. Hassan continued to laugh. Darren was still giggling and I was fuming. And when Hassan's slimy fingers reached for my pencil case, I violently moved it away.

'Buy your own stuff.'

'Quiet back there,' shouted Mr Philpot.

I gulped and slinked into my seat. This wasn't good. This wasn't good at all.

*****

The rest of the day's lessons passed in utter silence and in the shadow of my friends. They were quickly making new friends with the other girls from our class, whilst I was still sulking. Hassan had put rocks in that bag. Can you believe it, rocks? I had seen them being dropped into the flower beds during lunch time.

'She's a weakling,' Hassan had said. And when he saw me watching, his eyes had gleamed in impishness. 'What you looking at, weakling?'

'Shut your face you idiot,' shouted Ranjita in my defence.

And turning away from the not so nice exchange of words which followed, I made my way towards the tuck shop and brought the set of highlighters. The purchase made me feel better. Only momentarily. Because as soon as Hassan saw them during Art, he drained the orange and the green inks before I'd even had a chance to test them. And when I put my hand up to tell the teacher on

Parveen's insistence, Hassan apologised only to later tell me he hadn't meant it.

I would hate him until the end of the world. There was no doubt about it.

Chapter Nine

Lonely lamb chops…

'Beti,' said Uncle disturbing my TV time. Groaning I reluctantly left my cosy chair and went to our landing where he was putting on his coat.

'Dinner's in the microwave. Don't open the door to anyone and only use the home phone for emergencies,' he said as he picked up his keys. I rolled my eyes. He always said the same thing. Reading a prayer over my head to protect me in his absence, Uncle opened the front door. 'Allah hafiz.'

'Allah hafiz,' I replied closing the door behind him as he left me alone at home, like he did every night. But I was used to it and found myself retuning to the living room. I turned the volume up on the telly. Like my school books, the telly kept me company.

*****

It was later in the evening when I was warming my dinner and the house phone rang.

'You alright?'

'Yep I was about to have dinner.'

'What's Uncle cooked?' asked Habib.

'Lamb chops with rice.'

'Hmm nice. Have you done your homework?'

'Yes I did some extra too. Anyway did Yasmin like the film?' I asked hoping she'd enjoyed it as much as I had. On the big screen Mulan must have looked spectacular. I'd already seen it when Uncle had brought the cd home. Mr Lee was a regular visitor at the Cabbie, and Uncle always brought five discs for a tenner from him. Normally Uncle watched the over aged films in his room, and I'd be allowed to watch the ones suitable for me. And Mulan had been super.

'She liked it, yes.'

'Like you let me watch any of it,' said Yasmin giggling in the background.

'Didn't you let her watch it?'

Habib coughed. 'Ask her yourself.'

'Habib stop it…' squealed Yasmin into the phone.

I heard moaning and some weird sounds before Yasmin spoke. 'Hello, Mee, naaa, stop it Habib.'

'What is it? What's he doing to you?' I said because Habib could be silly sometimes. I hoped he wasn't speeding and scaring her.

'Err nothing,' said Yasmin still in her giggles. 'How are you?'

'I'm fine but why didn't he let you watch the film?'

'Oh we did see it...'

I heard the noises again, like somebody was chewing gum loudly.

'It was a great movie.' Yasmin was kind of out of breath. 'A very bevy hmmm great movie...'

'Did you like the bits where she fights like a hero?'

'Yeah, sure,' said Yasmin sounding a little dreamy. 'Meena sweetie what were you doing?'

'Getting my dinner ready,' I said as the microwave beeped.

'Habib stop it, I'm talking with your sister. You get your dinner ready yourself?'

'Yes.' Why did she sound surprised? I'd been warming my dinner since I was nine, as soon as Habib had taken charge of the night shifts with Uncle to control our minicab office. 'What are you stopping Habib from doing?'

'Err nothing, but tell me sweetie do you need some help? I can come over.'

My heart did a somersault. Yasmin had been bestowed the extra friendliness gene in extravagant amounts. She was always pleasantly nice to me.

'Yes, yes please come over,' I said. With the phone in my hand, I ran to the pot on the stove and clapped, rejoicing there was plenty of food.

Habib came back on the line, 'I'm taking Yasmin back home,' he said. 'Then I'm going to the Cabbie.'

'But she wants to come over. She said so herself.'

'Listen Baby,' he whispered, though I could sense he was vexed. 'Are you forgetting Uncle?'

'So... Can't I for once have my dinner with someone? Why do I have to be alone? Do you know how scared I am sometimes? Do you think I enjoy being on my own all the time? All my friends have dinner with their families. If for once I want Yasmin to join me, us, is that a crime?'

'Stop getting worked up.'

Yasmin gasped in the background. 'Oh my God is she upset?'

I threw the phone across the room. The battery flew out but I didn't care anymore. Banging my feet heavily on the steps leading upstairs, I made my way to my bedroom. Kicking open my door, I reached for the box on my top shelf and took out Mummy's picture from it.

My beautiful Mummy whose hair was long and silky and always braided like mine, stared back at me. Her eyes were dark, a dark caramel colour, like mine. Like Habib, Mummy had two dimples which appeared whenever she smiled.

Pressing my fingertip on her dimple in the picture, 'Mummy I miss you,' I said. Because I did. Being eleven didn't mean you didn't need your mum. I had needed her many times, and even though I cried lots for her to come back to me over the years, not once did she come, not even in my dreams.

But I loved her despite this.

When I was little Habib would always tell me stories about her. Habib was fifteen when she died so his memories of her were more vivid than mine. Having lost her when I was five, I had more fingers than any

41

memories. Not many memories at all but enough for me to miss her.

My last memory of Mummy was when I'd gone to see her at the hospital to bid her farewell. Dad had told me it may be the last time I saw her. It was therefore important for me to hug her nicely, making sure I didn't squeeze too tightly. Her body was full of pains and aches. In fact Mummy's body had completely shrunk. A few months earlier she'd been at home, healthy and well, holding my hand and walking me to and from school.

'My precious Baby...'

Mummy had tears in her eyes that day, as did my Dad. But I wanted Mummy to come home. I missed her food. I missed her reading my bedtime stories. I missed bath time with her, and I missed her brushing my teeth for me. I missed her playing with me and I missed her not being at home all the time.

Mummy combed my hair with her fingers whilst I had moaned the whole time. I was angry. She'd been at the hospital for too long.

'I want you to remember I'm always with you.'

'You're not,' I had cried. She was at the hospital and Dad had said something about her going away to a better place, where her suffering would end. But it wasn't fair for her to go on her own, was it? What about me, her little girl? She'd have to take me with her like she had when she went to Pakistan the year before. We'd left dad and Habib in London and Mummy took me with her because I was little, too little to be left without her for even a day.

'No come home now. Come home with me,' I had demanded.

'Baby I wish I could...'

Dad had pulled me away from Mummy. And he held me against his chest as I carried on crying.

'Promise me Kareem. Promise me you will raise her as a princess. Promise me she will be happy and well looked after...'

'I promise you. My love, both our children are precious. You don't worry at all,' Dad had said wiping his tears.

'Habib, my darling…'

Habib stood silently observing my tantrums on our mother's dying bed, knowing better not to demand things which were both selfish and impossible. He knew Mummy wasn't staying away from home on purpose. I remember him rushing to Mummy and toppling over her chest. He cried so much and seeing him like that, I had cried even louder.

Mummy died two hours later.

Her last words had been for Habib.

'Love your sister, always…'

*****

'Do not scare me like that, do you hear?' yelled Habib as he barged into my room and dropped to the floor besides me. Taking Mummy's picture from my hands, he wrapped me between his arms. 'Don't ever do that again.'

'I miss our parents,' I told him with quivering lips.

'You have me.' He kissed my forehead. 'I promise to spend more time with you. Don't be upset. Hush now.'

I pulled away from his embrace wiping my snotty, tear stained face with my elbow.

'Let me put this back,' said Habib with sunken eyes. I watched him put the photo back into my special box, and onto the shelf. 'Don't for once think I like leaving you alone. We'll work something out.'

'I'm okay,' I whispered knowing it wasn't his fault.

'Come here,' he sighed holding me tightly again. 'When the phone wouldn't connect, you scared me.'

'I got angry because you were rude to Yasmin,' I admitted remembering how this whole thing had started in the first place. I gently moved away from his embrace. 'You should go to the Cabbie, Uncle will get angry. He was assuming you were there before he left.'

43

'Ah let him stew for a bit, I want lamb chops with my little sister.'

And as my brother said this, a woman's voice called, 'Meena…'

'Shit I forgot she's here,' grumbled Habib.

But I jumped up and gave my brother a pat on his shoulder. 'Thank you, thank you, thank you,' I said before running down the stairs, forgetting my earlier melancholy altogether.

She stood in our kitchen near the sink, filling a jug with water. The dining table was made up and my plate of food was waiting for me. Hearing me enter she turned and set the jug on the side before holding out her arms.

Quickly I made my way into them.

'I don't blame you for being upset, dinner times are family times. Come on sit down and let me serve you.' Yasmin pulled out a chair and I sat down. She was smiling prettily. Her eyes dazzling like rare blue diamonds. 'Where's your brother?'

'Here,' said Habib as he entered.

'I've warmed you a plate too. Why don't you sit down with Meena?'

Something awkward lodged inside my chest watching Yasmin fuss over my brother and me. I wished for it to be always like this. My brother and her, they made the perfect couple. I swear they did.

And I decided Habib would have to marry her. She had to become a part of our family. As soon as possible.

It was all I wanted.

Chapter Ten

Wedding planners…

I had it all planned.

Yasmin would wear blue, solely because of her eyes. Blue looked stunning against her creamy complexion. And blue was certainly achievable when it came to Asian weddings. All we had to do was book an appointment with the people at number sixteen on Ilford Lane, to be allowed up their staircase and into the room where the business was conducted.

'Amandeep Wedding Services.' You chose the decor, the food, the colour scheme and they did the rest. Ranjita's grandfather had used them for her aunt's wedding and that wedding was the best I'd ever been to.

Uncle at first had been dead against the idea of me going. But when Parveen's mother, who wore a hijab, said she'd go with us, Uncle had agreed. He even commissioned the special S Class Mercedes belonging to Maqsood from Albert Road, to take us there in style. Habib had been surprised, knowing Uncle had a negative vibe about Sikh weddings. He said Sikh people drank and danced too much.

He was right.

It was my first rave ever. The food was good. The music was hip, and the dancing was fabulous. Ranjita pulled me and Parveen onto the dance floor and boy did she know how to move her body. It took a few tries and when I finally got the hang of it, Parveen's mother was pulling both her daughter and I home, saying it was enough.

As she handed me back to Uncle at the Cabbie I was rattled to hear her ranting about how solely I, minus Parveen, had danced all night like a Sikh girl would. She suggested I be told the true virtues of a Muslim girl more sternly.

'Muslim girls,' she said, 'aren't meant to dance amongst men. They have to be taught to respect and guard themselves from an early age.'

Uncle's face had fallen but she went on and on and I was hurt by what she was saying. I was rubbish at bhangra dancing, yet according to her I was a pro at it and Uncle ought to curb my viewing times of Bollywood movies to zero.

When she was gone I knew Uncle was going to be angry. I was about to cry because if there was one thing I didn't like doing, it was upsetting him. However Uncle did the unthinkable and seriously I couldn't believe it. He only went and turned up the stereo, and began pumping bhangra moves right there in the middle of our office. He was a funny dancer and soon enough I was dancing with him. We were fixing imaginary light bulbs whilst swinging our legs like Tarzan from one branch to another, laughing our heads off.

Soon passers-by on Ilford Lane stopped and watched and laughed at the uncle and niece team trying hard to break into bhangra. Though it didn't deter us. But when Uncle Dawood, my Mosque teacher walked past to make his way to the Mosque down the road, Uncle failed to see him and carried on moving like he was being attacked by a swarm of bees.

I had tugged at his arm. 'Uncle Dawood is looking,' I whispered being too afraid to yell it. In front of Uncle Dawood I was afraid to do anything to be honest. It was only when Habib sauntered through the door looking back at the Imam curiously, that Uncle stopped.

Uncle's face had never been so red.

Definitely music was a must for Habib's wedding. Bhangra and Bollywood. Uncle and I would have a ball.

'Ranjita you're in charge of the music,' I said loving the eager sparkle in her eyes.

'I'm like the best dancer in the world,' she exclaimed wiggling her hips in the middle of the corridor. Parveen was embarrassed, and I laughed as Saira tried copying Ranjita's moves. We were heading towards our Science class. I had my notebook out and was ticking my checklist for the wedding. Of course my friends all had important jobs.

Parveen was in charge of my hair because her sister Rehana was a hair dresser and a makeup artist. I would get her to style it in a fancy up do, like the women in the old type of movies had. Only I would have pearls and beads threaded into mine. According to Parveen, I would look amazing. I couldn't wait.

Saira was in charge of the seating and when she suggested I sit with them at the front table, which was to be reserved solely for my friends, I had kindly declined. It was my brother's wedding after all. I was going to be up on the stage all night looking like the Queen.

I wouldn't leave Yasmin's side. No way.

'Hey Saira, do you reckon you can also manage the little ones in case they ruin the decorations or bump into the cake?' I asked because at Jessica's cousin's wedding, the cake was knocked over by two bickering flower girls. I'd seen the video. Although Jessica and I had a good laugh about it and re-played the moment a hundred times before she had moved house, I wouldn't be laughing if it happened at Habib's wedding.

'I suppose so,' said Saira. 'Hey wouldn't Parveen be better since she has the scariest face ever?'

'Hey that's not nice.' I said. 'Parveen has a lovely face.'

'No I don't,' said Parveen growling like a monster. 'I think I'll like scaring little brats who can't sit still with their parents at a wedding.'

I laughed imagining her chasing frightened kids along aisles decorated with flowers and candles, when a pain on my scalp made me begin to see black and blue.

'Ouch...' I screamed holding onto my hair.

47

'Bloody flea bag get your hair off of me.'

'Don't move it's hurting,' I said as he deliberately moved away pulling my hair and me with him. 'Saira help me…'

'Oye Hassan,' shouted Saira. 'Stand still, her hairs stuck to your sleeve button.'

'What was she doing near me then?' said Hassan as he waved his arm in the air making me scream more. Darren his side kick laughed. As he always did.

'Hassan you're hurting me,' I almost cried, holding onto his arm so he wouldn't further pull it and tear half my hair out.

'Stop touching me then, you clingy cow.'

'That's it, get him girls,' said Parveen lunging at Hassan and grabbing him by his waist. Ranjita flung into action too, whilst Saira worked on releasing my hair.

When I was finally set free my eyes were tearing and my hair was a complete mess. This wasn't the first time he had pulled my hair. He had a thing for my braid. But where my brother did it as joke in his love for me, Hassan did it to mock me. 'Ding dong,' he'd say as he pulled it. Like my hair was a bell of some sort.

'You ugly bitches stop touching me,' shouted Hassan trying to get away from my friends, who were punching and kicking him, hard.

'I'm coming to your house today to see your new flat and I can't wait to tell your dad about you,' said Saira as she poked Hassan's belly with her pen.

'You know him?' Parveen asked with wide eyes as Darren tried to help him.

'Yes my mum and his mum are best friends unfortunately. I thought he was okay until I saw his true colours at school. I hate you Hassan for being rude to my best friend.'

'Who cares about you or your best friend?' said Hassan pushing her. She fell on the floor and winched.

Whilst Parveen and Ranjita helped her up, they cursed Hassan and Darren as they ran away in giggles. I stood

48

trying to calm myself and sort out my wayward hair, wondering why this boy was ever born. The answer was easy.

To sabotage my happiness.

Chapter Eleven

Tears at dawn…

'Where's Yasmin?'

'Who cares?' said Habib gesturing for me to sit at the front on the seat which had become Yasmin's over the past weeks.

I held a hand to my heart. There was no way I was going to allow my brother to do his usual on Yasmin as well. 'Yesterday she said, 'I'll see you tomorrow,' so what happened?'

'Shut up about her,' said my brother. 'I regret introducing her to you. She's loopy in the head. So do me a favour and forget about her.'

Now I couldn't breathe. I lost the ability to talk. And as Habib drove away from the school, I felt like ripping his hair out because he was the loopy one, not Yasmin.

'What do you want, MacDonald's or KFC?'

'Nothing,' I snapped as the odd October sun shone, blinding me through the glass. I glared back at it. How could it shine when my whole world was spinning in the wrong way?

'You're surely coming down with something because the little sis I know never says no to fast food.'

'I hate you Habib.'

I hated him even more when he laughed, pulled up outside KFC on Cranbrook Road, honked his horn and out came a pretty blond girl with a white cap on her head. Her uniform was too tight around her bust and her hips were wide. I frowned when she leaned over the window giving a full view of her massive boobs, and planted a bag of food between Habib's legs. He winked giving her the money and when the girl took a napkin out of her chest pocket and scribbled a long number on it, my eyes widened.

Habib's lips tilted upwards, and I stared at the girl as she pressed her lips to the napkin and gave it to my brother. She had left a lipstick mark on it.

'Two-ish tomorrow afternoon?' she said in a Russian-ish accent.

Oh my God. I wanted to be dead. This was not happening.

*****

The next day my three loyal friends and I had some serious discussing to do about the wedding and Habib's irrational behaviour towards my sister in law to be.

Imagine, I had only asked Habib when he dropped me to school that morning whether she'd be coming at home time with him, and he had bitten my head off.

'She's never coming,' he said making me the angriest I'd ever been. I wanted to dive into his brain and make him see Yasmin was the best girl for him. I was raging wildly, and forgetting all the lessons I'd learnt in good morals, from both Uncle and the Imam at the Mosque, I shouted 'Fuck' at him.

And I didn't say it once, I shouted it a whole six and a half times, whilst my brother smirked. His smirk made me furious and before I said it the full seventh time I got out of the car and slammed the door shut, leaving him to smirk all he liked.

As I made my way to class I was as red as a burst beetroot. And to make matters worse, when I sat down Hassan wouldn't stop staring at me.

'Why are you looking at me?' I said dropping my head on the table anticipating a horrid reply. Raising both his hands in the air, he shook his head. He was surrendering. At first I had glowered but I couldn't explain why out of all the things I could have done, I actually laughed.

To be fair on him he did look kind of funny.

51

I was giggling as Mr Philpot did the register, and when Hassan answered his name mimicking a girl's voice, I laughed some more.

'Yo Samina,' said Hassan from behind me as I rushed out of registration minutes later. Stopping to look at him, I tried not to laugh. The last thing I wanted was to encourage his idiotic mannerisms.

'I saw you,' he said as he caught up. 'I never knew you had it in you…'

I raised my brow and shook my head. What was he going on about?

Holding my freshly made plait he swung it around my neck whispering, 'I saw you swearing at your dad. Control that anger or it'll get you in trouble one of these days...'

Holding my braid in my hand to stop it swinging, I bit on my bottom lip as my eyes fixed on his twinkling blue ones. Sea blue they were. No sky blue. Dolphin blue. A mix of night time blue, or…

'Ding dong...'

No, his eyes were not special, they were disgusting.

Like him.

*****

'If Yasmin was interested in your brother she would have at least been in touch with you once,' deduced Parveen over our Friday lunch stroke picnic on the school bench outside the canteen.

I opened my bag of ready salted crisps and offered my friends some.

'It makes sense,' said Ranjita taking a handful of my crisps. 'I bet she's interested in somebody else.'

'Don't say that. I'll be heartbroken.'

'Well maybe you can tell your Uncle to go to her house and ask her dad for her hand in marriage for Habib then.'

'That's a great idea Ranjita,' I said popping a smile, seeing a new ray of hope. Uncle would definitely agree.

He was forever praying Habib would settle down. And what could be better than marriage as a means to do so.

*****

Uncle always said, 'Every bad moment is soon followed by a good one.' He was wrong because my moments kept getting worse.

Early Saturday morning I woke up feeling weird. My tummy hurt and a sharp pain forced me to the toilet. There I realised my life would never be the same. In a panic I began to cry. It was horrific. My eyes couldn't even look at it. I swear it was scary stuff. I had no idea what to do and where to go. I couldn't call Uncle and definitely not Habib. I was mortified. I wanted Mummy.

My panic was quick replaced with sadness.

Reluctantly I went into Habib's bedroom where the upstairs phone was kept, to ring Uncle. I had no other choice. However on his bedside cabinet was also his mobile phone. Without a seconds thought I unlocked it, scanned through his contact list and dialled Yasmin's number.

'Hello,' I said helplessly, at the same time guilty for disturbing her sleep. It was four o'clock in the morning.

'Why are you calling me now? Is there anymore left for you to say?'

'It's me,' I said trying to stop myself from crying.

'Who? Oh Meena. My God is Habib okay?'

'Yes he's fine.'

'But sweetie you're crying...' The softness of Yasmin's voice was making me feel better already.

'I need you.'

'You should be asleep. Why are you up?'

'I've got a problem.'

'What problem?'

'I, I have a tummy ache and there's blood...'

Immediately she gasped. 'Oh dear is this the first time?'

'Yes.'

'Don't worry,' she said in such a soothing voice. 'This is normal. Listen do you have any pads or…?' Yasmin paused and then clucked her tongue. 'Of course not, I forgot you're living with a brother who wouldn't know the needs of a girl. Is he home by the way?'

'No he's at the Cabbie. So is Uncle. I'm by myself.'

Sighing she said, 'My parents will kill me if they found out but I'll pop over. Will you be able to open the door for me, in say ten minutes?'

'Yes,' I answered wiping away my tears. I knew I could count on her.

'Great. Until then relax, it happens to us all. Just pray my folks are fast asleep and don't wake up as I sneak out of my flat.'

My heart warmed. She was the best.

*****

'I come bearing yummy hot chocolate,' beamed Yasmin as she came back into my bedroom. She had arrived earlier and her help and presence humbled me and only served to strengthen my wish to have her as my sister in law.

'Drink up,' she smiled giving me my mug as she glanced at the alarm clock. 'Oh is that the time? Your brother comes home around five, doesn't he?'

'Yes and please don't tell him about this. I'll die if he found out.'

'You need to tell him,' she said. 'As much as he is a pain sometimes, I know Habib is a very loving brother to you. He loves you more than life itself and I admire him for it...'

'Enough to marry him and to become my sister in law and live with us in this house forever?' I said in one breath.

Yasmin held a hand to her chest and stood up.

'What's wrong?' I said slipping out of my bed.

She shook her head and the whites of her eyes became a shade of red. 'Listen I think you're all good now,' she said smiling with difficulty. 'I've left two packets of sanitary towels for you in that bag and there's one in the bathroom closet. Just keep changing yourself regularly and if the pains get worse, I suppose you can have some Calpol. You're good because you've got two days to rest at home without school being a bother. Take a few in your bag to change during break times anyway.'

'Why are you upset?' I placed a hand on her arm. 'I'm sorry I woke you in the night. You were the only one I could tell. Are you scared your parents will know you were out at night without telling them?'

Cupping my cheeks in her palms she said, 'You're an innocent girl Meena and I know you are too young to understand me but Sweetie, always remember this one advice, when in the future you think you've found the one, don't trust him right away okay. Sometimes it's wise for us silly girls to save our dignity and...'

She removed her hands from my face and pulling me close to her chest, she began to cry. And because she was crying, I started to cry too, even though I didn't truthfully understand why?

'Oh Meena, I want nothing more than to be Habib's wife. But he doesn't like me. I went against everything and everyone for your brother...'

'What do you mean?' I said pressed against her motherly embrace as her sadness shook her body.

'Girls in our culture and religion, Pakistani girls, Muslim girls rather, they don't go out with boys Meena. I've been extremely wrong to spend all this time with him. If my parents find out, they won't be happy.'

Gulping I asked, 'So why did you go out with him if you knew it was wrong?'

'I don't know how it happened. Maybe my silly heart forced me,' she said releasing me and sitting on my bed. I sat beside her. 'When you fall in love, your heart won't listen to logic, or right or wrong. Regardless of the rules you're bound by, it finds a way of escaping. The same happened to me, I guess.'

'Do you really love my brother that much, to disobey your parents and your religion?'

'I know it's wrong, and it's why I'm hurting,' she said nodding her head.

I bit my lips and she got up and paced my room with both her hands on her head.

'Look at me being an emotional wreck in front of you.'

'Please don't be mad at Habib. I'm sure with a little sorting out from my Uncle, he'll be a perfect husband to you.'

'Oh Meena,' she said turning to look at me. I felt awful, her eyes were so red. 'I wish I could explain. Let's just say I'm waiting for Habib to grow up...'

I felt bad for her. My brother didn't love her. Every time I mentioned her name, he would blast my head off.

'Can I tell him you came? To let him know how much you love him. He'll marry you right away, I promise.'

'No. I don't want him to feel I'm using you to get close to him,' she said wiping at her eyes. 'I came here because I don't like the fact you're always on your own. If for an hour or so I brought some ease to you, helped you out, it makes me happy.'

'I think of you as my big sister,' I told her truthfully.

'You are too kind.'

And as Yasmin gathered her things and hugged me goodbye, I was determined I wouldn't give up. I would make Habib love her back if it was the last thing I did.

He'd have to marry her. End of.

Chapter Twelve

Mission: Getting home.

Habib was mad at me. Whenever I tried speaking about Yasmin, he didn't like my interfering. And despite knowing full well I was suffering from the dreaded periods, he didn't care to listen to me, even once.

How Uncle and Habib had come to find out in the first place was beyond me. Maybe the pack of sanitary towels in the bathroom cabinet had given my game up. What had followed were two open mouths belonging to two speechless men.

Thank God for Yasmin.

A whole week had passed since, and it was Friday home time again. I was waiting outside the school gates looking at each passing car. Habib had always managed to get here on time before. I wondered why he was late. Walking further up, I checked both sides of the road. It was about thirty minutes since the buzzer had sounded and the streets were clear of the school run cars. Sighing I went back inside the school, hoping he'd taken the car inside.

I searched the whole car park. He wasn't there either.

I shivered at the uncomfortable breeze blowing against my ears. The school didn't look right without the usual hustle of children. The teachers weren't coming out of the gates either anymore. If only I'd had a mobile phone. All the other kids had one. But Uncle disapproved and hadn't allowed me one for my last birthday, saying it would come in the way of my studies.

On the verge of crying, I decided to walk home by myself. I knew becoming a woman would have these side effects. Habib probably thought I was a grown woman and didn't need him anymore. Well I would show him…

'Boo!'

'Oh my God Habib,' I jumped.

'It's me you idiot.'

'You scared me,' I said coming face to face with my tormentor.

'What are you still doing here?' he asked. 'You're alone?'

Ignoring Hassan's questions I looked over his shoulder at a black car coming down the road. But as soon as the car neared, my heart crawled back inside my chest.

'Samina…?'

'My brother hasn't come to pick me up yet.'

'Oh, so why are you crying?'

'I'm not crying,' I lied.

'I'm not blind Samina.' He flicked a tear from my cheek with the pad of his thumb. His tongue was poking out from the corner of his lips and his eyes were shining dark blue. My eyes watered, he would do something horrid to me I knew it.

'Don't cry,' he said softly, surprising me. 'I'll walk you home.'

'What if he turns up and I'm not here?'

'Let's go to the office and tell Mrs Brown to phone your mum then.'

I should have done this already. Waiting for Habib out here and watching every passing car with hope, the thought of going to the office hadn't even crossed my mind.

'Or have you heard of a phone?' said Hassan as he pulled one out of his bag. 'It's something which looks like this.'

I bit my lip and watched him press some buttons on the fancy looking phone.

'Who are you calling?'

'My sister, she was supposed to be here to take me to my kick boxing club.'

'You kick box?' I asked wiping all remnants of tears, as he made impatient faces waiting for whoever he was calling to pick up.

'Yeah, how else would I be so strong?' he said showing me an imaginary muscle on his bicep. I smiled a little and Hassan decided to phone his mum, as his sister didn't answer his call.

'Mum… No, she's not here. One hour's detention for P.E. I told her twenty times,' he yelled. 'You need to sort her depressing problems quick time. Okay, okay, I'm sorry. Okay bye.'

'What?' he snapped glaring at me as I stared at him holding his phone out to me. 'Do you know his number?'

'Whose number?'

'Your brother's of course.'

'You want me to phone him?'

'Girls, you're all the same,' he said, waving his hands in the air. 'Just call him will you, I need to rush to my club. I don't have my water bottle or any money because of my dumb sister.'

I gulped but dialled the Cabbie's number. On the first ring the phone went blank.

'Shit the battery died,' said Hassan snatching the phone from me.

I bit my lips harder. It was dark now.

Hassan picked up my school bag from the floor. 'Don't worry I'll take you home first. I bet your brother will be in trouble for ditching you. My sister will be too. My Dad's going to kill her tonight.'

Hassan started to laugh at the thought of his sister getting in trouble but how was I to tell him, my brother was both my mum and my dad?

'What is it now?' said Hassan giving me my bag. 'Alright I'll wait here with you then. Just don't worry okay.'

'Don't you have to be at your club?' I whispered touched by his offer. In fact for the first time, I was glad he was here.

'I do but I'd lose my sleep if something bad happened to you if I left you alone, isn't it?' he said. 'And I kind of love my sleep.'

I smiled whilst debating my options.

'Come on Samina tell me where you live?' he said. 'I hope it's not in the North Pole.'

He was trying to make me feel better and I must admit he was succeeding. 'Ilford Lane.'

'No way, I live there too.'

'Really…?'

'We moved here recently,' he said as we began to walk. 'It's a right dump compared to my old house in Manor Park.'

'I like it. We also have an office on Ilford Lane.'

'Yeah and us. And my dad decided to move us in the flat above it so he could put our old house on rent. He's such a loser,' said Hassan with a roll of his eyes. 'Ilford Lane has rats everywhere.'

'I can't believe you called your dad a loser.'

'He is one. He's always angry these days and has gone to Manchester to fix my sister up. He wants her to get married to some poor guy there.'

'Fix her up, why what's broken of hers?'

Hassan pushed my arm as he laughed. 'You're funny as well as stupid.'

'And you're mean,' I grimaced rubbing my arm.

'Mean? I don't see anyone else helping you out in your time of need.'

'Yeah don't remind me,' I mumbled as I began to skip to keep up with his hurried steps. 'At least slow down.'

'Why missing me, are we?' he said wiggling his brows.

'Yes in fact I am,' I countered sarcastically.

'Aw you should have said Sweetheart,' he said in a really teasing tone as his eyes glittered like a cat's would in the dimness of the evening. 'Come hold my hand. Promise I'll stay real close so you won't have to miss me ever.'

'Ha ha funny.'

'I always keep my promises,' he said as he stopped so I could catch up with him. I took a step back though when he held out his hand, which of course I wasn't going to hold.

'Suit yourself then...'

'Hey I never saw them,' I said not noticing the half packet of Starburst sweets he was offering to me on that hand.

'Too late,' he said. My smile dropped. 'Only kidding.'

My smile returned and I took the sweets.

'They're my favourite.'

'Mine too,' I said as I stuffed two in my mouth and I was impressed when Hassan stuffed five different flavours into his mouth. All in one go.

*****

'Which part of Ilford Lane do you live at?' said Hassan once we turned into Mortlake Road.

'Barking end, near the Mosque.'

'I live in the busy part where all the shops are. I normally take a left from here,' he said pointing towards a side road. 'But we can walk this way to get to your house first. Do you live upstairs your shop too?'

'No we live in a separate house. Our shop is really a minicab office. It's on the Ilford end too.'

'Lucky you don't have to be in a flat above it,' he snorted. 'My moron dad has so many houses but had to dump us in a flat.'

I frowned. 'Are you ever nice to anyone? Stop calling your dad names. It's rude.'

Hassan grinned as he reached to pull my plait but I moved away in time. 'He isn't really a moron. And Samina I am being nice to you. I'm taking you home. I gave you my sweets and I'm probably going to be late for kick boxing.'

'Thank you. I like this nicer Hassan much better than the horrid Hassan I see at school every day.'

'Well I like both Hassans,' he said as he took off.

'Hassan you promised,' I reminded him when he ran too far ahead.

'I am keeping my promise, you cry baby.'

'I'm not a cry baby,' I shouted hurrying my steps towards him.

'Really?'

'Yes,' I said freaking out a little as I ran. Mortlake Road was scary and dark compared to Ilford Lane. This was a perk of living on a busy street like Ilford Lane. It was always packed and bright, even during night times.

'Last one to the end of the road is the world's fattest pig,' said Hassan as I almost caught up with him. 'Hurry up fatso.'

'Hassan Iqmal one of these days I'm going to kill you,' I said breathlessly.

A few times I did manage to catch up and laugh, as we gave each other a light shove. Soon this game of run and catch became fun, and we ran all the way down the road.

'I won,' I said completely out of breath when I stopped seconds before him on Ilford Lane. Hassan was equally out of breath and I gave him my water bottle from which he drank thirstily.

'My house is that one, the corner one,' I told him pointing at the end terrace across the road.

'I'll come and play knock and run for sure now. Darren lives near here too. It'll be fun.' Hassan's whole face lit up in anticipation of the mischief. 'So watch out Samina, you kameena…'

'Hey that's an Urdu word,' I scowled knowing it didn't have a nice meaning.

'Yeah and it suits you.'

'You're so mean. Anyway is your shop on this side of the road or that?'

'That,' he said pointing to the other side and when he said, 'Let's walk to the zebra crossing together,' he had taken the words right out of my mouth.

I couldn't help it and grabbed hold of Hassan's arm as we crossed the main road. When we were across he called me a, 'chicken.' I decided to let it go. He had called me many things which were far worse and I was still alive.

'Go straight home Samina, your mum's probably waiting.'

I shook my head and was about to enlighten him that only Uncle or Habib waited for me but he had already moved on in the opposite direction of Ilford Lane.

'Bye,' I shouted.

He turned and gave me a mischievous smile holding up my water bottle, 'Thanks for this and see you on Monday Samina kameena.'

'Go safely,' I whispered wishing him well despite the horrid name he called me. And believe it or not this was the first time when I felt Hassan wasn't all that bad after all.

He was quite lovely.

Chapter Thirteen

The great fire of Ilford Lane…

It definitely wasn't my evening. Normally Jessica's mother would've always kept a spare key to our house for emergencies at her place. But now with them gone and the key returned, I was stranded.

Habib would get it real bad from Uncle.

With this thought, I began to stomp back up Ilford Lane towards the Cabbie. I was fuming and my stomach was growling. Carrying my tired feet onwards, in what was an extremely dark hour for me despite it only being five o'clock; I marched until I stood on the opposite side of the office, staring at it.

I had to cross the main road. A hurdle I'd never managed to do on my own since my father's death. However thanks to the slow approaching car in the safe distant, and a man carrying heavy shopping bags from his spree at the Indian supermarket, I took my chance and discretely held onto one of his bags in order to cross with him.

Desperate times…

Safely across though and thanking the man in my heart, I rushed to the Cabbie.

The bell at the door which always pinged and ponged whenever someone opened it, pinged and ponged, and ignoring Uncle Ilyas lounging on the settee in the waiting room, I barged behind the glass cubicle and shouted, 'You forgot about me.'

'Beti…?'

'Habib didn't come to get me. No one was home. I was scared crossing the road and, and...' I couldn't speak no more. Crying was easier.

It took a few seconds for Uncle to process this information before he stood up from his swirly chair. 'You walked home alone?'

Looking up at him, I said, 'After waiting hours outside school I walked home with Hassan. But when I got home no one was there to let me in.'

'Hassan, who Hassan?' asked Uncle cupping my face.

'He's in my class. He said he'll walk with me because I was scared.'

Uncle stared at me weirdly, so I shouted, 'It was dark outside and I was scared. I'm still scared. Look I'm shaking all over.'

I was.

I pushed his hands away and plumped myself on his chair. 'I'm hungry,' I sobbed.

'Habib,' roared Uncle into his mobile phone making me look up. His face was red and his forehead had a hundred creases. 'No she's here you irresponsible boy. Yes she's very happy. No you buffoon she came in crying. Where are you?'

I was still crying when Uncle threw his phone on the counter.

'The stupid boy is stuck in traffic,' said Uncle shaking his head. 'Whatever he's up to these days is beyond me. Last night he disappeared leaving me on my own after that shameless girl came in asking about him, and today he forgets his own sister. Tomorrow he'll forget me and this business altogether and Ya Allah…'

'I'm hungry,' I said not interested in a speech.

Uncle shook his head again as he pulled out a few pound coins from his pocket. 'Go get what you want,' he said. 'And stop shouting.'

'No,' I yelled. I was too angry to go to the Dixy shop next door to buy my own food. Normally I'd be there in a flash. Munna who worked there was a Bengali immigrant and he always gave me extra chips and free sauce. Apparently I reminded him of his little sister in Dhaka. He used to work for the Cabbie once but stopped when Uncle found out his licence was a fake. My Uncle was a man of rules. He made certain his drivers were all legitimate.

Reputation and honour was something my Uncle lived for.

'My beautiful beti is angry?'

I huffed and looked the other way.

'Oye Ilyas,' said Uncle as a grin began to appear on his familiar features. 'Jaa eik chicken burger aur chips to leh aa yaar, with Fanta.'

'No Strawberry Miranda,' I said wiping any signs of tears away. In fact on the thought of getting some proper food, I managed a small smile as my Uncle gave orders to Uncle Ilyas, a driver and good friend of his, to get me my meal.

'Not good for you,' growled Uncle Ilyas through the glass separating us. He always made me laugh.

I roared back like a lion. He hated fast food but went to get it for me nonetheless.

*****

'Where is she?' said Habib as he rushed into the cubicle where Uncle was on the phone to a customer and I half asleep with my head resting on the counter.

Uncle hissed, 'Shut up,' and pointed to me.

'Where were you?' I shouted pushing him away when he came near.

'Samina,' sissed Uncle impatiently, 'I can't hear the nice lady. Sorry did you say Romford Greyhounds?'

Rolling my eyes at Uncle and his boring job, I stomped into the back room. Habib followed.

'I lost track of time. I can't believe I forgot.'

I shrugged pretending not to care.

'You got home alright, didn't you Baby?'

However before I could blow his head off with my grievance, a loud commotion coming from outside had us both hurrying out to where Uncle was.

66

'It's a fire,' said one of the drivers stood by the door looking outside.

I gripped onto Habib's hand, momentarily forgetting my upset with him.

'A fire, where?' said Habib with tense brows. The grip on our hands tightened as we both stepped outside onto the pavement.

'Further down the road,' said Uncle as sirens began to scream in the near distance.

There was an awful lot of smoke and I could smell the odour in the air. In a matter of seconds, I could even see the disaster.

'Habib it's getting bigger.'

Swirls of red and orange had begun painting the dark horizon in an art I didn't find attractive. The vicious sounds the fire was causing were deafening and the fiercest I'd ever heard. Despite it being further down the road, the recently arrived rescue workers pushed everybody away. There was a crowd of spectators.

As Uncle said, 'It's quite serious,' Habib let go of my hand and saying he would be back in a second, ran towards the source ignoring Uncle calling him back.

Sensing my discomfort over this, Uncle pulled me against him and stroked my hair. 'Don't worry they'll have it under control soon.'

'Habib?' I whispered because although my brother was a grown man, he too could get overwhelmed when Ilford Lane witnessed scenes resembling the images from our past.

Firemen were everywhere, as were the police and paramedics. I kept hold of Uncle's hand and tried not to freak out. I mean I was eleven and all woman now. What I saw when I was six, shouldn't have really bothered me.

But it did.

These people, this crowd of shop owners and late shoppers and residents and passers-by who were gasping and sighing, both sombre and surprised, resembled the crowd which had stared at us, on this same street a year after Habib and I had lost Mummy.

Dad had promised Mummy he would look after us forever. Yet that day when that stupid car ran into him, he left us too. Just like that.

Without even a goodbye.

The rescuers later had to take Habib and me out of our own car, from where we had witnessed our father smiling one moment and the next being plunged away to his death. He had only gone to buy us ice cream from across the road.

The same road I was too scared to cross on my own, till this day.

A woman wearing a green uniform had carried me on her lap as she had tried making me talk. But I was numb because I knew Dad had gone. I could see blood on his face and blood all over his clothes. He was lying in an awkward position in the middle of the road.

Lifeless.

Habib wasn't numb though. He was shouting, banging, kicking and punching. And when the loud sirens and the chaos around us overpowered any emotions he had left, my brother too had numbed.

We were orphaned.

'Beti,' said Uncle wakening me. 'It's okay,' he reassured. 'The fire men have it under control.'

I hoped so. Because I didn't think I could deal with more tragedies on this street.

Chapter Fourteen

When tender hearts crack…

Having woken after midday the following day to the smell of eggs being prepared downstairs, I dragged myself out of bed and began getting ready. After the fire was tamed and the road re-opened for traffic and pedestrians, Uncle had brought me home because I was pretty shaken up. Although he had stayed at home with me, I hadn't stopped worrying.

Habib didn't return to the Cabbie. No one knew where he was.

Mehmet his friend, who'd come in early to take over from Uncle, had said something about a girl being trapped in the fire. Apparently he'd seen her being pulled out by the firemen and being rushed away in an ambulance. I hoped she was okay.

As I made my way down the stairs, I could hear Habib's voice. He was home. A smile graced my lips as I hurried my steps towards the kitchen.

'Don't ever mention her to Samina…'

I paused upon hearing Uncle say my name.

'And don't tell anybody it was you who the girl darkened her honour with either. She wasn't as good as she made out to be. What she did with you was un-Islamic and wrong and as much as I'm disappointed in you for taking advantage of this, she should've known better. You need to look at this incident as a wakeup call. Turn to Allah my son. Ask for forgiveness. Be an example for your sister. Imagine if our Samina did what the girl did with a boy we didn't know. Imagine the dishonour. Imagine our...'

'Samina would never,' said Habib with a voice laced with fury.

I stepped into the kitchen. 'What would I never?' I asked frowning. 'And why is your hair so messy?' As Habib ran a hand over his head, I wondered why his shirt was creased and his eyes swollen and red.

'Good, you're awake for some hot brunch,' said Uncle, ignoring both my questions. 'Sit down.'

I sat down next to Habib and scowled when he reached over and kissed my temple tightly. I pulled away but he pulled me back by cupping my head tightly in his hands. He brought my face close to his and stared me out, making me look back at him with knotted brows.

'Listen to me,' he said. 'Whenever a boy tries getting near you, you think of me and what I'm about to say and I swear Samina you'll know what I meant, and you'll think twice about your actions.' My brother's eyes darkened. 'Decent Muslim girls don't hang out with boys and they certainly don't go anywhere with them.'

I gulped, afraid and a little guilty for coming home with Hassan the day before. It never crossed my mind he was a boy, and in my religion it wasn't allowed for me to be with him since he wasn't family.

'You weren't coming that's why I walked home with Hassan. I was scared,' I whispered in my defence.

'What, who's Hassan?' said Habib releasing his grip on my head.

'The boy in my class who's always nicking my stuff. He had a detention and when he saw me waiting for you he said, he'll walk me home because he lives on Ilford Lane as well.' And because Habib's eyebrows creased more, I added, 'Promise he's not my boyfriend. I don't love him.'

'No. Oh God, I know,' said Habib as he shook his head looking tired with drooping eyes. 'Not about that. This isn't about yesterday. I meant in general. When you're older. Don't break my trust, that's all.'

'I won't,' I said awkwardly as Uncle sat across us. He too looked pretty serious. There wasn't a trace of a smile on either of their faces.

'Good now make your brother another promise.' Habib held my pinkie finger in his but he wasn't playing nor was he in a joking mood. I glanced at Uncle and his expression was just as hard.

'Promise me you will never tell anybody about Yasmin and me. Promise me you'll forget about her.'

'Why?' I said as I looked at Uncle.

'Because no one should know she spent time with a boy. With Habib. It will hurt her family,' answered Uncle pushing a plate of food towards me. 'They'll be disappointed in her and it isn't nice for them to find out now, so it's best we kept his involvement in their daughter's life a secret.'

'But she's going to marry Habib,' I said wondering how Uncle had found out about this. 'She told me she loves him.'

'Stop this talk,' shouted Uncle making the cutlery rattle, as he tapped his fist on the table. 'You are too young to be speaking such terms. Boyfriends. Girlfriends. Love. What is this?'

Uncle's coldness irritated me and I pushed the plate of food away. I turned to Habib. 'She's willing to fight to be with you. Her parents will find out eventually.'

My brother closed his eyes tightly as he gripped the back of his neck.

'She told me she loves you.'

'Samina!'

I stood up scraping the chair on the tiled floor, hurting my own ears.

'Sit back down and eat the food.'

'No. Make Habib marry Yasmin first,' I shouted back. What was it with these two shouting at me all the time?

'I warned you didn't I?' yelled Uncle pointing his index finger at Habib. 'I warned you to keep my beti away from your antics. How come I never knew this girl was close to her? Have you been teaching your sister to hide things from me?'

Before I could get in more trouble, I ran out of the kitchen and into the living room, glad the telephone chose the exact moment to ring. I rushed to pick it up.

'Hi, it's Ranjita.'

I replied a greeting back and plopped onto the sofa, still annoyed.

'Did you see the fire last night?' she exclaimed. 'It was ginormous. I could see it from my window, and my dad said it was near your Cabbie. It didn't burn down did it? I was well worried for you lot.'

'We're alright. Our Cabbie didn't burn down,' I reassured her. 'It was the new estate agents and the florist further down the road.'

'Yeah Saira told me. She was crying when I phoned her. I couldn't believe it though.'

'Wait a sec, why was Saira crying?' I said as Habib entered the living room and sat beside me. I shifted a little away from him. He made me so mad.

'Oh my God Sammy,' said Ranjita. 'Didn't you know it was Hassan's flat which caught fire and his poor sister died in it? Because Saira's family are close friends with them, she told me as soon as it happened.'

'And Hassan…?' I managed to ask as my grip on the phone tightened, despite my fingers which began to be pricked with pins and needle like sensations.

'Oh unlucky for us Hassan didn't die. He wasn't even home when it happened. Only his sister died…'

The phone fell from my hand and because Habib was sitting near, I dropped my head onto his lap, and seriously I tried not to but I couldn't help it. My breathing became harsher and my eyes began to flood. Though I was small when my parents died, I knew from experience the heartache Hassan would be going through. How would he overcome the loneliness which comes when someone you love leaves you and there's no chance of them returning?

'What's wrong?'

I couldn't reply.

'What did you say to her?' said Habib to Ranjita, who was still on the phone. 'Hassan's sister…?'

I looked up despite my anxiety.

'Oh Yasmin…' my brother whispered in a shaky voice whilst putting the phone down and holding me.

'I want to speak to her,' I said. She'd make me feel better. She and I were special like that and perhaps she could accompany me to lay some flowers for Hassan's sister.

'You can't,' said Habib as his eyes watered and his voice broke. 'She's gone.' His red eyes moved from me to the skin he was known to peel on his thumbs when troubled. 'She won't be coming back,' he cried.

'Why?'

'I'm sorry.'

'Why?' And because Habib wasn't looking me in the eye anymore, I knew he had hurt her and made her go away. I got off the sofa and pushed him against it. 'I'm telling Uncle all about her and he'll make you marry her tomorrow, just you watch,' I shouted.

But Uncle was already standing in the room watching with a blank expression and when I tugged at his arm demanding him to tell Habib to get Yasmin back, Uncle remained silent. However Habib's next words opened up doors to a place where I'd thought I would never be going again.

'She's dead Samina. She's the girl who died in the fire.'

'No,' I said as a fear engulfed me making my breathing difficult to manage. 'Hassan's sister died, not our Yasmin…'

'Baby Yasmin was Hassan's sister.'

'No,' was all I could whisper.

And the door which had been closed for many years opened and sucked me right inside it.

Chapter Fifteen

Shades of grief...

Dr Patel said I would snap out of it in my own time.

'It happens,' he had said. 'Dealing with bereavement is different for everybody and with what Samina went through when she lost her parents, we don't want her relapsing into the nightmares and illness she experienced then now.'

Doctor Patel was afraid. Little did he know, I was already seeing those nightmares. When Dad died I would see his body being flown into the air. I would see his bloodied face and I would hear my brother's cries all around me. I had spent weeks, maybe months in silence then, watching the scenes from the disaster replaying over and over. And the nightmares would always follow a splitting headache.

Although I couldn't remember much of this, Uncle had told Dr Patel my ailments and confirmed I was having the same now. My head was constantly throbbing and my silence was haunting.

I was sat by the dining table in the kitchen and Uncle was trying to get me to eat my lunch.

'Beti,' he said, gently like a feather. 'Please eat something.'

When I didn't reply Uncle fed me. Something he'd been doing for days. He had made pilau rice, one of my favourites, which he'd been making almost every day since. I didn't like it anymore.

Nothing was nice.

'You need to go back to school. It's been three weeks. You'll lag behind from the rest of your classmates,' said Uncle as he rubbed his forehead.

I wouldn't allow him to go to work. I was following him like a shadow. I panicked if he as much as left the room to go to the toilet.

'Both Habib and I are worried beti.'

I knew Habib was worried. He had come into my room the previous night and had taken Mummy's photograph out of my special box. He had stared at it the way I often did. And when I woke up in the morning he was asleep on my bed, still wearing his coat and trainers. The photograph resting on his chest.

'This isn't healthy. You need to talk about this. That girl, Iqmal's daughter, let her out of your mind now. She's gone. You have us. We are your family. Why are you…?'

I didn't let him finish. I got up from the table and walked away.

*****

The third week arrived and so did a worried looking Aunty Asma from Blackpool. All three of her children and her husband also came. Normally I would have been happy to see them but this time, I wasn't.

During this visit Aunty Asma rearranged my bedroom. She bought furniture and a new set of curtains and bedding. It was a grown up theme, blue and yellow stripes. She made her sons Faisal and Faizaan, paint the walls in matching colours and she even changed the carpeted floor to a new laminated one. According to her, my purple pony stuff was babyish.

I let her do the changes. Who cared anyway?

However six days into her visit, she forced me to dress up in a new outfit she'd bought from down the road. Apparently there was a surprise for me, a surprise which would make me feel better again.

Nothing could make me feel better.

*****

Dressed in the itchy, blue shalwar kameez underneath my winter puffer jacket, in ant like steps I walked next to Aunty Asma as she led me and Farah her daughter, towards the Mosque. Some relatives of ours were waiting outside it, freezing to death.

Habib was there too. He had shaved and combed his hair and was looking his normal self. Faisal was standing next to him and they were laughing. When Habib saw me he came over and took my cold hand in his warmer one.

'You okay Baby?'

I looked at everybody. Why were they gathered here?

'Come on, let's go inside,' said Uncle Murad, Aunty Asma's husband.

As I spotted Uncle, I relaxed a little. Letting go of Habib's hand, I slowly went and held Uncle's hand instead.

He looked handsome dressed in a brand new black suit with a satin trim on the collars. His hair was gelled back nicely and I thought Faizaan may have helped him with it. Because Uncle never used gel, only Jasmine oil.

'Beti, this I am doing for you,' he said kissing my hand. 'I want you to get well. If bringing this mother home for you is going to make you happy again, then I will do it.'

'Mother...?' I said. The word hurting my throat as it made its way out.

Uncle beamed down at me and dropped my hand to cup both sides of my face. 'Yes a mother. For you. For your happiness.'

I stared into his eyes. A mother. For my happiness.

'Are you okay about this beti?' he said with a smile so wide. 'We still have time to run away. Your Aunty Asma can be pushy sometimes and she has me convinced this marriage will be best for our little family.'

I looked at Habib. When he smiled, I too somehow managed to break into a small smile of my own.

'You look pretty like this,' said Uncle leaning down to kiss my cheek. 'I wish I had done this before. But I was always afraid a new mother wouldn't love you like I do. I was selfish to think I'd be able to care for you and raise you on my own. Beti you made me realise what a fool I was. I should've married and brought home a mum for you many years ago.'

'Jawed,' came Auntie's voice from the entrance. 'Come on in, the Imam is waiting.'

'Should I do this?' said Uncle releasing my face and untying the scarf around my neck. He began to wrap it over my head to cover my hair, something girls were supposed to do to before entering a Mosque.

I managed a nod and with my hand in Uncle's, went inside the Mosque.

Chapter Sixteen

Along the path of recovery…

She wasn't as pretty as Yasmin or Mummy was. Her nose was slightly pointed and her lips were super thin and her eyes were narrow. I overheard Aunty Asma telling an elderly aunt she had sharp features and men liked those in women.

Bushra. Her name was Bushra.

She was Aunty Asma's husband's long distant cousin, who'd arrived in the country only recently. Her nails were long and painted in shiny red polish and her hair was a brown, chestnut colour. I think it was dyed and she was fair. When she stood up after the Nikka had been conducted, I noticed her height was quite small compared to Uncle's.

I was sitting on my own when the woman, Bushra, came and extended her henna tattooed hands to me. Her bangles jingled along her wrists and her clothes were glistening under the beams from the many chandeliers in the room.

'Samina, am I right?' she said as her thin lips tilted upwards and her heavily made up eyes looked at me.

I gave a shy nod and flinched a little when she cupped my hand and kissed my forehead. She wore too much perfume. Looking away from her, I searched for Uncle, and released a long held breath when he was approaching us.

'Ah Bushra this is her. This is my princess,' said Uncle as he released my hand from hers and intertwined it in his familiar one. 'This is my daughter, my special girl.'

'She is beautiful Mash-Allah,' replied Bushra showing me her teeth as she tilted my chin to look at me properly.

'That she is. In my life these two kids mean everything to me.'

'I shall bear that in mind,' said Bushra as she blinked her lashes.

Uncle cleared his throat and Bushra looked up at him smiling bigger. Uncle murmured something and took small steps towards her. I followed closely beside him. The sides of my head were beginning to throb again. My hand dropped to my side.

'Uncle,' I said holding my hand up for him, but before he could take it again, Bushra had already placed hers in his.

*****

We were on our way to the restaurant in Seven Kings where the wedding reception was to be hosted. I wanted to be in my bed. Faisal, Faizaan and Farah were travelling with us and their silly antics were annoying me.

'So little Sammy girl,' said Faizaan. 'What do you think of our new Aunty?'

I shrugged, I didn't know her. She was a stranger to me.

'She's alright you know,' chirped Farah not looking away from her mobile phone.

Habib looked over his shoulder. 'You feeling okay?'

I didn't reply but stared out of the window.

*****

'We'll join you in a tick,' Habib told my cousins as he grabbed my wrist stopping me from following them into the restaurant.

I watched my cousins disappear.

'Get back inside the car.'

I opened the back door and when Habib got in next to me, I had to scoot away from him.

'You're angry I know that but how long are you planning to keep this up?' he said with tight lips. 'I've apologised to you. I've killed myself over and over about what happened but it's time to move on.'

I pursed my lips.

'Everyone's worried about you. Uncle even got married for your sake. I know you're hurting, but you need to understand she's gone. You need to move on.'

My eyes watered.

'This wedding is happening so you can get better although I don't see you looking happy. You're only eleven for crying out loud. You need to get out of this. Be a child again and let me do the worrying. When you don't look at me and never want to talk...' He closed his eyes taking a harsh breath in. 'Come here.'

I pushed him away. And without thinking, I opened the door, got out of the car and ran.

'Stop!'

Ignoring his command I kept running until the sound of a loud horn honking and the screech of rubber alerted me of where I was.

'Fucking control your kid you arsehole,' came the driver's startled yet aggressive voice.

I trembled at his words, and the horrible face he was making scared me. In a panic, I ran back to Habib who was halfway on the road himself.

'Don't have them if you can't control them...'

'Just fuck off,' Habib shouted back as he hurried me off the road, ignoring the abuse the driver was still yelling at him.

Once safely on the pavement Habib pushed me against a wall. 'You idiot, you silly idiot,' he spat. His face was red and sweaty and his eyes were wet and his body was shaking. 'You stupid girl...' His fingers gripped my arms tightly and he shook me. 'Why did you do that?' he shouted. 'Do you know what I was going through when you ran onto that road? Do you have any idea how I'm feeling right now? Do you?'

His eyes were dropping tears at high speeds as he shook me like I was a lifeless rag doll. But I wasn't lifeless. Finally I could feel something other than self-pity and anger towards him.

'Habib,' I cried and as soon as his name left my mouth, a whirlwind of emotion forced me to trap myself against my brother. I couldn't even breathe because my cries were that severe.

'Never do that again,' said Habib as he kissed my head holding me close. 'I won't be able to cope if anything happened to you too. I regret ever bringing her with me to pick you up from school that day. Everybody we love just leave us don't they…?'

I cried more when I understood the depth of his words. He was hurting too. I pulled away to look into his eyes and all I could see were the many shades of grief he'd hidden behind his hazel disguises so well.

'You're all I have,' said Habib as he pulled me against him again. 'We'll get through this together like we always do. Believe me Baby, I miss Yasmin too. I wish I could bring her back but you know I can't do that. If I could, we'd have our Mummy, and Dad, and Yasmin, all of them with us. That day when I didn't come to school to get you, I spent the day at our parent's graveside trying to come to terms with stuff Yasmin had told me the night before. I then went to see her. I told her I was going to send Uncle to her Dad to ask for her hand in marriage, but within an hour of her going home, this disaster happened. I wish I'd kept her away from home for longer,' cried Habib like a helpless child. 'I hope you can forgive me. And I hope she will too...'

'You loved her?' I asked and when he confirmed he did with a nod of his head, I felt a burden being eased. 'She loved you too,' I said as I wiped at my tears.

'I know but she won't be at peace until you get better. If not for my sake for hers get over this. I can't bear to see you like this anymore. I want you to go to school on

Monday without a fuss and I want you to be you again. I want my Baby back.'

He returned my watery smile with a dimpled one. I reached for his hand. Hearing his confession brought a peace to my young heart. My Yasmin died with the knowledge my brother loved her. Her anxieties about him not loving her had been removed by him. She died as my brother's soon to be wife. She died happy.

This made me smile.

Chapter Seventeen

The gap in the garden fence…

Uncle was reluctant to go but Aunty Asma had convinced him I'd be okay whilst he went on a honeymoon around Scotland for a few days. They couldn't go anywhere else like Venice, or the Seychelles, because Aunty Bushra had restrictions on her Visa and couldn't leave the country.

When Uncle had initially refused the trip, I'd been proud of him. But Aunty Asma as much as I adored her, could be a right pain at times. She packed Uncle's bag, helped Aunty Bushra with her makeup, and set them off right after breakfast.

The house seemed too quiet. Habib was asleep after his night shift and Aunty Asma's family had returned to Blackpool. Aunty Asma remained to look after me. She was watching an Indian serial on the Star Plus channel, and I was bored. I needed something to do.

'It's raining.' Aunty Asma shifted her attention from the television and glowered at the windows. 'It's the third time I've brought the washing in.'

'I'll go,' I said hurrying out of the room before she did. The prospect of getting drenched in the rain was something exciting to do.

'Wear your coat then. I don't want Jawed complaining I didn't take care of you in his absence.'

At her request I pulled my coat from the hook in the landing and clumsily weaved my arms through it. I rushed into the kitchen to let myself out of the back doors and relished in the light drizzle falling on my head.

I busied myself in my chore by aiming and throwing the wet clothes from the rotary line inside the house, hoping for them to land on the dining table. But a loud noise of something smashing made me look over my shoulder. The sound came from a neighbour's house, and was followed by a woman's shouts. This particular house, the one our garden was directly connected to, and separated by a flimsy fence, had been empty for weeks. Maybe somebody had moved in.

The voices got louder. It sounded like a child was getting told off. And I decided to do the neighbourly thing and poke my nose through the gap, which Jessica and I had purposely made in the fence in order to trespass easily to get our balls back.

The woman's voice which I assumed belonged to the mum, was asking the child to come back inside the house.

'Just leave me alone…'

I flinched at the child's aggressive response. The slam of a door made me quickly step back inside my own garden. From behind me though, I heard a football being kicked against a wall. Then cries...

'Why did you have to die?'

I stopped in the middle of my garden. I knew that voice.

My slippers dug into the wet tarmac as my toes curled inside them. My eyes closed tightly, as did my lips. And as his cries intensified I held my palms over my ears. But I could still hear him.

'Yasmin come back. Please come back for me...'

Emotions are a strange thing. When a person is overcome by them, the heart, the feet, the legs, the arms, the face, the brain, the whole body does things it normally wouldn't.

Emotions are like that. They make you weak and strong. They make you numb and responsive and helpless and brave all at the same time.

I swear I didn't know how but one minute I was standing in my own garden and the next I was slipping through the gap in the fence and in a matter of a second I held his head against my shoulder, and I whispered words to him. Words I couldn't make any sense of despite me being the one saying them.

84

His breaths were mingled with his cries as he too blabbed words which sounded like he was speaking in a foreign tongue. He wasn't though. He was speaking the same language as I. The language which is used to let emotions out.

A release of words to bring some ease.

However once the words had been let out and he had cried as much as the moment required, Hassan realised he was using a random girl's shoulder to cry on. He pushed me roughly against the wall, resulting in a sharp pain shooting up my elbow.

Wincing at the impact, I panicked when I saw his fist move up high in the air.

'Hassan no…'

The punch was about to land on my face when thankfully he recognised me in time. Now I was the one crying even though I'd promised Habib I wouldn't anymore.

'What are you doing here?' shouted Hassan, his eyes looking red and puffy yet annoyed at the same time. He wiped at his tears and I could only stare back at him as my own tears fell and my body trembled.

It was getting colder.

Hassan took a step closer to me. I closed my eyes, ducked my chin against my shoulder and pressed my body against the wet and icy wall.

'I asked what you're doing here…'

'Please don't hit me,' I pleaded like a scaredy cat. 'I'm sorry I won't ever come here again.'

'I won't hit you.' I felt his voice soften. 'How did you come here anyway?'

I opened my eyes. He was standing too close. If I attempted to run he'd be quick to stop me. And if he hurt me what would Aunty Asma say? Uncle had asked me to be good for her. I'm sure trespassing and getting beat up was not on his list of good things.

'Samina…?'

'I live there.' I pointed at my garden. 'I came through that gap in the corner.'

Hassan turned towards my garden. Curiously he stepped in between the gap in the fence and when he looked back at me, I caught a glimpse of amusement appear on his face.

'We're neighbours?' he asked turning back to size up my house.

'Yes. I guess.'

'We moved here two weeks ago,' he said. I wiped my eyes. 'How come I never saw you before? And how come you've not been at school for like forever?'

I sucked in my lips. It had started raining again. This time heavier.

'Saira said you've been ill.'

My nod confirmed this and Hassan stepped back into his own garden. He came near. The rain had soaked his hoodie through. I watched a series of drops of water drip from its drawstrings onto his shoulders.

'Are you better now?'

I nodded again and shifted my attention to the rain drops falling from his hair down to his forehead and rolling along his face. Perhaps he was doing the same thing to the drops streaking down my face because his eyes were staring at me too. I was drenched through.

I began to zip up my coat.

'You're going to get ill again. It's cold. You should go inside now.'

His voice was the gentlest I'd ever heard it. It felt weird. Nonetheless I nodded my head and took small but shaky strides towards the gap.

'…Because school is boring without you.'

I turned to look at him. He was smiling. An emotion much better than the sounds of sadness I'd heard him cry only moments earlier. I smiled back regardless of the ache in my own heart remembering his pain. He was missing his sister. It was as clear as the rain water falling from the sky. But I had promised Habib and Uncle I would never talk about Yasmin to Hassan or to any of my friends ever again. It was to remain a secret. Her relationship with my brother was taboo, dishonourable and wrong.

'Yasmin's family,' Uncle had said, 'are already going through hell coming to terms with the way she died, and this secret is best kept locked away in our hearts forever, where it will be safe.'

It was for the best.

'I can't believe it but I missed you too,' I told him wiping the water from my face because it was the truth. I had thought about him all the time.

Hassan chuckled as he shook his head spraying the water from his hair. He looked like a cute puppy enjoying a mischievous shake after a bath.

'I never said I actually missed you Samina Kameena.'

My smile grew wider. 'Whatever you say, Hassan Iqmal. And for your information, I'll be at school on Monday.'

'I'm glad to hear that.'

Slipping into my side of the garden I shouted, 'Hassan, please go inside. It's cold and I don't want you to fall ill either. Because I don't think school will be any fun without sharing my stuff with you.'

'I never thought I'd be happy my dad chose this house. Living here won't be so bad after all.'

And I couldn't have agreed more.

Hassan and I, yes we could be friends.

Friends forever…

Chapter Eighteen

'Hun you need to stop here.'

Confused and slightly drained I turned to Seb who had somehow changed into his tee shirt and joggers, and had placed on the coffee table an impressive breakfast of gooey pancakes, French toast, and berries.

'As eager as I am to learn more about the sweethearts of Ilford Lane, I need you to eat something first.'

'Sweethearts of Ilford Lane...?' I asked leaning forward to pick up a strawberry. Indeed I was famished.

'You and your bully boy. However much I regret not being there those first weeks of your new school to punch him silly, I can't help gush at how cute you two were,' said Seb stuffing a forkful of pancake and cream between his lips.

'Cute? It was all a mistake,' I said wiping the juice from the fruit dribbling down my lips with my sleeve. 'Sometimes I wish I'd never gone into his garden and befriended him that day. Maybe my life would have remained simple.'

'Your life was never simple to begin with. I'm proud despite being orphaned and vulnerable from an early age; you did extremely well for yourself.'

I shrugged not convinced. He didn't know half of my vulnerabilities but noticing his swollen eyes I said, 'Why are your eyes red?'

He too shrugged.

'You cried?'

'Just because I'm immune to many female qualities,' he said. 'I still ache for the ones close to me. I'm not afraid or shy to admit I couldn't bear some of the moments where you broke down totally immersed in your childhood grief. Even my desperate attempts to make you stop talking and bring you back to the present failed, until now.'

'I couldn't help it either. It's been many years.'

'I won't pity you. I'm going to admire you instead.'

'I admire you Seb,' I said choking back my own emotions.

He chuckled, humbled no doubt, as his ears pinked.

'Come on eat up Doctor Jones,' I said softly. 'This delicious food is getting cold.'

'On one condition...'

I raised a brow.

'After eating you will continue to tell me how the sweethearts of Ilford Lane later came to be Mister and Misses.'

'You have work?'

'I've been naughty and phoned in sick.'

'What?' I said knowing the extent of dedication he had towards his job. 'Why?'

'Never you mind why, hurry eat up and tell me how that blue eyed kid became to be who he is to you.'

Taking a deep breath in, I accepted.

Ten years earlier

Chapter Nineteen

Virtue and vice…

I could do this. I'd been doing it for years. Although I mentally cursed myself for gobbing down a giant bag of Minstrels. Now I was too fat. Normal girls my age would have been able to revise for their final GCSE's without pigging out on volcanic amounts of chocolate, and strawberry Miranda. Not me. The key to my brain's ignition was junk food.

Pulling in my stomach I tried one more squeeze and almost toppled over as I tumbled into the garden on the other side.

'Hurry up…'

'Hush,' I warned in a whisper looking back over my shoulder. Thankfully no one had seen me. I ran towards the patio doors and stepped inside his house.

'What took you so long?' he said as I locked the door shut behind me.

'Aunty was taking forever to sleep,' I said rushing to the downstairs loo. Climbing onto the shower tray I began washing the mud from my feet. The water came out boiling and I squealed, which made Hassan laugh.

'The water's too hot.'

He carried on laughing.

'I stepped in a muddy puddle in my haste to get here I'll have you know. I took my sandals off because they were noisy and walked bare feet.'

'Oh and here I was thinking Samina's about to shower.' He wiggled his brows and when I turned the shower cap his way, he was quick to move outside.

'Samina I'm all wet.'

Chuckling I said, 'The things I do for you Hassan Iqmal.'

'Just get out already.'

'Okay grumpy bones. I'm all done.'

Hassan threw a towel at me and I used it on my hands and feet before tossing it on top of the laundry basket.

'Come on,' he said pulling me by my arm, urging me up the stairs faster. Once inside his room Hassan pushed me onto his bed.

'Careful,' I said sucking in a sharp breath and holding a hand to my back.

'Look,' said Hassan, not noticing my discomfort.

'It's the You Tube video of Darren at Ola's birthday party.'

'No way, who uploaded that?' I leaned forward to look at his laptop. Darren was on the screen singing, and he had creamy cake smeared all over his face.

'Yours truly,' said Hassan saluting as he drew his face near.

Smacking his head away I said, 'You can't do that.'

'I can and Darren is pleased. It's had over ten thousand views. Anyway you should have been there to see for yourself. Everybody from our class was there.'

'Hmm,' I murmured remembering the lecture I got from Aunty Bushra about parties. Not finding Darren's song funny anymore, I went over to the window and looked out at my house. Through it you could see into my kitchen, and directly into my bedroom upstairs, as well as the whole back garden. Hassan called it his, 'five star view.'

Although it was only midday and I couldn't see anything inside my house because the lights were off, I shivered. I hoped Aunty Bushra hadn't woken up. She always napped at midday. And I always made sure I was home before she realised I wasn't there.

'You should've seen your little gang. Parveen and Saira were wearing traditional clothes. They looked like they were at an Eid party, not a sixteenth birthday bash…'

Noticing my quiet he came over to me. 'What are you looking at?' he said as he whacked my back to pull me out of my reverie.

'Hass,' I recoiled. His light action made me wince and hold a palm over the small of my back.

'What…?'

'Nothing,' I said trying to move past him. I should've stayed at home because Hassan knew me too well. Grabbing my hand he gently pulled me to him. And as I took a step closer to him, he sucked in a deep breath and did what he always did whenever I felt like this.

'She hit you again didn't she?' he said wrapping me snuggly against his chest. 'How much more shit are you going to tolerate? Why can't you tell your stupid Uncle, huh?'

Tell Uncle. Tell him since Habib had moved to Dubai, his wife had taken it upon herself to make my life hell. Besides if I said anything against Aunty Bushra, Uncle wouldn't have believed me anyway. He would've thrown me out onto the streets, because he wasn't my real dad.

Something Aunty always said, over and over.

And I knew Uncle could do this. He worshipped his wife. She was the God of our house. What she said went.

'I'm going to kill her one day. I swear Samina I hate her so much. And I fucking hate your brother for what he did by leaving you with her. Fucking arse...'

Moving out of his embrace I decided to head home. Despite my grievance with Habib I couldn't tolerate anybody saying a word against him. He'd been fed up with his life here. That was all. I mean who wasn't fed up. Ilford Lane was crap. End of.

Habib had needed to get away from Aunty and her persistent pestering for him to marry one of her dumb cousin's from Pakistan. He had told me this himself. Yet he failed to mention he would get up one day and leave. I'd waited all night for him when he left two years earlier. And because I'd fallen asleep on the stairs whilst doing so,

Aunty had gotten a fright when she came down the next morning, thinking I was an intruder.

That morning, I received my first blow.

'What was it this time?' said Hassan as he stopped me from leaving his room by standing in front of the closed door. 'Your Uncle called you his princess again which the hag couldn't tolerate, is it? Or did you forget to do the dishes or play mum to her dumb kid?'

'Ayaan is not a dumb kid,' I retorted. Ayaan was my Uncle's three year old son and I adored him.

'Oh yeah because you're his freebie nanny, you're the maid of that household and fucking…' he punched his fist on the door. 'Show me what she did to your back?'

In a quick motion he turned me around and was lifting my sweater up against my wishes. And as soon as he saw the purple bruise, he went to sit on the edge of his bed.

'It's not that bad.'

He snorted but he would keep this a secret like he'd been doing for years. He wouldn't tell his parents, or the teachers at school, or my friends, because he had promised he wouldn't.

And Hassan always kept his promises.

His silence grew uncomfortable and I took my Science folder from his desk, deciding it was best I went. From the corner of my eye I saw Hassan reach for something from his school bag.

'Did you finish copying these notes?' I asked closing the topic of my abuse.

'Hmm,' he murmured.

'I best be off. Your mum will be back soon and I've…' My eyes widened and I forgot what I was about to say when I saw what he was doing. I'd heard from some kids at school he smoked but hadn't seen him doing it and it didn't look right to me. It didn't suit him. It wasn't good for him.

'Hassan you're smoking?'

'And,' he said staring at me blankly, something he did quite a lot these days.

'Stop it right now,' I demanded. It was bad enough Habib used to do it all the time but I wouldn't sit back and let Hassan ruin his health like this. He was only sixteen. He shouldn't be smoking.

'Please,' I begged dropping the Science folder and closing the distance between us. Daringly, I took the disgusting thing from his fingers and trembled as I looked around for something to destroy it with, and when I couldn't find anything, I put it out on the laminated floor by stomping on it.

'I've got more,' he said flashing a whole box of them in front of my face.

'Give them here,' I shouted. My body shook at the thought of what could happen to him if he smoked the whole lot. 'They're not good for you. Throw them away before it turns into an addiction.'

'Shut up with your mothering me. I'll do what I want.'

He pulled another stick from the box and lit it with a plastic lighter. I rushed to him again. Hassan held it up high and at almost six foot, he knew I wouldn't be able to reach it.

Giving up, I simply watched him indulge in the vice.

'What?' he scowled.

'I'll never talk to you. It's either the cigarettes or me.'

Taking a long drag Hassan waved a dismissive hand in the air. I crossed my arms over my chest hating how he still managed to get under my skin.

'Easy, peasy, I choose this,' he said blowing a mouthful of smoke in my face.

I coughed.

He laughed.

*****

Leaving Hassan to smoke all he wanted I slipped through the garden fence and ran back inside my home, only to hear my name being called.

'Eh Samina…'

'Yes Aunty.'

'Bring me a cup of tea.'

'Yes Aunty.'

'First come here for a minute.'

Wiping a hand through my hair and clothes for any tell-tale signs of my recent misadventure, I hurried up the stairs and into her bedroom. She was lying on her bed. Ayaan was napping beside her.

'Come,' she gestured with a tilt of her index finger.

On slow steps, I neared her. And although her eyes were closed, I could feel the tiny hairs on my arms stand. Her body shifted on the bed before she opened her eyes, and a shocked gasp left my mouth as her palm connected to my cheek.

'I called you twenty times,' said Aunty rubbing the hand she had slapped me with. 'I suppose you were using those headphones again. How many times have I told you come on my first call?'

'I didn't hear you...'

'Bring those headphones to me now.'

With my palm held to my cheek, trying my hardest not to shed any tears, I went to my bedroom to fetch the headphones which Uncle had given me on my birthday. Seconds later I watched Aunty snap them and throw the loose cords at me.

'Useless orphan girl… Well don't stand there looking, get me my tea.'

I went to make the tea.

Chapter Twenty

Strangers in the night…

People speaking downstairs woke me from my sleep. Glancing at the clock I sat up on my bed. It was three O'clock. Rubbing my eyes I wondered what was going on.

Was Uncle home? Odd. He always came home for breakfast with us around eight in the morning. He was shouting. Curiosity made me leave the warm bed. I covered Ayaan who slept next to me with the duvet properly, threw on a hoodie and hurried outside into the landing. The voices were getting louder.

Tying my hair in a messy bun, I stopped halfway down the stairs. In the passage was somebody's luggage, a couple of large suitcases and some smaller bags. One I recognised.

Habib?

'When did you ever listen to me?' shouted Uncle coming out of the living room. Muttering something, he began climbing the stairs. When he saw me, he stopped.

'Is it really him?' I said as I wrung my hands together.

Uncle's eyes narrowed on me and his forehead creased more. Ignoring my query he touched a side of my face and said, 'What happened here. Why is it red?'

Choking with disbelief I said, 'Habib is really here?'

'Yes he is and he has a surprise for us. I've already seen it. You go and see for yourself too. What is this mark on your face?'

'It's nothing. I must have slept on my phone or something,' I whispered as familiar footsteps began to come closer.

'Welcome your brother home,' said Uncle. After rubbing his hand on my head, he climbed up the rest of the steps and disappeared across the landing.

'Baby…'

I shook my head. How dare he call me that?

And what of the promise he made to Mummy on her death bed? He hadn't thought about me in two years. After abandoning me why was he here in the middle of the night calling me his Baby?

'Look at you.'

'No,' I said denying him an embrace. I didn't want to look at him. Not yet. Not ever. 'Don't touch me.'

'Baby…?'

'No,' I cried unable to hold in my emotions. He had hurt me beyond belief when he'd left. The only reason I'd kept myself sane was because of Hassan's friendship. And now even he felt cigarette smoking was more valuable than our relationship.

'Don't cry,' said Habib blocking my way to escape him by standing in front of me. 'Won't you look at me? Won't you let your brother hold you?'

Again I nudged his hand away when he attempted to touch me. But inside me, my heart was beginning to rejoice at seeing him again.

'I've missed you.'

'Liar…'

'Samina is this any way to talk to your brother?' said my heavily pregnant Aunty as she waddled up the stairs and took hold of my hand and placed it in Habib's. 'Sorry. She's just shocked to see you. She's still half asleep.' Auntie's lips twitched and I felt a tight pinch on my side.

Habib cupped the un-bruised side of my face and I was forced to lean into him.

'Forgive me,' he whispered with watery eyes as he kissed my forehead.

I nodded despite the long list of conditions and punishments I'd drawn up in my mind for this occasion. But seeing him in the flesh, hearing his voice, feeling him being close and inhaling his familiar fatherly scent was enough for me to shower my mercy a billion fold on him.

'Bibi darling…'

97

'Ah Maryam, allow Habib to have his moment with his sister. Surely you can see how much she means to him,' said Aunty Bushra stepping away from us.

Habib drew away first. I wiped at my tears with the sleeve of my hoodie and followed him down the stairs into our living room.

'Meet Maryam,' smirked Aunty as she stroked her baby bump having placed herself on the single sofa.

Uncovering my eyes from my sleeve, I looked at the chubby woman standing next to my brother. She wiped his eyes with her scarf. I pursed my lips and tilted my head to one side.

'Oh Bibi,' said the woman.

'Seeing my Baby again has made me emotional.' Habib pulled away from her and held out a hand for me. When I didn't make any attempt to take it, he came to me instead.

'Maryam this is her,' he said kissing my head. 'This is my beautiful baby sister.'

'Bibi the way you go on about her, I was expecting a child of nine or ten years,' said the woman as her fringe fell over her eyes. 'She's grown up.'

Habib wiped at his eyes again. 'You have grown up Baby.' He kissed me again. 'Look at you, so pretty. I can't believe my little Samina is all grown up.'

'Well introduce her to your wife then,' said Aunty. 'Samina your brother is married with a child on the way. Can you believe that?'

So this woman, Maryam, was his wife. And she wasn't chubby. She was pregnant. Like Aunty.

'Hi,' said Maryam holding out a hand for me to shake. I never imagined I would be introduced to my brother's wife with a formal handshake.

With a heavy heart, I shook her hand.

'I've heard a lot about you,' she said.

I smiled at her before looking up at Habib who still held me close. He had a goatee beard now. His hair was much shorter too. And he was wearing a red button down shirt.

Habib never liked red. It had always been a pet hate of his.

'You been okay?' he asked and I nodded my reply.

'Well I'm too tired to do anything at this hour. I need to lie down. Samina see if you can make something to feed your guests. There's some lamb in the fridge.'

'We're not hungry,' said Maryam. 'Just a cup of milky tea will be good. And a bed.'

'Samina also check everything is in order in Habib's old bedroom. And bring me up a cup of milky tea also. Actually make it hot chocolate.'

'Yes Aunty,' I replied as Habib looked from Aunty to me with his eyebrows stretched.

'Be quick okay and then get back to sleep. If Ayaan doesn't see you when he wakes up, he gets upset,' added Aunty before waddling out of the room.

'Do you take sugar?' I asked Maryam awkwardly, who had made herself comfortable on the same sofa Aunty vacated.

'Only a little honey please. And Habib will want tea with…'

'Less milk and two sugars.'

'You remember?' said Habib.

'You're the one who forgot.' My answer wiped the smile he was wearing but I didn't ponder. I had tea to make and a bedroom to set up for the strangers.

Chapter Twenty One

It's not right…

Monday morning revision notes in one hand and permission slip for the leaver's Prom in the other, I bade Uncle good bye at the school gates. At sixteen most teenagers were allowed to walk to school by themselves and held some degree of independence.

Not me.

Where Habib had pampered me in the form of his protectiveness, Aunty Bushra had taken over from his school run duties when he'd left to prove a point, that she could be as much a mother to me as my own brother had been. However with her having only a couple of weeks until her new baby arrived, Uncle had been doing this duty instead.

Technically secondary school was over. It was June, exam period. After this I had a long summer break before college started and I wasn't looking forward to the holidays at all. Long gone were the days where I'd spend my sunny summers up in Blackpool. Aunty Asma was too busy looking after her own grandkids, to ever have me over.

'Earth to Samina...'

'Gosh Ranjita you scared me,' I said as she hugged me from behind.

'Well get your ears checked because I was calling you for like forever. Mr Philpot even told me off for shouting when I walked past our old classroom. Can't believe we won't be sitting in there again. I'm actually sad.'

The feeling was mutual. I didn't want to leave either. Despite my problems at home, my friends and classmates were special to me. I felt I was losing a huge chunk of my life by moving on.

'You got it signed at last,' squealed Ranjita noticing the signature on the form in my hand. 'This is the best news. Wait until the others hear about this. We are so getting you the same dress we're all wearing. Actually you're my size, I'll get my sister to buy one tonight.'

Ranjita's sister worked at Debenhams inside the Ilford Exchange. And Aunty Bushra was especially glad about this. Where she gave Ranjita's mother discounts on her orders of rich moisture cream from her trusted Avon brochures, Aunty received huge discounts on clothes and knickknacks from the department store in return. Aunty had a thing for silver and gold coloured ornaments. She was Ilford Lane's own queen of bling.

'Anyway I'm off to French. You've got Biology right?'

'Yes.'

'Good luck, I'll see you after the exam.'

'Okay. Good luck Ranj,' I said waving as she went.

I was about to enter the office but looked back when Ranjita shouted, 'Oh your boyfriend was looking for you earlier.'

'He's not my boyfriend,' I shouted back, something I'd spent years explaining. But for some reason even my closest friends felt Hassan and I were much more. I swear we weren't.

We were only best friends.

*****

'What's up your arse today?' said Hassan grabbing my arm and pulling me away from my friends. My Biology exam had finished and we were waiting to be allowed in for the next one. History.

'Why are you ignoring me?'

Scowling, I reminded myself why he was my friend in the first place. His arrogance and his wit, he was famous for these. And since Year Ten, his good looks and his tall, lean build had many swooning over him. And he knew it. He was cocky. He was rude, and he still tormented me.

101

'Your cheek?' he said pointing at it.

Consciously I cupped my palm over the said side of my face. I had concealed the bruise this morning with makeup. I bet the stuffy hall topped with the warm June weather had melted it off.

'Again?' he said poking my shoulder with his finger. I looked around us afraid of what the others would think. 'The fucking bitch.'

'Hassan,' I warned fidgeting with the strap of my shoulder bag. Ranjita and Parveen were making their way towards us. 'Please calm down, everyone's watching.'

'Like I care,' he said giving me a slight shove. 'You're beginning to annoy me with all your shit. Why can't you fight back? Why can't you show some guts for once? Why are you such a fucking weakling?'

My mouth hung low and by the time Ranjita and Parveen came over, Hassan had weaved his way through the crowd of pupils and disappeared out of my line of vision.

'You okay?' said Ranjita placing her hand on my shoulder. 'What was he saying? He looked angry.'

'Nothing important,' I whispered trying to get my breath back. This was a lie. What he said wasn't what I had expected from him.

'Oh, quick lets queue up, the doors are opening.'

I followed my friends, offered them good luck and completed the exam, all the while conscious of the boy sitting directly behind me.

*****

With the exam over and the next one not due for another week, I was with Ranjita and Parveen as we went over some answers. Saira appeared and I shielded my cheek with my loose hair. I had already re-applied concealer borrowed from Ranjita, using the excuse Ayaan had thrown a toy car at me whilst playing. My friends had seemed convinced.

'What's up?' I asked when she clicked her fingers near my eyes.

'Huh, no,' said Saira slumping down next to me. 'You looked lost in thought. Anyway Hassan told me to tell you he's waiting in the Tech Room.'

'Samina,' Parveen said looking up from her notes. 'I've been noticing you two getting really cosy these days. Do I need to remind you he's a boy and in Islam you're not even supposed to be talking to him? Your Uncle will kill you if he finds out how touchy touchy you are with him. I saw you hugging him the other day, what was that about? Everybody saw you. And Somia Ahmed from 11rt even asked me if you're going out with him. She called you a slut. Do you know that?'

'Parveen shut up,' frowned Ranjita. 'Sometimes you can be so heartless. We know Samina's not into Hassan like that. You should have kicked Somia up her fat arse for saying that.'

'I'm just stating a fact.'

'What, that I'm a slut?' I stood up and grabbed my notes from the bench. 'And Parveen you don't need to worry about me being too cosy with Hassan anymore. Because I think even he's given up on me now.'

Saira got up too. 'What do you mean by that and where are you going?'

'Saira I'm going home.'

'But he's waiting for you.'

Waving a hand in the air, I began to walk away.

'It's not right,' Parveen yelled after me. 'He's a boy. It's wrong. I'm only telling you because it's my duty as your best friend to lead you in the right direction. He's a bad influence on you. This friendship isn't healthy. It's not right Sam.'

'She doesn't mean that, Samina come back,' yelled Ranjita.

'I'll see you next week,' I shouted back despite Parveen's words which kept echoing in my ears.

Chapter Twenty Two

No one messes with our Princess…

Surprisingly the atmosphere at home was brighter than the previous night's. Habib was fussing over Ayaan like a doting elder brother, and his wife Maryam was forever chatting away with Aunty about everything and anything Dubai. I believed the gold bracelet which she'd brought back for Aunty had helped in gaining her full acceptance. Aunty Bushra loved her jewels which explained the super smile on her lips as she showed it off to everybody.

Uncle seemed oddly happy too. During the drive home from school he had told me the strangers were staying. Maryam was going to have the baby here. It was a boy. I would soon become an aunt to a nephew.

'I can't believe I'll be a granddad,' he had said. 'Habib has done well finding a girl like her.'

A lump had formed in my throat. So Uncle had given his nephew his blessing. A year. They had been married a year and we'd only just found out, yet Uncle was okay with this. I was not willing to accept it as easily though. I was deeply upset and sweet memories of a special girl with blue eyes and a warm smile kept clouding my mind.

And standing in my garden looking in the direction of Hassan's window, I couldn't stop imagining how wonderful life would've been with her presence filling that home and ours.

Why wasn't it her having my nephew?

A loud thumping noise followed by Ayaan's cry made me jump out of my thoughts. He had fallen from the wooden swing he was playing on. I ran to him and screamed. He had blood on his head, but he wouldn't let me pick him up.

'What happened?' said Habib as he came running from inside with a worried looking Uncle behind him.

'He's bleeding,' I said as my panic rose.

Uncle picked him up.

'Uncle is he okay?' I cried. Ayaan may have been my Uncle's but I had loved him from the second he came into the world. And seeing him on the floor screaming in pain covered in blood was not a sight I could witness without my heart spinning on a violent carousel.

The blood, his cries and then Aunty Bushra coming outside, and pushing me against the concrete wall whilst shouting profanities at me for attempting to kill her baby...

I can't remember much after that. All I recall is an overbearing pain taking my breath away and Habib's voice shouting back at her.

*****

Habib was furious. Maryam was shocked. And Uncle after bringing Ayaan and Aunty back home from the hospital had eaten his dinner, and rushed to the Cabbie. Ayaan had needed stitches on his head. A bit of his hair was shaved and the wound would leave a scar.

When they returned, Ayaan had been asleep and Aunty laid him in her own bed despite knowing he hadn't slept without me since he was one.

'Has she done this before?' said Maryam as she pressed a bag of frozen peas to the huge bump on my forehead later that same night.

I shook my head. 'I wasn't looking after him properly. It could have been worse. If anything happened…'

'Nothing happened,' said Habib. 'He's a child. Children get hurt. You didn't do it on purpose. But what the hell did she do to you? Maryam did you see how she attacked my sister?'

'Bibi I did tell you, Aunty Bushra is quite shifty looking,' said Maryam as she peered at my forehead, giving me a whiff of her strong Arabian Oudh.

Habib took the pack of peas from her and I moved his hand when he tried holding it to me. 'Tell me has she hit you before. This other mark on your face, it wasn't because you slept on your phone was it?'

I stared at my brother. Why did he care all of a sudden? I mean two years. I'd been tolerating this shit for two years because he'd left me. The bump on my forehead was nothing in comparison to what I'd already endured. And frankly his sympathy wasn't needed nor appreciated.

I got up. 'I'm tired. Goodnight Maryam.'

'Baby your dinner...'

Ignoring him, I went and curled up in my bed. Without my baby brother Ayaan, next to me.

*****

I woke up much earlier than anticipated for the holidays the next morning because I needed to catch Uncle before he went to sleep. When I went downstairs Uncle was drinking his tea and there was a plate of uneaten cake rusks on the table. On shaky legs I went and sat down on the chair next to him.

'Aslaam Alaikum Uncle.'

'Walaikum Asalaa…' he stopped mid greeting when he fixed his gaze on the horrible gash on my forehead. Apparently Aunty in her anger had pushed my head against the concrete wall and had Habib not come in the way, she would have done it again.

'I'm sorry,' I said. The thought of Uncle being displeased with me sent shivers of anxiety up my spine. 'I didn't mean to hurt him. One minute he was swinging then the next…'

'Chup,' said Uncle asking me to hush and pulling my head against his shoulder. 'I don't want you feeling sorry for anything. And beti, Bushra will never touch you again. If she dares then I'll make sure it'll be her last day in this house as my wife.'

I took a long breath registering his words. He was angry at his wife. Not at me. He would throw her out. Not me.

'It was an accident. And at the hospital when Ayaan was being stitched, he was asking for you to come and hold him. He wanted you and not his own mother.'

'But Aunty said I'm not allowed near him…'

'Hai, you haven't even stepped inside the house yet and here she is filling your ears against me already,' moaned Aunty as she waddled into the kitchen and sat on the nearest chair to her.

'Bushra that is enough,' said Uncle using a tone I'd never heard him use before. And I think Aunty sensed the offish-ness in his voice too, as her eyes narrowed on him. But they quickly widened when he pointed a firm finger at her.

'Never lay a finger on my beti again. I tolerate much in this house but never for once think I will tolerate you raising a hand to her. When did you assume it was fine to call her an orphan? How dare you? I am her father. I married you to be her mother first and my wife second. However somewhere in my leniency you seem to have forgotten this. I am never going to say this again so listen carefully, Samina is my jaan and you will not strike her or call her the names you did yesterday.'

'Ja…wed,' Aunty stammered and as she attempted to say something, she stalled and closed her thin lips.

'Beti eat breakfast and get ready by eleven. Let me rest a little then we're going shopping to buy you an outfit for the Prom. It's this Friday isn't it?'

I nodded despite being scared of Aunty as she glared.

'We'll take Ayaan as well.'

As Uncle left the kitchen I saw Maryam standing by the door. Her eyes were wide and as she came in, Aunty Bushra began to weep.

I sat glued on my chair. Uncle had told her off for me. He still loved me. He cared.

'See Maryam, see what I have to endure in this household,' wept Aunty into her scarf. 'Look at me, heavily pregnant and he, my husband is chiding me. Oh Allah if in the spur of the moment I lost my senses seeing my child hurt and raised my hand to his precious daughter, I will have to tolerate such abuse from him. Never did I imagine caring for someone else's child would result in such consequences…'

'Relax Aunty Jee, relax.' Maryam rubbed her hand up and down Auntie's back as she tried consoling her, all the while staring at me. And when I wiped at my own tears Maryam shook her head.

Seeing Aunty crying in her state wasn't easy for me either. I knew she had a baby inside her. I knew she wasn't feeling too good these days but what she was saying wasn't right either.

Nothing she was saying was right.

'Oh you are incredibly lucky Habib chose the right time to leave her and marry you. If you were here you'd be going through the same thing; trying to pine for your own husband's affection.'

And as Habib came into the kitchen minutes later, Aunty excused herself and sniffling on her way out, went towards the living room.

'What was that about?' he asked Maryam.

'Your Uncle was angry at her for hitting your sister.'

'Damn right he would be. No one touches our princess and gets away with it.'

'She's heavily pregnant Bibi. He could have been a little gentle.'

'Yeah whatever,' snorted Habib and when he began fiddling with a gauze he had in his hands and asked me to sit still while he tended to my broken skin, I saw how Maryam was looking at us.

'Bibi…'

'Not now Maryam,' said Habib kissing my head as he finished. 'You scared me yesterday. Your brother can bear the world's pain but not yours. I'm feeling so sorry I left you the way I did. I hope one day you can forgive me.'

I took comfort in his words when he pulled me against his side.

'I forgive you Habib,' I said.

'Didn't I tell you Maryam, my Baby's a diamond? I love her with all my being.'

'I love you too Habib,' I told him not caring about the two eyes which were staring at us. At that moment I wouldn't have cared if a tiger hungry for our meat was glaring at us because I was too consumed in my emotions.

My Uncle and Habib still loved me.

Chapter Twenty Three

Touchy touchy…

Uncle carried the bags and I held a sleeping Ayaan against my shoulder as we entered our house. I was knackered. Our shopping spree at Lakeside had been fun. Uncle hadn't stopped me buying stuff. He bought me three tee shirts, a new pair of trainers and a teddy bear. And after looking in about twenty shops he finally found something he thought was fit for me to go to the prom in.

I must admit what he chose was special. A champagne coloured fit and flare dress, which came down to my ankles. It was made from a shimmery silk fabric, which glistened as it flowed along the body. Because it was sleeveless, Uncle had asked the store assistant to help choose a shrug with it which could cover my arms. He also bought me matching diamanté sandals, and the whole outfit screamed pretty.

Once inside our living room, I put Ayaan down on the sofa and Uncle asked for a nice cup of tea. I wondered why the house seemed calm though. In the kitchen I noticed there was no pot of food on the hob, which was strange because Aunty always cooked the main dish for dinner by now. It wasn't in the fridge either. If there was one thing Aunty did with pride, it was cook our meals for us.

Maybe she was asleep upstairs. I filled the kettle deciding to make her a cup as well. I couldn't wait to show her the shiny broach I persuaded Uncle to buy for her. However movement in the garden shifted my attention and soon enough the source of the racket revealed himself and knocked on our back door.

I rushed to open door and frowned to see him grinning.

'Go away my Uncle's home.'

'So?' said Hassan peering inside. 'Why do you have a plaster on your forehead?'

I pushed his hand away and tried closing the door. 'Get lost. I'll phone you okay.'

'Beti,' Uncle's voice startled me and I moved away from the open door. 'Who's there?' Without waiting for me to reply Uncle went outside to have a look himself. My body trembled. Uncle had warned Hassan not to come in our garden on many occasions. Since the Yasmin episode, he had a dislike of the Iqmal's. He had even forbidden Aunty in the past from going over when she was quickly becoming good friends with his mother.

'What are you doing here?' roared Uncle and I held a hand to my chest as I stepped into the garden behind him.

Hassan was picking a football up from the flower beds. 'I called so many times for someone to throw it back. Sorry… I jumped over to get it myself. It's a limited edition you see, I didn't want your Ayaan spoiling it. Oh hi Samina, how's the revision going?'

Uncle turned his glare around to me and I tried keeping my face as straight as possible. Hassan, why did he do stuff like this?

'This is our garden,' I yelled at him despite my fear. 'You can't come in here. Next time your ball comes over, Ayaan won't spoil it, I'll burst it myself.'

Hassan started to laugh.

'Beti go inside.'

Uncle's cold stare forced me to do as he said but as I stepped inside I heard, 'Why does she have a plaster on her forehead?'

I smiled to myself.

'She has a cut not that it is any concern of yours. Next time your ball comes over don't trespass.'

'Yes sir,' said Hassan and I couldn't help but laugh a little too.

*****

The home phone rang as soon I stepped inside the house.

111

'Baby call Uncle, Auntie's in labour. We're at King George. Send him here now…'

Dropping the phone I ran back into the garden shouting, 'Uncle, Uncle...'

'What is it?' he snapped looking at Hassan's retreating back.

'Habib just phoned saying he's at the hospital with Aunty Bushra and the baby is coming,' I said in one breath.

Uncle quickly moved inside the house. Leaving me instructions to lock the back door and tend to Ayaan when he wakes, Uncle picked up his phone and keys and left right away.

I stood watching after him in the landing, worried sick.

'Please Allah look after my Aunty Bushra and give me a cute little sister this time…'

It wasn't a second later when I felt warm hands touch me from behind and pull me back.

'Beti go inside…' he whispered mimicking Uncle.

I squirmed in his arms and managed to free myself from his hold. But remembering how horrid he'd been lately, I pushed him. He fell to the floor. Looking both confused and cheeky, he held out his hand for me to help him up.

Instead I rolled my eyes, slipped to the floor against the wall and brought my knees up against my chest. He moved to sit next to me and began looking around, obviously wondering if anybody else was at home. Let's just say Hassan knew his way around my house too. He'd been here many times before, sometimes when Aunty was asleep and sometimes when I was alone.

'You're still ignoring me.'

I shrugged my shoulders.

'I'm sorry,' he said taking my hand in his. 'I saw Habib coming out of your Cabbie earlier. When did he come back?'

'Two nights ago.'

'And who's the fatso I saw with him?'

'She's not fat, she's pregnant and she's his wife.'

Hassan smirked and said, 'What is it with the women in your family and being huge?'

'I'm not.'

'You're the exception.'

I removed my hand from his and Hassan was quick to cup one side of my face making me look at him. 'Damn I had to see you. Your phone's dead. You do know you're meant to charge it on occasion. I've left hundreds of messages and why didn't you come to the Tech Room? I waited ages for you.'

'You were rude to me,' I said staring into his eyes as they darkened.

'I was pissed off okay. When I saw the mark on your face I just lost it. I was fuming as it was because my dad has booked us tickets to go to Pakistan for the holidays.'

'What the whole summer?'

'Yes. I won't go though,' he said as his thumb began to softly stroke my cheek.

'It might be fun to get away before college starts. Lots of people are going away. Ranjita's going India and Ola's going to Nigeria.'

'What about you?'

'What about me?' I whispered. 'I'm not going anywhere.'

His eyes studied my face a little too closely. 'I don't see you for a day and your forehead has a huge plaster on it and you're asking me this.'

'Habib is here now. I'll be okay. Besides do you have a choice?'

'Fair point,' he sighed as he moved closer and placed my head on his chest. Wrapping his arms around my neck, he began to gently comb my hair with his fingers. 'I've quit smoking by the way.'

Fiddling with a button on his tee shirt collar I said, 'It's not good for you. It gives people cancer.'

'I only did it a few times and I've quit so don't stress.'

113

'I'm glad… Hass…' A knock and the rattling of the letterbox at the front door made me grip his shirt. Someone was coming.

'Relax,' said Hassan finding my worry amusing. 'Look it's only a pizza pamphlet.'

Sure enough it was some junk mail.

'Chicken…'

'Shut up, what if that was Habib or Uncle?'

'Then what?'

'Did you see the way Uncle looked at us in the garden?'

Hassan grinned. 'That was funny.'

'It wasn't,' I said patting his cheek lightly.

Taking my hand away from his face, Hassan intertwined it between his fingers, 'Saira said something about you having a fight with Parveen.'

'It wasn't a fight,' I replied relaxing against him.

'What happened?'

'She was saying stuff about us. The same old. About people thinking we're together like that. How many times do I have to tell everybody you're my friend and that's all?'

Hassan moved me off of him and stood up. Going into the living room, he spotted Ayaan sleeping on the sofa and kept his gaze on him as I followed him.

'What happened?'

'Nothing,' he shrugged. 'You're right, we're only friends.'

'Despite this Parveen warned me our friendship isn't allowed in Islam and said I'm too touchy touchy with you.'

His eyes shot back at me, 'Touchy touchy?'

'Yeah we don't touch each other,' I scowled.

'Of course we don't. We never touch each other,' said Hassan agreeing with me as he shook his head. 'We're only friends. I wonder how people can possibly assume you and I are together. Whatever gives them that idea?'

'I know right, how dumb? Anyway look I saved you some samosas from last night. They're delicious.' I grabbed his hand and when he wouldn't move, I put my arms around his waist and forced him into the kitchen. Once there I quickly opened the fridge, took out the plastic box I'd put them in and warmed up the snacks in the microwave. I also took out the ketchup because he liked it.

As he devoured them, I sat next to him wondering how Aunty was doing at the hospital.

'Thanks they were yum,' said Hassan and I grinned noticing the dollop of sauce on his lips. The tissue box was empty though and not being bothered to fetch another one from the cellar, I used the pad of my thumb to clean his face.

Hassan stared at me the whole time.

'You're so quiet,' I observed.

'Huh, no, anyway I best be off,' he said breaking out of his thoughts and getting up.

Not wanting him to go despite knowing it was best he did, I rushed up to him and cuddled against his chest, 'I don't like it when we fight.'

'Samina before I go can I say you've touched me like twenty times in the last ten minutes. And right now you're hugging me like a wife would hug her husband, so I wonder why people are thinking we're more than just friends.'

I pulled away. 'I never touch you like that,' I frowned, mortified.

He cocked his head to the side and laughed. And I huffed crossing my arms over my chest.

Pinching my cheeks he said, 'I adore you for your innocence.'

'Leave off,' I scowled.

Raising his hands in the air Hassan said, 'I'll see you at the prom now. I'm going Manchester for my cousin's wedding with Mum tomorrow. And Dad wants to bore me to death by taking me to his offices there.' He rolled his eyes. I bit my lips. A lot of Hassan's holidays were spent in Manchester. His father practically lived there.

'Anyway I'll see you at the venue. I doubt your family will let me take you in the Limo we're all hiring. In the meantime don't miss me too much.'

The kiss he left on my cheek before he left that day, for some reason lingered on my skin more than it had ever done before.

Chapter Twenty Four

Fancy frocks…

Baby Aneela, Annie as we were all calling her, arrived at ten minutes past midnight, weighing a healthy eight pounds and seven ounces.

My own baby sister. I couldn't believe it.

The following day at the hospital, Aunty Bushra had looked dreadful. I swear her hair had been all over the place and her bed side table was a complete mess of baby products and fruit. But the baby in her arms was adorable. I couldn't stop holding her and planting kisses on her soft chubby cheeks. I loved her already. I even held her car seat as she entered our house for the first time. I was over the moon.

As I was taking her to Aunty for her feed later, I accidently overheard a conversation Maryam was having with someone over the phone. And what she said unsettled me and ruined my wonderful day.

'Habib insists we stay longer. I've never seen a brother love his sister this much. It's irritating. He's thinking of taking her with us to Dubai. 'Over my dead body,' I said. No of course not, she's nothing like my Bibi. She's awful looking. Don't compare my man to that ugly thing…'

*****

The night of the Prom arrived and having sent a text to Hassan confirming I'd be there for the hundredth time, I rushed to Aunty who was heating the curling tongs in her bedroom.

'Aunty, Uncle said I need to hurry. He needs to be back at the Cabbie.'

'That man and his Cabbie. I sometimes think he's hidden another wife in the flat above it, where he leads a completely separate life from us.'

I laughed imagining it until she turned around and held a hand to her chest as she looked at me up and down.

I pursed my lips. When Uncle had seen me downstairs he'd been happy and had taken photos on his phone, gushing over how pretty I was looking. But he would obviously say this because he was my Uncle.

'Maybe the makeup and curls will make me look nice,' I said remembering Maryam's words the other night. '*Ugly thing…*'

'Ya Allah,' beamed Aunty. 'Why did I not realise you had grown up into a beauty before?'

I shook my head. The dress was stunning. Not me.

Holding me at arm's length Aunty looked at me properly. She was admiring the dress no doubt. It looked even nicer flowing from a body than it had on the hanger at the store.

'You don't need makeup to look nice. Believe me your natural skin tone is radiant enough. I'll outline your eyes and add some baby pink lip gloss and that's all okay. You know your Uncle doesn't like you wearing makeup so let's keep you looking like an angel.'

I watched nervously as she took out her expensive tiara from the drawer, and after fiddling with my hair she fixed it on top of my head. I stood as still as I could while she expertly curled some loose strands of my hair.

'All done,' she said. 'And tell Ranjita you couldn't wear the red dress her mum brought over. We'll take it back and get a refund. I didn't like it anyway. But you have to admire Jawed's great taste. Listen remember what I said earlier, we trust you to use tonight as a last chance to see your teachers and friends before you all go your own ways. So stay away from the boys and especially that Hassan. Jawed told me he saw him in our garden again. The boy is trouble and I will be having a word with Sheila about this.'

I smiled. Hassan was cheeky. 'I won't do anything to break your trust Mummy.'

'What did you say…?'

So I repeated myself, 'I won't do anything to break your trust Aunty.'

'…Oh I thought you said something else,' said Aunty shaking her head. 'This baby is making me lose my mind. Anyway come stand here let me take a picture of you to send to Asma and the family in Pakistan. Just let them see what a beauty I have raised.'

'Samina are you not ready yet?' called Uncle.

'Coming.'

*****

Ranjita, Saira, Parveen and Ola were wearing the same red dress with the laced sleeves. They looked mean. I swear they did, especially Ranjita. She was pissed off because I came in wearing the wrong dress, a dress which according to her made my boobs look huge. It didn't because if that was the case, Uncle would never have allowed me to wear it.

'Another Limo's pulled over,' said Saira. 'Why didn't we think of doing something lavish like this?'

Everybody was showing off for some reason. There was a big buzz around arriving in a fancy car and having pictures taken next to it, to the extent that Ola had asked Uncle if he could step out of his Range Rover, so she could have a photo shoot drooling over his car. My Uncle hadn't known where to look. And I had to pull my friends away telling them he was in hurry. Which was the absolute truth; he had a Cabbie to run.

'Oh my God would you look at that?' exclaimed Ola as her eyes blinked repeatedly.

We all turned to see for ourselves. It was a Limo alright. A huge Hummer one, glistening like it had been sprayed with a thousand white stars. And I must admit, parked amidst the massive display of fairy lights on the trees, it did outshine the other cars.

And there were loads.

'Why are you smiling all of a sudden?' said Saira nudging my shoulder. 'It's only Hassan and his dweebs. Just look at the clowns.'

Suppressing the urge to kick her, I smiled wider. Hassan was coming over. I hadn't seen him in almost a week.

'Twins are we?' he smirked as he neared. I laughed.

'No way Hass, I see more,' said Darren pointing between Ola and Ranjita. 'I can see Triplets, no quadruplets.'

'Oh so why are you guys wearing the same white shirts then?' said Ranjita playfully, pushing Darren away.

'Careful this is an expensive suit I'm wearing,' he said fixing his jacket. 'Come Hass lets go check out the real chicks. This gang of red hot chillies are vicious.'

'I'll catch up in a bit,' replied Hassan gripping my hand.

Darren rolled his eyes but when he looked at me, he took a double take. 'You're not wearing red. I swear you were in the same dress as them a second ago.'

'No Samina decided to be an outcast today,' said Saira giggling.

'I say you do look different tonight,' said Darren wiggling his brows. Consciously I began fiddling with my shrug hoping it was covering me properly.

'Stare at her like that again and I'll pop your eyes out,' said Hassan tightening his hand around mine. Nevertheless the sheepish grin Darren gave before he rushed away had my friends laughing.

I wasn't laughing though. Neither was Parveen.

'Let go Hassan,' I whispered feeling awkward at the way she was twisting her lips in stroppy angles while she stared at us. The other guests had started going inside the hall and I knew my friends were eager to get good seats before the crappy ones were left. It was best we went inside too.

'Come with me,' Hassan whispered back.

Parveen heard him and said, 'No Samina comes with us. I'm sure you have other friends, I mean girls who are more than willing to hold your hand for you all night.'

'What is your fucking problem?' scowled Hassan. 'And Samina I can't believe you allow her to boss you around all the time. She's so…'

'Hassan…'

'What?'

I pursed my lips. 'Please. I'll see you later okay.'

For a second he stared at me but when Parveen took my hand away from his and held it in hers, his lips tightened. Waving his hands in the air he quickly walked away.

'He's got the hot's for you. He's all hormonal over you. I'd definitely give him some tonight if I was you.'

'Shut up Ola,' snapped Parveen. 'Samina knows she's a Muslim. And Muslim girls don't have boyfriends. Its best she kept her distance from him.'

'Well you can't blame him,' said Ola taking a sip of her cola. 'Our Sam looks gorgeous tonight. No wander he couldn't take his eyes off her.'

'It's her boobs,' screamed Ranjita as she giggled.

'Shut up alright,' I said wishing I'd gone with Hassan. Maybe I could find him. I took a step in the direction he went but then stopped.

'Promise me you will stay away from the boys and that Hassan…'

I took the same step back and spent the rest of the night mingling with my ladies in red instead.

*****

Uncle had phoned and was sorry he hadn't managed to come and pick me up on the agreed time. He did however reassure Habib was on his way to me, for which I was glad as all my friends had already gone home. I wasn't completely freaking out yet though because lots of us were still hanging around the gardens and posing with the cars some more.

'You know I could kill you sometimes…'

Spooked I turned around. 'Don't creep up on me like that,' I complained.

'And I don't appreciate being ignored. I don't know what game you were playing tonight but whatever it was, it wasn't yours,' said Hassan grabbing my wrist. 'Why do you allow those bitches to boss you around like that?'

'I don't,' I whispered looking into his eyes.

'Fuck you, you don't. I haven't seen you in a week and when I do you're all dressed up like a beautiful fairy of some magical kingdom and all you can do is push me away like I'm some sort of dirt bag and not your soul mate…'

'Soul mate?'

'Sorry I take that back, I'm your friend. The one you're ashamed to talk to in front of your best friends these days.'

'I'm not ashamed of you.'

'You are.'

'Am not,' I said as my lips began to quiver and maybe he noticed because as he opened his mouth to say something else, he shut it again. However he did take a step closer and brushed a curly bit of my hair behind my ear.

'Come here you idiot.'

This time I didn't not do as he said, I obeyed him and stepped into his arms.

I was so sorry. I didn't mean to hurt him. I could never hurt him.

Never.

Chapter Twenty Five

Family muddles and cuddles…

Maryam was driving me mad. I honestly failed to see her through the same eyes my brother saw her with. It was as clear as the summer heat which had been boiling us recently, that Habib had lost his marbles when he'd fallen in love with her. She was rude, lazy and demanding.

Every day she would get me in trouble from Habib.

'She's feeling low,' he would later justify handing me a chocolate bar. Treats and gifts may have worked when I was younger but now I felt offended each time he did this. I mean, I did all her washing, all her ironing, served all her meals and still she moaned I wasn't doing enough for her.

She was pregnant not ill. She managed to eat, sleep and rest well. And she could also spend hours shopping at the Ilford Exchange buying stuff to take back to Dubai. Yes it was confirmed, they would be leaving as soon as my nephew was born.

To get away from her demands, I had taken some lunch over to Uncle at the Cabbie. Albeit Uncle disliked it, I sat behind the counter and controlled for a bit whilst he ate. Over the years I'd managed to learn the trade quite well. However neither Habib nor Uncle liked it when I was at the Cabbie. I think it was because I was older now and there were so many drivers working for us. Uncle definitely wasn't comfortable when I had to unnecessarily talk to any of them.

'Uncle why don't you sleep, I'll handle things for a while?' I suggested. His eyes were red and the weather being sticky and humid wasn't helping either. He had yawned many times since I'd been there.

'No beti you go home. I'll be okay.'

'Uncle,' I said crossing my arms over my chest. He smiled.

We had renovated the top storey a few years back. There were now two flats above the Cabbie, one which was rented to an Albanian couple. And the other was only recently vacated and Aunty had been adamant to keep it that way. We kept all our spare stuff in it, much to Uncle's dismay. He was missing out on a lot of rental income.

'You are too persistent.' Uncle stood up and he was about to go up for his rest when a man wearing a suit and carrying a leather briefcase entered.

'Hello, where do you need the car too?' I asked, as Uncle would.

'I don't need a car,' said the man. 'I'm looking for a Mister Jawed Ismail.'

Uncle came over to us. 'Yes. How can I help?'

'I'm Martin from Abbott and Margaret Solicitors,' said the man shaking hands with Uncle. 'I'm here to discuss a matter concerning my client, Mr Habib Ismail.'

Uncle's face paled and an hour later when both men returned from the back office, one look at him had me biting my lips.

The man from the solicitor's walked behind the counter and without any warning began pulling out the control cords.

'Excuse me,' I shrieked as the whole system shut down. 'What do you think..?'

'Let him.'

'But Uncle…'

'I said let him,' yelled Uncle and I took a step back both mortified and embarrassed.

Less than ten minutes later we were heading home in Uncle's car.

In utter silence.

*****

By law the Cabbie was Habib's. My Dad had left it to him. Every bit of it. Uncle had no right over it. And Habib wanted it back. Not the actual Cabbie but the whole value of both the flats above it and the commercial property below them.

Uncle was fuming. Aunty Asma and her husband were already on their way over from Blackpool to help sort the mess out. And Habib and Maryam after having said their bit justifying their actions had gone upstairs.

The dynamics of my family were about to change again and somehow I knew I'd be caught up right between them.

Habib had already explained how he needed the money for a house and to set up a new business in Dubai. With a child on the way he had no other option. Apparently he had already asked for the money and Uncle had refused, saying the Cabbie was his own blood and sweat. At this Habib had reminded him the terms of our father's will. Habib told me he had even offered Uncle to buy it at a discount so the business could go on as normal. But Uncle was stubborn.

Habib had been left with no choice but to consult a lawyer.

'Why can't you stay here?' I had said.

'Baby I can't, I have a family now. I need to take care of their welfare.'

'What about me?'

'Uncle has adopted you. I can't take you with me until you're eighteen. Trust me as soon as you turn eighteen, I'll come back for you.'

Closing my eyes I leaned back onto my headboard.

Nothing was making any sense.

*****

The day of the results arrived and my nerves were all over the place. The recent mood in the household wasn't helping, neither was the fact a certain someone had completely forgotten about me since he went on holiday. In this day and age how hard was it to phone, text or email someone from Pakistan?

125

I was standing on our drive, anxiously waiting for Habib to come home. He had to take me to school to pick up my results. Apparently Aunty Bushra was too busy with Aunty Asma to take me. Aunty Asma's stay had been prolonged and I couldn't imagine what was so important to them that they were always consumed in deep conversation. They'd been phoning Pakistan a lot as well, and their heads would be glued to each other's for hours afterwards.

'Phone Habib,' Aunty Bushra had frowned. 'It's about time he took some responsibility for you. Jawed and I do all the hard work and he just reaps up the rewards.'

Uncle was paying up. He bought the property from Habib and was waiting for the paperwork to come through. The Cabbie was open for business again. Truth be told, Uncle got a fair deal. If the property had been put on the market, Habib could've got almost double the amount for it.

Maryam wasn't happy about this but I knew Habib was contented. My brother's heart was huge. Well it had to be to fit somebody like Maryam in it for starters.

*****

'Habib I got all A's,' I yelled running into his arms. I was ecstatic. Eleven A stars and one A.

'Woo hoo my genius,' cheered Habib kissing my forehead. I carried on jumping and when I saw Ola running over to me, I jumped some more.

'I can't believe it,' I said giving her a hug and waving my result sheet. The teachers inside had been overjoyed at what I got. 'Wait has anyone seen Hassan? I wonder what he got. Has he been in? Is he back from Pakistan?'

'No Sam I haven't seen your lover boy,' grinned Ola. 'Ask his sidekick Darren if you're missing him that much. He's still inside crying over his grades, I bet...'

'Who are you taking about?' said Habib grabbing my shoulder roughly. I stopped giggling. 'Hassan, the Iqmal lad…?'

Ola knowing about our culture, and belonging to a set of strict Catholic parents, froze, like me.

'What were you saying?' he asked Ola, twitching his jaw as his grip tightened. 'Lover boy…?'

When neither Ola nor I responded, Habib snatched my result sheet, shrugged his grip away from my shoulder and went to the car.

Leaving Ola biting her nails, I also went and sat in the car. Habib looked serious. His eyes were focused on the road and he began to drive, too fast. When we reached the Cabbie, I panicked. Was he going to tell Uncle?

'Hassan isn't my boyfriend if that's what you're thinking. He's in my class and I was curious what he got because I helped him revise for science and maths and English and food tech because Mr Philpot paired me with him because his marks were way crapper than mine. I don't know why Ola said he's my lover boy. He isn't. It was a joke and besides I haven't seen him since June. He's gone to Pakistan you know. He'll be there all summer and I for sure don't love him. In fact right now I hate him so much and I hope he's failed all his exams. But please don't tell Uncle. Uncle hates him and he really isn't even that bad. Uncle hates all his family. But I promise you he isn't my lover boy. Ola was just being silly and joking…'

'Will you shut up?'

'Promise me you won't tell Uncle because I don't lo…'

I was silenced as Habib placed his huge palm over my mouth. 'Is there something for me to tell him?'

I shook my head.

'Good. I shouldn't have to remind you of what I've already explained to you. Muslim girls do not hang out with boys and the day I hear otherwise about you,' he pointed his finger at me in a threat and I gulped. 'I know very well that kid is a moron and you've always disliked him, so keep it that way. I'll never forgive you if you disrespected me or my honour.'

I shook my head agreeing and Habib removed his hand from my mouth letting me breathe again.

'I'm proud of you today,' he said, finally flashing his dimples. 'You've done so well in your studies, something I never managed to do. I've hurt Uncle. Always disappointed him. Baby I've hurt everybody in one way or another. But the guy in that Cabbie, he deserves to be proud of at least one of us. And you've done that. Just you see his face when I tell him your results. Thank you for this. Eleven A stars, is that even possible?'

'Habib,' I said wrapping my arms around his neck. 'You're the best brother ever.'

*****

Nobody in my family had done as well academically. Aunty Asma's kids had only made it as far as college and even then they had dropped out. Perhaps this explained the sour look on her face when Uncle had come home singing my praises, and stuffing everyone's face with laddoo and cake.

Uncle was smiling again. And to top that, Habib was treating us to a fancy restaurant on Edgware Road. Here Uncle gifted me a full two hundred pounds to spend on whatever I wanted. Habib and Maryam gave me a pair of golden hoop earrings with a diamond ball dangling below them, and Aunty Asma had promised to take me shopping on Ilford Lane to buy me a nice Pakistani outfit.

'I don't know what the fuss is with getting girls highly educated these days when at the end of the day they are to sit at home and have babies,' said Aunty Asma as she bit through a piece of chewy lamb.

I wondered why she had changed so much. When Farah got married and left her with two daughters in law and five grandkids, all in one big house, she kind of turned ratty. I liked her better when I was younger.

'No Asma, my Samina has made me a happy man today,' beamed Uncle as he tapped my head. 'Kareem and Ayesha Bhabhi would have been as much if they were amongst us. May you achieve even higher my jaan,' he said swinging my new earrings admiringly. 'My daughter is going to become a doctor and make me the proudest man alive. Just wait and see.'

'I will Uncle. I will be a doctor one day,' I told him thumping my fist on the table.

Because I wanted nothing more in this world than to make his dreams come true.

Chapter Twenty Six

A taste of freedom…

Baby Salman my nephew arrived three weeks earlier than expected and with the wait for his passport, Habib and Maryam had already started packing to go. I couldn't imagine living without Salman. I was in love with him. He had these tiny hazel eyes which stared at me whenever he was awake. He hardly cried and at two weeks old, he was already smiling. Believe it or not Maryam was also beginning to grow on me. A lot of her weight had shifted and her chubby cheeks had shrunk. Habib had joked the extra weight had made her cranky during the pregnancy. Maybe he was right.

They went a day before my college was due to start. Uncle, little Ayaan and I went to see them off at Heathrow airport. It was hard but at least this time Habib said goodbye properly.

When I got home, the house was hauntingly quiet despite Annie whingeing due to her teething. I hugged her to me and took her into my bedroom. Yet I still felt lonely.

I stared out of my bedroom window. The light in Hassan's bedroom hadn't been switched on for weeks. Leaning my forehead against the cold glass, I yearned for the moment it would be bright again and I could see him waving my way, like he always did.

'Where are you Hassan?'

*****

It was agreed I could go to college in our neighbouring borough of Newham. The Sixth Form College there had impressed Uncle when we visited for an open day. And due to her own commitments towards Ayaan's new nursery and Annie's care, Aunty had finally admitted she couldn't juggle giving me a lift anymore.

Therefore I should've felt liberated walking through the college corridors on the first day. Far from it, I was nervous and scared.

The September sun was bright but a chilly breeze had me snuggling my neck against the denim of my jacket. Overwhelmed at the sight of so many excited young adults, I hurriedly dodged my way inside the foyer, wishing I'd gone to Barking Abbey where most of my school friends were going.

Reaching the Science department I began searching for my form class hoping I wasn't going to be late. The college was like a maze.

'Do you know where room B12 is?' asked a boy as I walked along the same corridor for the umpteenth time.

'I'm actually looking for the same room,' I replied with a nervous smile before moving onwards but the same boy skipped towards me.

'I'm going to the reception to ask. You can come with me if you want.'

'Err, okay.'

'Great my name's Ravi,' he said holding out his hand.

I bit my lip. I knew Parveen and Saira never shook hands with boys. And Aunty had lectured about how wrong it was to talk to boys millions of times. She had also warned if she found out anything out of line about me, she would send me to Aunty Asma's without delay. And Aunty Asma would gladly hitch me up to some random boy from Pakistan, like she'd done with her own kids when they began going off the rails.

Gulping I shook Ravi's hand despite this.

'Normally when someone introduces themselves they start by sharing names,' said this boy Ravi, rubbing a hand behind his neck.

'Huh? Oh, my name's Samina.'

'Samina. Muslim?'

'Yes.'

'Oh,' he said as his grin dropped.

I didn't say anything else. Perhaps he didn't like Muslims.

Maybe he thought I was a terrorist.

*****

By lunch time I had slowly drifted away from Ravi and made a new friend. Her name was Libby. She was Kenyan and had moved to London only recently. I found her pleasant. Her stories about her past had me intrigued from the word go.

'So do you know lots of people here?' said Libby as she punched her phone number into my mobile phone. We were at the bus stop waiting for our busses to arrive to go home. She lived in Mile End in the opposite direction from me.

'Actually no, none of my friends came here,' I sighed, missing Parveen and Ranjita already. We'd been together since primary school.

'Oh I thought you were friends with that guy, what's his name, Ravi?'

'No. I don't even know him.'

Libby raised her brows and flicked her braided hair over her head.

'Seriously, I don't know him.'

'Well, I think you have an admirer on your first day here.'

'No chance.'

*****

The bus was packed. Finding a gap to stand along the aisle, I glanced at the windows hoping they were open, it was boiling. But my eyes caught the back of someone's head as he hurried into the college building.

The bounce in that walk.

No it couldn't be. When he eventually returned from his trip, Hassan was going to go to Barking College.

The bus rolled and took me away from the scene. The whole way home my mind reminisced that first day of secondary school. How I wished I was sitting in Mr Philpot's classroom again.

Watching the twinkle of Hassan's blue eyes.

Chapter Twenty Seven

Fishy dealings…

After dinner I was helping with the washing up and little Annie wouldn't stop screaming. Aunty was desperately trying to settle her down. Ayaan was stood by the back door tapping the glass, trying to scare the cat away. For some reason our garden was a haven for all the neighbourhood cats. Aunty was forever moaning about them spoiling her flower beds.

'No,' shouted Ayaan but leaving my chore incomplete, I rushed to open the front door. Somebody was ringing and knocking impatiently. Surprised to see Aunty Asma so soon, I moved aside to let her in.

'Don't be too happy to see me,' she muttered as I greeted her and looked out into the drive expecting to see either one of my cousin's or Uncle Murad with her. There was no car. Who did she come with?

'Go upstairs right away and put something decent on. Why do you always wear such clothes? Go wear shalwar kameez. And wear a scarf over your head. Go…'

I frowned following her into the living room. 'Why?'

'Bushra why is the house so messy?' she said not even greeting her. In a frenzy she began fluffing the cushions and straightening the rug under the coffee table.

Aunty Bushra with her mouth hung low said, 'What are you doing?'

Aunty Asma waved her hands in the air and grimaced, 'They are here. They were adamant to see her today. I had no choice but to jump in the car with them and come.'

Aunty Bushra's small eyes had never looked larger as she stared at Aunty Asma, who was now wiping dust from the television with her own scarf.

134

'I know it's sudden but what could I do?' said Aunty Asma. 'They return to Pakistan in two days. It was now or never.'

Annie began to cry again and Ayaan's screams for the cat to, 'Go away,' in the kitchen got louder. I was still frowning.

'I haven't spoken to Jawed yet,' said Aunty Bushra handing the baby to me. 'He will never approve. You should have spoken to him first. And a phone call would have been appreciated before turning up like this.'

Aunty Asma pulled the net curtains aside and looked outside. 'I think they've gone to buy sweetmeats from Nirala. They'll be here any minute, and don't worry I'll deal with Jawed. It's not like they will do anything today. They're only here to see her.'

'See who?' I said and I didn't know why my simple question caused both Aunties to look at me with awkward expressions. 'Who are you talking about?'

'Go to your room,' said Aunty Asma with a small tilt of her brown lips as she rushed over. She kissed my cheek and bent down to take Annie from me. 'Be a good girl and put on the black shalwar kameez I gifted for doing well in your exams. Yes, don't you agree Bushra her fair complexion will look striking against the black chiffon?'

'Why should I dress up?' I asked but the doorbell rang and flailing in a panic, Aunty Asma grabbed my arm and hurried me up the stairs, amidst me whining about all the fuss.

One hour and a half later, with both babies fast asleep and me rocking back and forth trying to stay awake, Aunty Bushra came into my room. She was smiling, widely.

'Why was I not allowed downstairs?' I said a bit pissed off. Aunty Asma had said I mustn't because some far away relatives from Pakistan were here to discuss something important and it wasn't something for children like me to hear. Although she said she'd call me down later, I had to wear the Pakistani clothes as opposed to my tee shirt and leggings. I also had to be extra polite and speak to them in my best Urdu.

'You may come and say salaam now,' she beamed fixing the scarf to my outfit over my head. 'Do as Asma said and everything will work out perfectly.' Aunty cupped my face. 'If this goes well, all will be good. Smile prettily and keep your mouth closed and only speak if they ask you something.'

Shrugging my shoulders, I rose and followed Aunty down the stairs and into the room.

Three women, two old and one Auntie's age, and one old man with a white beard, sat in our living room. They had eaten. The dining table was messy with food trays and plates.

'Oh here she is, our lovely daughter,' said Aunty Asma holding her hand out to me as I came further into the room. 'Samina say salaam.'

I did to the lady nearest to me.

'Walaikum Asalaam,' she, as well as the others replied. With a little smile, trying not to laugh at how they were all gawping, I sat down and began fiddling with the scarf when it kept slipping down my shoulders.

'So Samina, do you like Shahrukh Khan?'

I looked up and swallowed. I hadn't expected the man with the beard to ask me that. Shahrukh Khan was a famous Bollywood star who was the best…

'Err,' I stammered thinking how to reply. I adored the actor and his movies. But Aunty Asma was quick to answer for me.

'Bhai Saab our Samina doesn't watch any of that rubbish. She recently got twenty A Star grades for the GCSE exams. Did the best in the whole of Ilford. Was photographed by the Ilford Times and had a whole page printed in her praise. She will be a doctor one day.'

She was exaggerating. My picture wasn't ever in a newspaper. And I got eleven A stars, not twenty.

'She's too consumed in her studies to watch Bollywood movies. And the filth they show these days is far from the films of our times anyway,' continued Aunty Asma. 'No our Samina wouldn't even know who Shahrukh Khan is.'

Why was Aunty Asma fibbing? I had watched a Bollywood film on B4U Movies as soon as I'd come home from college earlier. I'd even eaten my dinner on my lap to catch the ending.

The guests however seemed satisfied. They were nodding and looking at me real carefully. And when one of the women called me over to sit next to her, I began to get uncomfortable. I hadn't seen these people before and the way they kept their eyes focused on me wasn't funny anymore. It was annoying and putting me on edge. But Aunty Bushra's eyes were narrowing on me and when she twitched her lips motioning me to sit next to the woman, I quickly got up and went and sat next to her.

The woman kissed my head and gave me some money. I looked up at Aunty again and she nodded her head. I kept the money in my palm. Next the man stood up and gave me a pair of earrings and asked if I liked them.

I didn't reply. They were huge. Chandelier like. Something someone like Aunty Asma would wear to a wedding.

'I can't believe it,' said the younger woman embracing both my Aunties like she had won the lottery. 'My brother Feesh will be delighted. Samina is perfect for him.'

'Mubarak ho. Congratulations everybody,' the old man danced, before forcing a brown, gooey gulaab jamun into my mouth.

I pushed his hand away letting the sticky juice from the Indian sweet drip along my chin and onto my clothes. And what the man did next had me mentally gagging. He ate the same gulaab jamun which I'd bitten into. And pinching into another one from the plate, he bunged it into Aunty Bushra's mouth.

And as the youngest woman snapped a picture of me on her phone, and the other one hugged me, I felt my chest splitting open.

Were these people fixing my marriage to somebody called Fish?

Chapter Twenty Eight

Missing soul mate…

As soon as the idiots had left, Aunty Bushra happily counted the money they'd given me. Five hundred pounds. And the earrings were genuine Indian gold and would have cost another five hundred. The huge basket of sweetmeats was the best the shop sold. But for some reason Aunty lied she and Uncle had diabetes, and she had forced Aunty Asma to take them for her family in Blackpool instead.

'Why?' I had only asked, and Aunty had come near to striking me. Fuming I had phoned Uncle at the office because he had to know. But he snapped for phoning when he was busy and said whatever it was I wanted to tell him could wait. I'd also Skyped Habib and his wife had blatantly lied when she answered his phone and said he wasn't in. She had disconnected the call and Habib's status had immediately changed to offline.

My luck sucked.

*****

I skipped breakfast and left home an hour earlier the next morning. On the bus, I regretted this. I ought to have stayed at home and waited for Uncle.

Reaching college in ample time for my Biology lesson, I went and hid in the furthest corner of the library. Here I took deep breaths as my heart kept skipping beats. This wasn't happening. I'd heard stories of girls being married off at an early age. In forced marriages. Illegal marriages. Which went against both culture and religion.

My Aunts were up to no good. If Uncle had been at home when the stupid guests were there, he'd have thrown the money and the ugly earrings back at them. He would

139

have thrown them out too. Aunty Asma's actions had been sly and Aunty Bushra loved Indian sweets. She would have eaten them all within an hour, but because she didn't want Uncle finding out, she sent them away.

It had to be this.

What if Uncle agreed though?

No he would never do this to me. He had promised he would keep me with him forever. I was his princess.

*****

I must have spent hours in the library that day, hidden away, lost in the thoughts of my fate, until a librarian jerked me back to the present. The table I was sat at was needed for a group session in life skills. Perhaps I should've asked to join the group. I needed skills. I needed skills to stand up for myself.

Picking my bag up, I headed out towards the lobby. There was free Wi-Fi there. I needed to talk to Habib. There was no way he would tolerate this.

I dialled his Skype ID.

'Hello,' I said as Maryam answered again. 'I need to talk to Habib. Isn't this his phone?' She made a stroppy face and I seriously tried my hardest not to cry. The lobby was busy with students and teachers. It was time to go home, meaning I'd missed both my morning and afternoon lessons.

Way to start the academic year!

'Please Maryam get Habib, I need to tell him something very important.'

Rolling her eyes Maryam waved her hands through her messy hair and within seconds the screen went blue. And as my fingers itched to press reconnect, my throat felt too dry and everything around me felt too clammy, as if the world was closing in on me.

I needed a drink. Rubbing a hand to my neck, I urged myself to cross the distance to the vending machines.

A group of boys were gathered there. Tall boys. Rough looking. All wearing hoodies over their heads, and baggy bottoms. I debated whether I should forget about the drink. But one of them, the one wearing a huge chain around his neck, moved aside and as he smiled he asked, 'What would you like?'

Blankly I took a pound out of my pocket and dropped it in the slot in the vending machine. I waited for the Fanta bottle to come out at the bottom. It didn't. The boy chuckled and took my pound out of the slot. I took a step back and despite me looking like a total freak, he said, 'You want Coke?' as he put the pound in the machine again.

I shook my head rasping, 'Fanta.'

He smiled. A friendly big smile. A smile you wouldn't expect from someone like him with a piercing in his brow and a tattoo to give, but he did. He handed me the Fanta and the twenty pence change and he told his friend to get off the bench in front of the well-kept shrubs, so I could sit down for a bit.

I knew I looked like a weirdo, that's why. Because of people like my Aunty. Always smiling in front of others. Always living up to expectations in the community. Always dressed immaculately. Always extra polite and careful in their manners in the presence of others. Praying, fasting, and giving charity, doing stuff, good stuff. But on the inside, as mean as the most vicious meat eating dinosaur to have ever lived.

The boys moved away. I stayed on the bench. The Fanta in my hand. Unopened. The phone in my other hand. The screen still blanked on Habib's details.

Maryam. My sister in law.

I remembered a time in the past of that gentle woman, the kind soul I dreamt would marry my brother one day. Her beautiful smile, her sweet voice and her soft, blue eyes. She shouldn't have died. She should've been here fighting my corner for me. She would've made everything

141

better because she was the kindest, most caring person I'd ever known.

Oh how I missed her. And how I was yearning for that bit of her heart she'd left behind for me in the form of her brother...

'Nah mate, I couldn't find her. Darren you sure she's at this college…?'

I looked up and everything around me came back into focus. I gripped both the phone and the drink firmly in my hands as I stood and followed the sound of that voice.

And there he was, walking swiftly towards the exits, engrossed in a phone conversation. A smile found its way to my lips and brushing my eyes to wipe away those silly tears which had fallen in his longing, I rushed after him.

'Hassan…'

He carried on walking.

'Hassan…' I croaked pushing myself past the few students who remained in the building to get to him.

He stopped.

I stopped.

He turned.

I waved the bottle of Fanta in the air acknowledging him. He slowly pulled the phone away from his ear. A couple of pupils came in between my view of him and wiping my eyes of more tears I craned my neck and saw him standing a couple of yards away with his eyes closed and his mouth tilted upwards.

I pouted my lips and took small steps, stopping inches from him. I reached to touch him with a quivering finger. His eyes were now open and twinkling as they stared at me. His lips were wide apart in a handsome smile.

But I was weak. An emotional wreck. The instant my finger touched the familiarity of his stubbly jaw, I realised he wasn't a mirage I'd seen. He was real. The real thing.

My arms went around his waist and I pulled him against me, hoping to never let him go.

*****

I don't recall how long we stayed like that however when I did gain some sense of where we were, Hassan had already started walking us back inside the college. Coming to a courtyard we sat on a bench. He wiped my face and brushed some of my loosened hair by tucking it behind my ears.

'What's the matter?' he said staring into my face. 'Tell me why you're crying?'

'I'm not,' I said leaning onto him.

He moved his head back to look at me and raised a brow.

'I'm just happy to see you.'

I felt his chest muscles constrict, 'I'm happy to see you as well but you're kind of scary like this. Did somebody say something to you?

Not knowing why, I shook my head and denied anything was wrong. 'I'm better now,' I said letting him kiss the side of my head.

Kissing it again he said, 'I was looking for you yesterday and that little monkey of yours piss me off so much. Did Ayaan not tell you I was in your garden?'

I drew away from him. 'It was you he was telling to go away.'

Cupping my face he said, 'I missed you Samina. I threw my ball over four times, risked my life, just to see your beautiful face.'

He was teasing, I knew it.

'And I cut my arm in the process.'

Letting go of my face he rolled the sleeve of his polo shirt up. On his muscled bicep was a red scratch, the size of a cumin seed. I smiled as he cringed at his hurt. Despite being a champ in his kick boxing, Hassan was a total wuss. The minute a small cut or bruise touched his skin his stomach would roll over. The sight of blood would make him faint.

I kissed the tiny graze on his arm before rolling his sleeve back down and resting my head against it.

'Here's another cut,' he said tilting my chin to look at him point to his lips. I blinked my eyes but before I could react, he playfully shoved my shoulder and rested by pulling me against his side. Growling into my head he said, 'I missed you badly.'

'You didn't even phone. I waited for at least a text telling me how you are. You can be so unfair sometimes.'

'Hear me out before sending me to the gallows,' he said. 'My phone got nicked as soon as I got to Pakistan. It had all my numbers and believe me I did try calling you, hundreds of times, but for fuck's sake I couldn't remember it properly. I swear not even Darren's. He must have told you, I didn't call him either. And my dad wouldn't buy me a new phone saying it was my fault I'd lost it in the first place. And the net just sucked...'

Intertwining our fingers, I accepted his reasons.

'I was a jerk to everyone in Pakistan. The family there were fed up with my attitude. By the end of the first week I was adamant on coming back. My Dad wouldn't have it though. He made Mum and me stay there for eight weeks while he returned to Manchester, to open up another office selling rat infested houses. He reckons I'll be taking over soon. Fat chance of that,' he snorted.

'So long as your here now. That's all I could ever ask for.'

There was a silence next.

My gaze followed a bee as it hovered over a geranium bush in the centre of the courtyard when I asked, 'How did you know about this place?'

'I saw it yesterday when I came to enrol. Lucky I did. It was the last chance to get in. And I'm glad I brought my exam results with me because seeing what I genius I am they let me join straight away. I couldn't get myself to go to Barking, not without you anyway.'

'Really?' So it was him who I'd seen from the bus the day before.

'Of course,' he whispered pulling our hands up and kissing mine. 'Now tell me what's wrong with you?'

'Can't you and I escape to somewhere?'

'You can marry me,' he joked. 'I'll take you on a honeymoon around the world. We'll travel by first class to all the most exotic countries and have our babies on the planes to get to travel free...'

'That's not even funny,' I said cutting his ridiculous thoughts. 'What is it with people wanting to get married all the time?'

'Samina I was kidding.'

I pulled me hand free. 'I best get home. It's getting late.'

'Habib picking you up?' he mumbled crossing his arms over his chest and kicking a large stone away.

'No he went back to Dubai. My nephew was born you know, Salman.'

'Congrats. Why did he leave so soon though? Why did he even come back? Let me guess, he probably only returned to pick up the crappy stuff he'd left in his wardrobe, idiot.'

I remained silent. I didn't want to admit it but deep down I had realised Habib's visit wasn't because he had missed me, it was to get his money.

'What time does Aunty Cow Dung come to pick you up then?'

'She doesn't,' I said trying not to smirk. He always came up with rude names for her. 'I'm taking the bus.'

A grin appeared on his face making him look more handsome. His face was all tanned and radiant. It must have been sunny in Pakistan.

'And it's late. I'm going home,' Getting up I picked my bag from the floor whilst fastening the buttons on my coat. Despite everything I hadn't told him yet, I was relieved and extremely glad to have him back. And I was even happier he was going to be with me at college every day.

'You can't smile at me like that and...'

'Huh? Hey...' I squealed as he grabbed my wrist and pulled me back down. Clumsily I fell on top of him.

Our faces were inches apart.

145

'Hass…'

But Hassan hushed me by pressing his lips over mine.

Chapter Twenty Nine

Confused hearts…

We sat staring at the same patch of geraniums which had a dozen bees dancing around them, sucking out the last pollen drops of the season before the stems lost flower and they starved. However the sound of my breathing was much louder than the songs the bees were buzzing in their frenzy to eat while they could. Even the sound of the aeroplane racing into the sky at the nearby City Airport, wasn't louder than me.

He shouldn't have done that. It was damn out of order. Not only did he kiss me, he crossed a line. My relationship with him wasn't like this. We weren't meant to be kissing each other on the lips like two beasts starved of any prey for months.

No, Hassan shouldn't have done that.

And I should've stopped him much sooner.

'Oye love birds, scarper. I'm about to lock the doors.'

We both turned to see the caretaker jingling a huge set of keys by the door.

'We're going,' replied Hassan.

We got up and as soon as his hand clasped mine a sensation I'd never experienced at his touch before, made me purse my lips.

Why was I feeling this way?

'I'll call us a cab.'

'No the bus,' I croaked. He looked odd for some reason. All grown up. Actually why hadn't I noticed his new hairstyle and when did his chest grow so broad? He appeared taller too. He was almost like a giant compared to me.

'It's almost six, the bus will take forever.'

'I'm bussing it,' I said releasing my hand and walking ahead, aware he was close behind.

Three busses later the number Five arrived. I followed him up to the top deck. He found us seats together and reading the expression on his face, I didn't fight and sat down next to him.

Minutes into the journey he was the first to speak, 'I'm not going to apologize if that's what you're thinking. Not this time. No way. I don't regret what I did and neither should you.'

I did regret it. Habib's words. The promise I'd made him. My Uncle's warnings and Auntie's threats repeated themselves in my head. And it was wrong. I knew this. Muslim girls did not kiss boys on their lips like that. End of.

'I don't see you all summer, I miss you like crazy and feel stuff for you, and all you do is give me the silent treatment like this.' He grabbed my hand and oblivious to the crowded bus, he also thought it was okay to cup a side of my face so I would look at him.

I pulled away as an elderly man with a turban sitting behind us grunted his disapproval.

Respect. Girls like me had to show respect. Having your hand and face held by a boy on a bus wasn't respectful and neither was having words blown close to your ears.

'What is wrong with you?' I spat. 'People are watching, stop touching me.'

'What's wrong with me?' he hissed snatching my mobile phone. 'Seriously Samina, you've cuddled in my arms fuck many times, and I kiss your lips today and you go all mental on me.'

I opened my mouth to tell him otherwise.

I couldn't.

'Yeah… I thought so,' he snorted whilst adding my number to his new phone, leaving me staring at my trembling hands.

He was right.

Aunty fell for the library excuse and didn't say anything. I told her I had been studying from the reference books which we weren't allowed to bring home. She gave me my dinner accepting my lie and after taking a few morsels I pushed the plate aside. I wasn't hungry.

I was angry.

Later in my bedroom and cuddled next to Ayaan, my phone beeped. It was a text.

'Admit it for once we are not friends. You're my girl. Hassan x.'

I read over the same text until my eyes grew heavy and I fell asleep, exhausted. Completely forgetting I still had to talk with Habib and Uncle about the events of the previous evening.

*****

The next morning I was waiting for Uncle to come home. Aunty was still asleep, and I was praying he would return before she woke up.

A key rattled in the hole and before the door had opened, I was rushing towards it.

'Beti,' said Uncle slightly startled as he stepped inside the house.

'You said I'm your princess. You said I will stay with you forever so why did Aunty Asma bring those people here and get me engaged to somebody called Fish? I won't marry him you know. I won't…'

'Repeat what you said,' he scowled and I could see his eyes darkening. He was angry at me.

So instead of repeating it, I did what I was becoming an expert in doing these days. I began to cry and when I couldn't explain, Uncle led me to the living room and shouted for Aunty to come down.

'What happened?' she said when she appeared.

'Did Asma come over?' Uncle asked without wasting time.

'No,' lied Aunty, prolonging the o as she yawned.

'Yes she did,' I cried. 'Uncle she did come, with some people. They gave me five hundred pounds and gold earrings. They took pictures of me and said congratulations because I'm going to marry some idiot called Fish…'

'Calm down Samina,' shouted Uncle directing his anger at Aunty who by now was staring at me red faced. 'Bushra explain this.'

'Samina is mistaken,' said Aunty looking the other way. 'I was too tired to tell you when you got home yesterday and Annie was up all night and oh, I was too too tired…'

'Tell me Bushra.'

Aunty turned to face us again but also took a step back. Uncle's voice had risen.

'Yes Asma did come over bringing those people I had told you about,' sighed Aunty shrugging her shoulders. 'I myself was surprised when they appeared on our doorstep. You know your sister and how pushy she can be. She didn't let me call you from the office for you to talk with the family yourself. Ask her, ask Samina, I didn't accept the sweetmeats they bought. I didn't accept anything. Samina is mistaken. It's nothing. They only came to see her. Nothing else.'

Uncle cursed saying a word I'd never heard him say before. It was a bad word meaning something terribly vulgar.

'Samina go to you room.'

I ran out of the room. The shouting which echoed behind me wasn't healthy. Uncle was mad.

Not at me, but at his wife and sister.

*****

About an hour later Uncle came to my room.

'I won't do it. You promised me.'

'Forget everything,' said Uncle as he sat down on the edge of my bed. 'I've spoken to Asma and told her what to do with this ridiculous proposal. Concentrate on your studies and simply forget this.'

'I'm not engaged?'

'Of course not. I'm still alive you know,' he said rubbing his face behind his hands. 'Nobody makes decisions on your behalf. You're my daughter and no one will decide your future apart from me.'

The corners of Uncle's eye creased and I finally relaxed. 'But beti you are fast growing into a beautiful young woman. In a year or two there will be a line of proposals and one day I will have to consider one.'

I shook my head.

'It's the way of the world and it pleases Allah. Everybody has to settle. When your charming man comes along, I will eventually have to allow him to take you with him. But despite this you will remain close to my heart. Getting married and moving on does not mean a father stops loving his daughter now does it?'

Uncle pulled my head against his shoulder, his familiar woody scent and soothing words meant everything to me. 'The hardest thing a father has to do is give his precious baby away. Yet when the time comes, we all do it.'

'But I'm not getting married. Not ever. I want to be with you here forever.'

Uncle laughed into my head, 'Come on enough of this. You are making me emotional. And the next time your Aunties plan something like this, tell me sooner. Now get ready, I'll drop you to college before I go to sleep.'

'Can I stay at home today and go to the Cabbie with you later?'

'No your education is important. Get ready I will take you. You are already late.'

Chapter Thirty

A bad girl by night…

Half an hour later, I knocked on the door to my Maths class. I was fifty minutes late. Gavin, our tutor allowed me in. With my head down I went and sat on the only vacant chair I could see.

'You're quite the bad arse aren't you?' grinned Ravi as soon as Gavin had stopped lecturing and had set the task. 'When you told me you're a Muslim, I thought damn she'll be too pious to say yes to go out with me. But you bunked both Science lessons yesterday and you're late today. So, what have you been up to?'

'Listen,' I said as he wiggled his brows. 'I haven't been up to anything and you're right in thinking I won't go out with you because I'm a Muslim. But I wouldn't have gone out with you full stop, so let me concentrate on my work.'

He grinned. 'So where were you then?'

'Is that any of your business?' I frowned and when he kept on grinning, I shifted my chair away.

*****

My next lesson was Chemistry and it was the only class I shared with Hassan. Having spent the lunch break with Libby avoiding him, I had no choice but to face him now. When I walked into the classroom, he was gesturing for me to come and sit on the chair next to him. Libby and I both went over.

'Hey Samina,' said Ravi grabbing my hand as I walked past him. 'I saved you a seat.'

Prying my hand free and glaring at him for his nerve I said, 'No Libby and I are sitting over there.'

'Oh come on, we sit together in maths too,' he pestered.

'No, I'm good over here,' I said irritably as we both sat down next to Hassan and his friend Wajid.

'I thought you didn't hang around with boys. Is it okay to sit and play with the Muslim boys and not the others, hey?'

'What?'

'Are you deaf? She said no,' yelled Hassan making the others stare.

Shameless Ravi shrugged but winked at me nonetheless.

'I told you he fancies you,' laughed Libby finding it amusing. 'But what was he saying about Muslim boys?'

'I have no idea,' I whispered finding it hard to ignore the remark so easily.

*****

Our lesson had ended and I was packing my things when I felt Hassan squeezing behind me to get pass.

'I'll see you tomorrow alright,' he said ready to leave.

'Aren't we going home together,' I said as I quickly picked up my bag to follow him. He hadn't said much to me during the lesson either. And I had a feeling he was still in a hump.

'No you go ahead home, it's almost your bedtime,' said Hassan and I watched as he walked out of the room with his new friends, Wajid, Jatinder, and a pretty girl named Marjabeen, without looking back at me, even once.

Feeling a tad bit annoyed, I decided to head to the library to photocopy a page from a reference book for my homework before I headed home. However on my way there, I heard my name being called.

'Oye Samina, Hassan said you're a boffin. I need your help,' said Jatinder as he waved for me to come into the courtyard.

'I was heading to the library,' I told him looking at the huge clock hung up in the hall. I didn't want to be late again. Aunty Bushra was already angry for being found out as it was. I didn't want to further irritate her.

'Please be a mate and help me with this one sum,' pleaded Jatinder.

Dropping my shoulders I said, 'Okay,' and went over.

I had only entered through the open doors when I saw Hassan lighting a cigarette for Marjabeen, who for some bizarre reason preferred to be called Madge. Hassan lit another one and took it between his lips.

Seriously, I could have fainted.

'Hassan?' I shrieked the same way I had all those years back when I'd seen him do it the first time.

'Madge meet my friend Samina,' said Hassan emphasizing the word friend as he blew some smoke my way. I looked away. He was acting childish and quite frankly I wasn't amused.

Not one bit.

'You wanted my help,' I half snapped half complained turning to Jatinder who had some homework out.

'I got it wrong and Tony said I need to give it in before he goes home today. Help me,' said Jatinder earnestly. At the same time Wajid began whistling. I saw Madge walking away. Her backside was swaying and her skinny jeans were making her rear look huge.

'Like what you see?' laughed Wajid as he playfully elbowed Hassan.

Hassan laughed as well and seeing I was watching them, he winked my way, flicked the stub of his cigarette, and chased after her. I held my hand over my mouth as pretty Madge giggled sweetly and bobbed her perfect head with Hassan's. I continued to stare as they both sauntered away.

Before I broke down reeling in his betrayal, I busied myself by completing Jatinder's homework as fast as I could. I then hurried home all by myself.

*****

I couldn't rest. It was way past midnight and since coming into my room all I'd done was pace and stare at the window adjacent to mine. His light was switched off. He was sleeping and I hadn't stopped thinking over the events of the past few days.

My phone beeped. I dashed across my room to the window where it was on the sill and saw his text.

'Go to sleep Samina. At least Madge acts seventeen and not seven. And she never says, 'Don't kiss me. Don't touch me!''

I didn't like his reply. It was to the text I'd sent hours earlier asking why he'd started smoking again and what the story with Madge was.

Looking across at his house I could see his shadow standing by the window. His light had come on. He was staring back at me and he was holding something to his mouth. He was smoking.

I sent my next text.

'Are your parents in?'

'No.'

His reply was all the confirmation I needed. Grabbing my dressing gown, I tiptoed down the stairs. I knew it wasn't an hour I was comfortable going to the garden on my own. Nevertheless I had to see him. His recent behaviour was not on. I had to tell him this and sort him out.

A rush of adrenaline travelled up my spine and as I closed the back door leaving the latch unlocked for my return, which I anticipated would be within the next five minutes, I prayed Aunty wouldn't find out or I'd be dead meat pretty soon.

Our sensory garden light switched on and I cursed under my breath and hurried along. Outside was dark, cold and quite ghostly. Passing the gap in the fence using my phone as a torch, I picked up pace and within seconds I was knocking on Hassan's back door.

Shivering and with chattering teeth, I sent him another text,

'Quick, I'm in your garden. Let me in.'

'What the hell?' he scowled seconds later as he opened the door.

Pushing my way in and cuddling into the fleece of my night gown, I tied it up tighter and blew into my hands.

'It's so cold outside,' I shuddered as I sat on the edge of the sofa in his living room. He went over to the electric fireplace and turned it on. The glow from it illuminated his sleepy face straight away.

'What are you doing here?' he yawned switching the lights on in the room. He was wearing only his boxers. His chest was all muscled and swelling everywhere. Averting my eyes, I looked up at his face instead. 'I was asleep,' he said stretching his arms behind his head.

'Liar,' I gulped. 'You were smoking standing by the window texting me.'

He crossed his arms over his chest and grinned. When did his biceps get so huge?

'I saw you okay,' I scowled looking away at the rug on the floor.

'You peeping Tom. There's a law against that sort of thing. It borders on stalking, you know,' he replied mimicking my tone.

'I don't find that funny,' I said in a low voice as I fiddled with the belt of my gown. 'Anyway where are your parents?'

'Manchester, where else?'

'When are they coming back?'

'A couple of days,' he answered coming and slouching on the sofa next to me. And for some reason, I was too warm too soon. 'It's nearly one in the night what are you up to sneaking to my house at this ungodly hour?'

I craned my neck to look at him.

'A girl only risks doing this because she wants something,' he said and I swallowed as he began to gingerly brush my hair behind my ears causing the skin there to feel funny.

156

'Why are you here,' he asked moving even closer. Our chests collided. We were too close and sure enough he smelled of nicotine.

'You've been smoking. You lied that you quit,' I whispered, knowing his lips were hovering extremely close to mine.

'If a fag was all it took to get you here like this, I would've started smoking ages ago.'

'I've told you it's not good for…'

The next few minutes the only sounds which could be heard in Hassan's living room were the noises of transgression and dishonour being committed by none other than us two seventeen year old, clueless teenagers, who'd forgotten everything ever taught to them.

We had lost our way. Everything about that moment was wrong. The whole night was evil and corrupt. It was stupid and if I could take back time, believe me that night I would have stayed in my own room, fast asleep. Safe and chaste.

Not only the religious rules, we bypassed our culture, the values and norms which we had grown up learning and following. We crossed all the barriers set by family, set by etiquette and set by God.

We broke them all.

By letting Hassan near me, I was breaking my promise to Habib and Uncle and Aunty. I was committing the worst sin of all.

I was dishonouring my family.

But I swear I wouldn't have let anybody blame Hassan for any of this because it was me who went to him. It was me who allowed him to suck all the morals out of me. I allowed him to strip all the layers of dignity and modesty which I'd proudly worn until then.

That night I was allowing Hassan to rip each bit of cloth away from my guarded self, revealing only my shame, my nudity, and my obsession for him.

I regret that night. It wasn't meant to happen.

But it did.

Chapter Thirty One

Searching solitude…

'Wake up.'

I mumbled something lame in my sleep like, 'A few more minutes please…'

'Your Uncle will be coming home, come on get up.'

I opened an eye and seeing a shirtless Hassan drawing closer caused me to open my eyes fully. Realising where I was, I immediately pulled the duvet up to cover myself.

'Good morning my Sweetheart…'

A fear like no other overwhelmed me. His hand slipped inside the duvet and glided over my stomach.

'No,' I said as I flinched, moving away from his touch.

'How do feel?' he asked and despite my unease, he also kissed the side of my face.

My eyes watered and Hassan moved in between the covers. As soon as he wrapped me against his warm body, I used all my force to move to the edge of his bed.

'What's wrong?' he asked with knitted brows.

I shook my head unable to explain the turmoil brewing inside me.

'Samina, its okay…'

'It's not okay…' I shook my head as cries gushed from my deepest depths. I couldn't explain why my body was shaking uncontrollably. All I was aware of was my conscience, and the way it was striking me with lashes covered in nails, telling me I was not meant to be here. I was not in my bed. I was not home. I was going to die.

Sitting up on the bed making sure my nudity couldn't be exposed any further, I began looking around for my clothes.

'Where are my clothes?' I cried. 'Give me my clothes.' They were downstairs in his living room. That's where it had all begun.

'Why are you crying like this?'

'Just get me my clothes,' I sobbed pathetically.

'Samina…?'

'Hassan what have I done?' I screamed. 'What have we done?'

An entirely different emotion replaced Hassan's earlier cheer.

He left the room to fetch my clothes.

*****

He was downstairs standing by the garden door.

'Don't you dare regret last night,' he said sternly, in a tone a grown up would use for a child.

I fastened my robe tighter around me and slipped on my slippers. I walked towards the door. I tied my hair back and gripped the door handle.

'I'll see you at college,' he said as he helped pull open the door.

I stared at my house. If Aunty was awake, what would I say? In my haste to get here at night, I'd left our back door unlocked. She would know I wasn't there. What if Ayaan had woken up during the night? What if Uncle was home and having his breakfast in the kitchen? What would I do? What would I say?

'Why do you look so worried?' Hassan cupped my face. 'Sweetheart it's alright. Promise it is.'

'They'll kill me.' I said. Moving his hands off me, I tried wiping the evidence from my face of the tears which wouldn't stop falling.

I left after that.

And he knew it wasn't wise to chase me.

*****

I stepped inside my kitchen and locked the garden door behind me.

Seconds later the front door unlocked and I heard Uncle coming in from his night shift. I quickly opened the refrigerator and took out the milk, and I grabbed Ayaan's cup.

'Beti make me some tea whilst you are here. My head's hurting. We had a busy night.'

Uncle sat down on the dining chair and I hurriedly made his tea. When I put the cup in front of him, Uncle took hold of my hand.

'I was talking to Ilyas about you last night. About what an ideal daughter you are. He agreed I've done a great job raising you to be so well mannered and bright. You are my pride…'

I bit my swollen lips as I pulled the dirty hand of mine away from his clean one.

'Are you okay?' he asked changing his expression to one of concern and believe me, I tried hard not to give away signs of the deed I'd committed.

'You look pale.'

I shook my head and without saying anything I took Ayaan's milk as my reason to leave right away, and went upstairs. In my bedroom Ayaan was fast asleep. I left the milk on a high shelf to throw away later. That was dirty too now.

I showered by applying shampoo, gels and soap to my body as many times as I could until those tears of mine stopped. They didn't stop. And when the bottles had emptied, I stepped outside, still feeling disgusting and covered in filth.

I threw on a pair of jeans and a jumper. And leaving my hair wet to dry by itself, I stepped onto Ilford Lane and made my way to college, without facing my family.

I spent my time in the quiet corner of the library again coming to terms with what I'd actually done.

And all I desired was to die of shame.

*****

A little after lunch time knowing Hassan would be in our Chemistry class, I left the library and made a dash towards the gates. I wanted to get home before Hassan found me. How could I face him after what we'd done? How could I look him in the eye, knowing the extent of the shame? I couldn't face him. I was disgraced.

However as if he'd been expecting me, Hassan was already at the bus stop.

'I've been worried sick about you,' he said grabbing hold of my elbow. I moved his arm and seeing the approaching bus, I rushed to get on. He jumped on too. I stayed on the bottom deck refusing to follow him up and when he didn't come back down my silent tears betrayed the sense of relief I was feeling.

At Barking Station, Hassan got off behind me. I rushed ahead but he was too fast. He grabbed hold of my shoulder and flung me around.

'Leave me alone,' I frowned.

'What's your problem?' he asked releasing me. I didn't waste time and ran ahead, crossing the road into Fanshawe Avenue.

'Tell me what happened when you got home. Did they clock?' he asked catching up immediately.

'No they didn't and that doesn't make any of this easier.'

'You confuse the fucking shit out of me,' he cursed and because the elderly Asian couple crossing the road with us stopped to see what the commotion between us was all about, Hassan simply waved his hands in the air and walked back towards the station.

I watched him go. A part of me wanted to run after him and tell him I'd been happy with everything and I'd loved every second of the night we'd shared, but this would have been a lie because apart from the regret, I remembered nothing about it.

With my head down, too ashamed to face the skies where the heavens were, I carried myself forward in the direction of my house.

The sound of the Imam calling the believers of Allah to pray reached my ears and I looked around bewitched. The Azaan, the Muslim call to prayer was being said inside Barking Mosque. The doors to the holy place were wide open.

For a moment I stood outside in one safe corner listening to the mellow voice of the caller, my heart yearning to be closer to it.

My heart was restless and only to experience a moment of solitude I decided to go inside the Mosque and beg Allah to forgive me. I had done wrong. I knew I had committed something which was unforgiveable. But Uncle had always said whenever he went inside the Mosque, he felt a peace.

I needed to feel that peace.

'Excuse me sister you can't go in without a scarf on your head.'

I stopped and absorbed the burka clad woman's reminder.

Feeling guilt at not being appropriately dressed, I began retreating away. I wiped my face of a tear, maybe I wasn't worthy of being privileged the sacredness of the holy sanctuary anymore.

'Don't walk away from the house of God feeling dejected. You are welcome as you are…'

Turning to look over my shoulder, I saw my elderly Imam, Uncle Dawood gesturing me in.

I bit my lip before saying, 'Aslaam Alaikum.'

He answered my greeting with a soft smile. As I walked past him, I pulled at the hem of my jumper to cover my denim clad waist. My hair was tied in a messy pony tail and I wished I'd had a scarf.

'There is a basket in the women's section with spare hijabs my dear,' Uncle Dawood told me as if sensing my embarrassment.

'Thank you Uncle,' I said smiling at him weakly.

'Bless you beti Samina.'

'You remember my name?'

162

Uncle Dawood chuckled and the white beard on his face shone like a dove. 'Of course I know you're name. Jawed cannot stop talking about you whenever he visits. The Mosque committee were treated to a fantastic dinner when you passed your exams. The man was the happiest I'd ever seen him.'

The water I had been suppressing in my eyes rolled down to my chin and I quickly wiped at it. And as the Imam continued to talk about my Uncle, I buried my nails against my palms feeling not peaceful, but sorry. The respect he showed for him and his contributions to the Mosque was something I was completely unaware of.

My Uncle had always been a man who strived to uphold his respect and dignity in the community.

'Thank Allah for giving you a special Uncle who raised you as his own and taught you right from wrong. He is a good man.'

'Yes Uncle,' I choked and as soon as I got to the women's section, I grabbed a scarf, covered myself and went and prostrated in the furthest corner away from prying eyes.

I had to beg for forgiveness. I had made the biggest mistake of my life. I needed my Allah to forgive me.

And I also needed him to help me forget the boy who had also sinned with me. As hard as this prayer was, I prayed it.

I prayed it again and again.

Chapter Thirty Two

Finding solitude…

It's true when they say 'love hurts.' It does and I won't even begin comparing it to any other calamity I'd been through. Because what I was going through since realising I was suffering from this 'love,' was something I knew I wouldn't survive.

I was in love with Hassan Iqmal.

I had been on my lap top for hours on end Googling the actual meaning of this word 'love.' I had checked fifteen different textbooks and all the dictionaries in the college library for this word, and it was me and Hassan all over.

We fitted all the descriptions and all the emotions and were the perfect candidates for it. And then I was what they called, 'vulnerable in love.' The agony my heart's chambers were hiding was getting stronger by the day, making me less and less able to continue the way I had been.

I'd been ignoring, fighting and pushing him away for the previous four weeks. He had been persistent and pestering me to at least talk to him. He had sneaked into my bedroom half a dozen times already, and each time I had to threaten I'd jump out of the window if he didn't leave.

I was mental like that, loopy in the head, dopey in the mind, and worst of all my heart was all messed. Good and proper.

I wasn't eating. I wasn't talking much to anybody either. At home my family thought it was the pressure of studies. 'A level's are tough,' Habib had said on Skype one day when raising his concerns about my lost weight. And the others at college thought I was stuck up. I didn't even reply back when they said a simple thing like hello to me anymore. I was completely intolerable. And it was because of that one night which had changed everything.

I loved him. I was in love with Hassan Iqmal and I couldn't do anything about it, other than destroy myself by bottling my feelings up.

But this feeling, this way I was, it was wrong…

As his friend never once did I question our time together. Never did Habib's warnings, Auntie's threats or my Uncle's honour come and stand in front me like this.

Had I been stupid from the day go then? Yes. I'd been wrong from the beginning. Parveen had been right. My friendship with Hassan hadn't been right.

But how was I to cope without him? How could I go on living like this?

'Samina for the last time what's the answer?'

'Samina!'

'It was Hassan sir...'

The laughter which erupted at my reply shook me awake from those same thoughts to the present. Everybody, even Tony our tutor was laughing.

'Hassan so it was you,' chuckled Tony gesturing to the boy who now sat at the back of the room, alone and aloof.

I forced myself to turn my head to look at him. He had a pen between his fingers and unlike the others, he looked glum. He wasn't laughing.

Catching his gaze lock with mine, I found it impossible to breathe. I wanted to call his name. I wanted to reach him and feel the sides of his face in my palms. I wanted him to smile at me. But he shook his head and looked the other way.

'Settle down now,' said Tony. 'And Samina pay attention.'

Attention? I'd been using all of that to maintain this distance with the boy who wouldn't smile anymore.

With a guilty conscious, I watched him drop the pen on the table. He began packing his stuff. And ignoring Tony telling him to sit back down, he barged towards the door and left the room.

165

'Go after him,' urged Libby.

Without a second's thought, I mimicked Hassan's actions and left the classroom.

*****

I found him in the courtyard. His hands were in his jacket pockets and his legs were sprawled in front of him.

Breathless from my run looking for him, I went and sat down next to him on the bench.

It must have been a good ten minutes or maybe more as we sat in complete silence. It was the end of October. The bees were long gone. The flowers, the pollen all dried up. It was too quiet. The atmosphere around me didn't seem peaceful.

Crunching the autumn leaves under his trainers as he stood, Hassan began walking away.

'Hass…' I said desperate for him to stay where he was.

His feet stopped and I cried out as he strode back towards me. His eyes looked dark and dangerous. His stubble made him look older. The tightening of his jaw made me slip further back on the bench and I closed my eyes when his curled fist went up high in the air.

'Don't hit me…'

'Go fuck yourself,' he shouted gripping the back of my head in a tight hold.

My hair pulled and I opened my eyes and watched the same fist that was in the air fall to his side. Shoving my head back he released my hair and fell down beside me on the bench.

It was too much. I had done this to him. He was all over the place. He had yelled at Madge the other day. She had only asked the time. And he had also blown Wajid's head when he said he had acted 'out of order.'

Hassan was disturbed and I hated myself for it.

My breaths kept hitching as I tried regaining some control of myself. I must have looked a total freak.

'Sorry I scared you,' he said, his voice hushed but his fists were still curled.

I shook my head. I was the one who ought to have been sorry. It was my entire fault. I had been searching for peace since the morning we woke up together. I hadn't found it anywhere. Four weeks and three days, not an ounce of peace. Everything around me was chaotic and I was covered in a layer of discontent. I'd kept away from Hassan purposely. I had caused all this chaos. I had caused this aching and this longing.

Love wasn't a crime. In fact love wasn't considered a crime in anybody's religion. I might have sinned that night, but I'd been repenting ever since. I'd been releasing each breath of mine with heartfelt whispers pleading for mercy.

But I couldn't keep away from him any longer. It wasn't possible. I loved him. I loved Hassan with all I was. Staying away from him when he went Pakistan had been bearable because I didn't even know what love was then. I had learnt it now. I had felt it and I had done it. I knew each and every syllable of the word there was, and I was experiencing it in heights I couldn't handle on my own anymore.

'No I am sorry,' I said with a new found courage.

'…What?'

Slowly I looked up and gazed into his hopeful eyes. 'It's true. I'm sorry for ignoring you. Please believe me because I love you,' I voiced desperately. 'I love you so much Hassan.'

As if my words brought life into his limbs, he instantly pulled me against him and wrapped his arms around me. Breathing as heavily as me, he buried his face in my hair.

'I was scared of what we did that night. Allah will punish us Hassan,' I said as my voice shook. 'It was wrong. I was so scared of everything. Scared for you. Scared for me. But Hassan I can't stay away from you. I'm sorry, I'm sorry for everything…'

'Don't you dare try going away from me. Never again. Promise me you won't do this again.'

'I promise.'

Chapter Thirty Three

When something smells fishy…

The night before Eid Hassan and I were standing in our gardens, him on his side, and me on ours. He was helping to clasp the chain he'd gifted around my neck as I held the heart shaped pendent and smiled at it.

'I love it,' I said feeling giddy.

'It's also our ten month anniversary as a couple who are more than just friend's celebration, right?'

'Right,' I giggled as he tried tickling me. A clanking of pots coming from inside my house made me break away. 'I best go.'

Hassan grinned but nodded his approval. He was going to Manchester the following morning to spend Eid with his relatives there. We were on our summer break again and Hassan had convinced his parents to let him stay at home this year. His father hadn't been pleased. He wanted him to start taking the business seriously and to move to Manchester for the holidays, in order to learn the trade at the head office there. After all Hassan was his only child, and the group of estate agents scattered around London and Manchester were to be handled by him, eventually.

Actually deep down Hassan was thrilled by this. He couldn't wait to complete his studies and get his hands on some of his father's money. He had already started planning on what cars he would buy. A flashy BMW was all he dreamt about.

He was so cute.

Sneaking back inside my house, I laughed. Little Annie was sitting by the open cupboards with a wooden spoon in one hand and a colander in the other, and she was busy banging away.

'You trouble maker,' I said pulling her into my arms. She was adorable. Always up to mischief. We were celebrating her first birthday the following day. Aunty Asma's lot were coming and because it was also Eid, we had decided to make it a double celebration.

I carried Annie into the living room despite her whining to go back to the kitchen. Aunty was enjoying the Eid show on the Pakistani channel on telly, and Uncle was fast asleep on the sofa. Aunty had forced him to come home earlier than usual to help put the new curtains up in the living room.

'All done?' I asked appreciating the plum and gold coloured window dressing as I sat next to Uncle and jerked him awake. Annie jumped onto his chest and fiddled with his wrist watch.

'Yes,' groaned Uncle opening a corner of his eye and then closing it again.

'Your Uncle has turned old too soon,' said Aunty.

'He's not old,' I smiled snuggling next to him like Annie was. 'He's my cuddly bear.'

'No mine,' grumbled Ayaan charging at us from out of nowhere and climbing onto Uncle's legs.

'No mine,' I teased trying to push him off.

'Kids give the old man some rest,' said Uncle. And as his eyes opened he pulled us all in for a huge hug.

I had never been this happy. Everything was perfect.

*****

I had finished eating the delightful treats Aunty had cooked for our Eid breakfast when the doorbell rang. Despite feeling stuffed, I raced Ayaan to the door. Knowing he wasn't allowed to open it, he stepped aside, happy in claiming his win for getting there first.

I ruffled his silky hair and opened the door expecting the early bird Aunty Asma and her clan.

'Eid Mubarak.'

170

'Khair Mubarak,' I replied cheerfully but not recognising the man who stood there, I tried closing the fully ajar door a bit to stop him peering inside. Unfortunately, Ilford Lane wasn't as safe as it once was.

'You must be Simmi,' he said almost breathlessly. I imagined whoever he was had run the length of Ilford Lane, twice.

'Err no,' I said. 'I'm not Simmi. You've got the wrong house.' I began closing the door more forcefully but the man pushed at it stopping me.

Freaking out I called, 'Aunty...'

'I am assuming you have not recognised me,' said the man in an accent which told me he'd arrived from Pakistan recently.

'Huh?' I gave him a brief look as I pushed at the door. If he was indeed a burglar, I'd need a good description. But his smile grew enormous and the way his eyes hovered over me wasn't appreciated. I was tempted to smack his face but Aunty came. She too eyed the grinning man with suspicion, and I think she also noticed the way he was leering at me.

Pulling me behind her, she pushed at the door ushering the man out, 'What do you want?'

'I am offended Aunty Bushra.'

I cringed as the stranger feigned hurt by shaking his head and lowering his gaze. But he looked up too soon, past my Aunt and at me again.

'I am Feesh,' he said. 'Fiancé to the lovely Simmi, I mean lovely Samina.'

Sucking in a breath and shaking my head in denial to his outrageous claim, I grabbed Auntie's arm and tugged at it. He most definitely was not a fiancé to me. He wasn't anybody. He was a strange idiot. He was a total nut case and I wasn't his fiancé. I was nothing to him.

'Oh, oh, Feesh. Forgive me, how silly I feel. My dear don't stand there come in, come on in.'

My eyes widened at Aunty as she moved aside and pulled me with her. The man, the Fish, or whatever he was, stepped into our home bringing with him a stink of suspicion and unease all around me.

*****

I was fuming. It was the first time Aunty had acted sly since the time Uncle had reprimanded her. Nevertheless she seemed completely unfazed with the fact I'd already told Uncle as soon as he came home from the Mosque after the Eid prayer.

And Uncle had reassured me not to worry. Our house for some reason had quickly filled up with guests. Amidst the chaos, Uncle had promised he would get to the bottom of it as soon as he got the chance.

The Fish boy who seemed to be the guest of honour, had taken away all of Annie's glory. I mean it was her birthday and Eid, not feed the Fish boy day with anything and everything. I swear everybody, excluding Uncle, was giving him the celebrity treatment.

Why?

There were people everywhere. And a whole heap of food had arrived from a local caterer's to feed them. Like me, Uncle was surprised by this. We had thought it was going to be a small family gathering with only Aunty Asma's kids and their kids, not everybody in the world.

Although I could see Uncle sitting between my Uncle Murad and the Fish boy, I knew he was boiling in anger inside. When Uncle was silent with his shoulders dropped, he was waiting to explode.

But I was going to remain brave and quiet like he had asked me to. I trusted him more than my own brother. Uncle would deal with this and I couldn't wait.

*****

For lunch the women were separated from the men and I needed a breather. I took Annie upstairs pretending she needed a nap. Annie fell asleep straight away. Pulling a

172

blanket over her small body, I rested my head against the headboard and closed my eyes.

I felt a dread settling in.

The door creaked open and opening my eyes, I couldn't believe Fish boy was there. With Aunty Asma.

'And this is her bedroom,' said Aunty Asma urging him to look around. I got off the bed and pressed my lips tightly together. 'You can of course change it later to suit your taste.'

'Aunty,' I snapped as I slipped my sandals on. How dare she bring him into my private space?

'Ah Samina you are here too,' she beamed. 'Isn't she pretty? My niece. Don't you agree Feesh, she is pretty?'

'Indeed, the prettiest,' replied the Fish boy spluttering spit my way.

Disgusted, I glared at Aunty Asma. How dare she say stuff like that? We weren't getting married. What was wrong with everybody? And for the first time that day unable to hold in my feelings any longer, I pushed past them and ran downstairs.

Uncle was in the living room still sitting on the same sofa with his head down. And the white bearded man, the one who fancied Shahrukh Khan and gave me those earrings, was sitting next to him, talking.

I didn't care. I went and squeezed myself in the tiny gap next to Uncle's other side and taking him by surprise, buried my head in his chest and began to cry.

'Beti?' said Uncle as he gently pulled me back to cup my face and look at me. 'Meri jaan…'

The endearment he used confirming I was his life, his darling, gave me instant relief. Once he had kissed my forehead, I dug my head into his chest and Uncle put his arms around my shoulders letting me hold onto him.

Everybody else could go fuck themselves. I was okay now. As long as Uncle was with me, no one could make these ridiculous lies about me and that lame Fish boy.

'Mash-Allah you have raised our Samina very cultured. The talk of marriage to my son has made her emotional.'

It was his voice, the bearded man's. So he was Fish boy's father. I felt his hand on my head and I cried harder. I didn't want him touching me.

'Be calm Samina beti,' he chuckled attempting to pull me away from Uncle, but I shrugged his hand away. 'Our Feesh will not be taking you away from your Uncle. He will stay here in this house with you after the marriage.'

'Please Bhai Saab,' said Uncle sternly as he straightened his back. 'You are talking in riddles. What even gave you the idea I will hand my daughter over to your son? I certainly did not agree on this proposal. Please stop talking this way. She is a child. It's upsetting her.'

'Jawed Saab all daughters get married one day. We understand she is precious to you, but sisters Asma and Bushra both assured me you had already consented when we blessed the engagement. Today we are here to set the date for the wedding. Our family members have travelled from Pakistan especially for this auspicious moment.'

'Who consented?' asked Uncle raising his voice and at the same time holding onto me more tightly.

'Jawed relax,' Uncle Murad, Aunty Asma's husband urged. 'Tabrez Jee is our elder. Let's talk about this more calmly.'

'*Calmly…?* Murad my daughter isn't a toy you can all use for your own benefits,' roared Uncle creating a silence around us. Even the children had hushed. I closed my eyes and kept telling myself I was okay now. Uncle was protecting me. Everything was going to be okay.

'Murad I expected a little respect from your brother in law,' Tabrez Jee, Fish boy's father spat. He sounded just as angry as Uncle now. 'You said to bring the family over on Eid to set the date.'

'Murad you had no right to do that,' shouted Uncle making the women in the room gasp. 'Samina is my daughter. How dare you?'

'Asma,' Uncle Murad now yelled. 'Is this the respect I get at your brother's house?'

174

And as the shouting and cursing and trying to get each other to understand each other continued, Uncle kept a firm hold on me and set everyone straight.

I wasn't anyone's fiancé. There was no upcoming wedding.

Everybody left without eating any of Annie's birthday cake. And as soon as they had gone, Uncle pulled Aunty by the arm and did something I'd never seen him do ever.

He raised his hand to her and left finger prints on her cheek.

It wasn't a nice scene for me to witness but I didn't blame him for doing it.

She deserved it.

Chapter Thirty Four

Revelations in the garden...

The night dragged. Morning was nowhere in sight. I wondered what the sky had in store for me, when inevitably the sun would rise and the darkness replaced. Was it going to be sunny again, or would it be grey and gloomy?

I could feel a storm coming.

Giving Hassan's window one last tearful stare, I turned to my bed, rather my empty bed because Ayaan wasn't in it. Aunty had taken both children to Blackpool. Faizaan had answered the distress call she had made to him and within minutes he had taken her away with them.

Uncle's smack had offended her deeply.

*****

The empty house was haunting me the next day and as Uncle was getting ready to go to the Cabbie, I asked if I could spend some time with him there. He agreed.

At the Cabbie, still feeling restless, I began doing chores which didn't even need doing. I mopped, I dusted, and whilst I was wiping a stain on the glass panels on the outside of the front doors, I heard my name being called by none other than Hassan.

His father's car was stopped in traffic outside our shop. A smile appeared on my face, glad he had returned so soon. I sent a small wave.

'Why haven't you answered my calls and what are you doing here?' asked Hassan poking his head out of his open window. I immediately frowned at his actions. He was sitting behind his parents in the car and as he spoke, they both looked over at me curiously. Especially his mother.

To my relief the traffic began to move but as he moved on he pointed at the door. 'You missed a bit,' he laughed.

I looked back at the door to see for myself. But all traces of joy at having him back home were replaced with something else altogether.

Uncle was standing by the window.

*****

My gut instinct was telling me Uncle was suspecting something. When Hassan's father had driven them away, Uncle had asked what he was saying. Obviously I lied and said he was merely asking about a college assignment. It was the totally wrong thing to have said considering Uncle wasn't even aware Hassan and I went to the same place. My answer made him rub his face behind his hands and when he released it, I swear he was a different person.

'I don't want you anywhere near that boy. Don't talk to him again or there'll be trouble for you too. Do I make myself clear?'

'Yes Uncle,' I replied with my head down.

*****

Less than an hour later, Uncle gave the controls to Mehmet saying he wasn't feeling too good.

'I'll make you some tea,' I said when we arrived home. 'Or should I just get dinner?'

'Only tea,' he replied in a low voice as he picked up the house phone. He didn't look well at all and looking at the way his shirt was rumpled and his hair uncombed, I felt a lump forming in my throat. I was responsible.

'Uncle, are you sad?'

My lips quivered as I looked into his red eyes. The house was empty and there was no noise. I hated it. Long gone were the days where I spent hours upon hours with only the telly as my companion. I hadn't had a lonely moment since Ayaan had arrived and I knew Uncle was

177

missing the kids as much as I was. They had never gone away, never ever.

'Beti,' sighed Uncle throwing the phone on the sofa and rubbing his forehead.

'I didn't want Aunty and you to fight,' I whispered.

'I don't understand her. It's not a little thing what she did. I can't forgive her for this easily. In fact I can't come to terms with any of it,' said Uncle.

'I'm missing Ayaan and Annie and I know you are as well. Please let's go and bring them back.' I pleaded, 'Please let's go.'

'Let her stew over there in Blackpool for a few days, she'll be back herself. Just you watch.'

After a few minutes of deadly silence, I decided to make that cup of tea. My stomach was rumbling, I hadn't eaten anything since the Eid breakfast. Leaving Uncle to his own thoughts, I went to the kitchen.

Within minutes I had Uncle's tea and a plate of leftover dinner for myself on a tray. As I entered the living room, Uncle began yelling over the phone.

'No I don't care what the family in Pakistan will say. Asma you can tell your husband I am not allowing this. Yes I have spoken to Habib. Of course he agrees with my decision…'

I pursed my lips. They were still going on about the Fish boy. And Uncle looked like he was about to murder someone. He was shouting loudly.

Leaving the tray on the coffee table, I went back inside the kitchen, my hunger all forgotten. As Uncle's voice loomed I had to take deep breaths. I was anxious. The most anxious I'd ever been. Why were they doing this to us? Why did they think I was ready to be getting married anyway?

Needing some air, I opened the back door and went and sat on our garden swing. The evening was a warm one and a tepid breeze brushed past my skin, yet I felt a chilly sensation. I shook my head, I was being silly. Uncle was putting them straight. I had nothing to be worried about.

But I was worried.

'Miss me that much did you?'

Two familiar arms snaked up behind me. One hand pressed over my mouth muffling my surprise and the other hand slipped around my waist pulling me closer as he sat next to me. The swing creaked and I held in my shock.

'I missed you too,' he whispered blowing his minty breath close to my jaw. For a moment I lost myself in his closeness but then as if sensing the lurking dangers, I pushed him away.

'You better leave, Uncle is home,' I said whispering my request.

'So what,' he moaned.

'Please go for now. I'll phone you in a bit. I need to talk about what happened,' I said as I moved away from him and looked towards the kitchen. The sensory light was on, and I'd rather die than allow Uncle to see me with Hassan.

'You look tired.' Hassan stood up and with narrowed eyes he said, 'You've been crying?'

It was all he had to say to make my heart race towards him and fall into his embrace again.

'Uncle hit Aunty and she took the babies away. Uncle is real mad right now. He's shouting at them and it's all because of me.'

'What are you talking about…?'

'Samina!'

Immediately I pulled away and ran towards the door. I was trembling. Believe me I was that scared. I didn't need to tell Hassan to leave because he too knew the drill. His hurried footsteps told me he was making himself scarce. Nevertheless I was still terrified.

'Who were you talking to?' said Uncle meeting me by the door and instead of allowing me inside, he grabbed my wrist and pulled me into our huge garden.

'No, no… no one,' I stammered making myself stiff unwilling to go further into the garden.

Uncle's red eyes scanned the entire plot and rested on me. 'I asked you something. Who was here?'

'No one,' I managed to repeat despite the steady beats of my heart. For a moment Uncle stared at me with fire blazing from every feature of his face and because he was holding my wrist too tightly, tears appeared in my eyes as I lied again. 'No one was here.'

Uncle dropped my wrist but he wouldn't stop looking at me with the same look of disdain he had presented the guests the day before. I stood there shaking, every cell inside of me both cold and hot.

'Hassan, come and eat your dinner…'

Uncle's head snapped towards the direction of the other garden where the voice of Hassan's mum echoed from.

And because I was a lost cause, I began to shake my head and cry out in false denial as Hassan's voice in the distance muttered, 'Shit,' and then, 'Coming Mum.'

'You better not be sneaking over there to see Bushra's niece again. Don't think I don't know what you two get up to…'

His mother's sentence hadn't even finished that Uncle yelled my name, instantly stopping my tantrum like reaction. Because when his heavy fist connected to my face, I was blinded immediately.

Chapter Thirty Five

A brick wall and an iron fist…

Before that evening if anyone had asked me who the one person who would never hurt me was, the answer wouldn't have been Hassan, because sometimes Hassan could still play the role of my tormentor perfectly. The answer would have been Uncle, my Uncle Jawed.

I wasn't too sure about that anymore.

My mouth was spluttering blood from a broken tooth and my nose was runny and bloody. The whole of my face was sore and my head dizzy.

He had hurt me.

I was lying on the floor on a muddy patch of grass. Maybe it was wet from my own blood. Who knew?

As expected from him, Hassan had come to my rescue as soon as Uncle had knocked me blind minutes earlier. He had yelled, and maybe he had even pushed Uncle away because briefly I had felt Hassan's body enveloping me. I may have lost consciousness next.

Coming back hazily I could see Hassan being restrained by his father at the edge of our garden, and his mum Sheila was begging my Uncle to stop saying stuff. My woozy state managed to make out he was talking about *my* Yasmin.

'Don't say things about other people's daughters Iqmal when your own daughter wasn't an angel,' said Uncle standing stiff. 'Your son is exactly like her. How many times did I tell him to keep away from my property and my daughter? This was exactly what I told your girl to do once.'

'Don't bring my daughter into this Jawed,' Rahese, Hassan's father hissed, gripping Hassan against him more tightly as he shuffled to escape him. 'That is out of order. She isn't here anymore. Don't slander her name like this.'

'Why?' sneered Uncle. 'She followed my nephew. Trapped him. Pestered him to run away to get married before you found out about her deed. And now your son is trying to stray my daughter in the same way as Habib was.'

'Habib,' cried Sheila holding onto her head. 'Your nephew Habib…?'

Uncle's lips tilted upwards and my blood boiled. I didn't like what he was saying. I didn't like how Hassan's eyes were closed and I didn't like the water which had started to streak down from the corners of his eyelids.

'Is it hard to accept?' said Uncle. 'Is it hard to imagine her and my nephew together? Hard to imagine she was expecting my grandchild. My bastard grandchild…'

'Be quiet about Yasmin,' I cried helplessly as I tried standing up. Why was he saying all this? Yasmin wasn't pregnant. She didn't die with a baby inside her. She died in a fire.

But before I could voice this, Uncle's fist assaulted me again and this time Hassan's arms didn't come over and cradle me.

All I felt was the storm I had predicted.

*****

Aunty Bushra returned home that same night. She came in a panic and one look at me and she had paled. It's true she had hurt me over the years, had smacked me, punched me, pushed me, beat me with the wooden spoon she cooked with, but I didn't think my face had ever bruised or blued to this extent before.

Ayaan began to cry and Aunty Asma who had arrived with them had to pick him up. Faisal, my cousin who had also come, reassured me it was okay and to stop crying. He cleaned me up and held a frozen bag of mixed vegetables to my jaw.

'Jawed, what have you done?' cried Aunty Asma. 'What is wrong with you? First Bushra and now Samina. Which jinn has possessed you my brother?'

Uncle ignored her. And taking the vegetable packet from my cousin he said, 'Faisal ring Habib. Tell him to get here by the time she turns eighteen. And tell the boy's family, I am sorry and I consent. Tell Murad to arrange everything with them. No actually I will go see Tabrez Jee in the morning myself and apologise. Samina is to marry Feesh. The engagement is on.'

A few long moments later where I had simply sat numbed, Uncle asked Faisal to get up. I felt the sofa dip. Uncle sat in his place. The bag of vegetables which he held was pressed to the side of my face.

He stared at me. I stared back.

His breaths began to hitch. His whole body trembled and when he couldn't control it any longer, Uncle pulled me against him and broke down on top of my head.

I had never seen him cry before and I couldn't help but cry with him.

*****

By midday the next day a brick wall was being built in our back garden. Uncle supervised the Polish labourers as they constructed it. Aunty Asma tried rescuing a bag load of spinach from Auntie's Bushra's vegetable patch, and I stood in my bedroom by my window, watching each brick define the border between the two houses.

My gum was aching. I had a hole in the back of my mouth. Aunty Asma reckoned the missing tooth would grow back soon. A side of my face was purple and black and my lip swollen and cut.

My eye was slightly black too. Thus a trip to the dentist was out of the question.

Habib as expected was mad. His face had burned red and his expression fluctuated between anger and disappointment as Aunty Bushra explained my deeds to him through

Skype. She had even resorted to showing him the texts Hassan and I had been sending to each other on my mobile phone, when he hadn't believed I could do such a thing.

Habib didn't yell at Uncle for punching me though, like he did the time when Aunty had hurt me. He didn't even comment on my appearance and I'm sure he could see me as clearly as I could see him on the laptop screen.

Realising he didn't care anyway, I kicked the coffee table and the laptop fell to the floor.

He hadn't cared for years.

Chapter Thirty Six

The bad boy bully strikes again…

Three weeks had passed and my yearning to see Hassan had never been greater. The wall was an ugly orange troll stopping me from getting to him. The front door was evil, as it was always locked and never let me through to the other side. The house phone, my mobile phone, the computer, the laptop, all the internet, everything and everyone around me had switched off and was hidden away from my reach.

Everything was evil for keeping me away from my Hassan.

I was stuck in my room, day and night. Refusing to eat. Refusing to change. Refusing to do anything. But everything else was going on as normal. Uncle at the Cabbie. Aunty Bushra and the kids going about their same routines. The only change was with Ayaan. He had started full time school. During the day he wasn't home, and at night Aunty had trained him to sleep in his own bedroom.

My college? The new term would begin soon and I needed to be there, so I could see him again. Most nights I would see his silhouette standing by his window. But I wanted to know why he had started drawing his curtains over the blinds now. He never did that before. Why did he not stand at the window looking back at me, making funny gestures, like he always had?

A knock on my bedroom door made me hug onto my knees. On the second knock, the door creaked open. A stench filled my room. It was Fish boy.

'May I enter?' he asked entering anyway.

He came and sat on my bed. Far enough but too close for comfort.

'Uncle Jawed asked how I feel about you returning to college next week.' His hand reached for mine and naturally I tried avoiding his touch. But he was a moron and grabbed it forcefully.

I felt disgusting and it felt wrong. I hated the fact he now lived in the flat above the Cabbie because since then this Fish boy had made it a habit to come over to the house every day.

This wasn't normal. This was a change I wanted to alter right away. Uncle had given him a job at the Cabbie. He was teaching him to control the business and I hated this. I hated everything about him.

'Why are you upset my dear?' he asked tilting his head to the side to look at me more carefully. 'What has occurred to make you this way? Tell me dear.'

I shook my head staring at his greasy thumb on my palm. He needed to move that. It wasn't right. He wasn't meant to touch me, end of.

'Tell me, I can feel there is a tension in the house. We were extremely shocked when Uncle Jawed came to my father apologising for his irrational behaviour on Eid, and fixed the wedding date. January first, what a nice day to get married.'

I turned eighteen three days before that date. I wouldn't do it though. No way. Never.

'Tell me dear, what worries you?'

'I want to go college,' I croaked, surprising myself.

He pouted his rubber lips and bounced his backside on my bed shifting closer.

'I want to be a doctor. It's always been my dream,' I continued.

'And my dearest, my most sincere Simmi, I will make sure your dreams come true.'

I tried to move him away as his slimy thumb left my hand and brushed my cheek.

'Always coy and emotional. I like that in you. You are delicate.' Tracing the same thumb along my forehead and flicking a strand of my hair behind my ear, he slurred, 'Do

186

not worry, I will speak to the elders and gain permission for you to return to college.'

A weak smile came to me thinking about Hassan. I would see him there. I would see him again.

'Pretty, extremely pretty...'

My smile dropped and when Fish boy had the audacity to squeeze out his lips preparing to kiss me, I got off the bed and ran downstairs.

I would never marry Fish boy.

*****

Uncle dropped me to college on the first day back. Obviously I'd lost the privilege of taking the bus on my own. He would be back later to pick me up.

However as I walked through the gates my heart began to beat too fast. Each step I took inside the college, I felt myself coming back to life again. A goofy smile found its way to my lips and it wouldn't go away.

I began looking here and there and dodging new groups of fresh students and teachers going about their tasks and endeavours, typical of any first day of a new term. I made my way to the courtyard where we first declared our love for one another. A sense of nostalgia hit me.

The courtyard seemed happy. The flowers were in full bloom and those bees, the ones which had disappeared for the winter were back and buzzing like anything. They couldn't be blamed because there was so much colour and pollen about. Even I had a bit of hay fever that day.

'Hey long time no see.'

I turned around coming face to face with Ravi. His hair was longer. He had it in a ponytail. 'Hello Ravi,' I replied finding my voice a little dry and crisp. 'Have you seen Hassan?'

His smile dropped and he shrugged his shoulders. 'No. I'll let you know when I do.'

'Thanks,' I said as I gave those bees one last look and went in search for Hassan again.

*****

I hurried to Chemistry. I could sense Hassan was there. And to my utter joy, he was. I almost skipped my way to him planning to tap his shoulder so he would turn around and see me. It would be the best surprise. To see me, his sweetheart again.

I tapped his shoulder and my hand came alive with sensations only he could give me by one small touch. I could smell his aftershave, the one I told him to never change, and I had to stop myself from putting my arms around him and losing myself in his familiarity.

His body shifted to look at me.

Choking on my voice which sounded like a silly laugh, I said, 'Hass.'

His eyes twinkled as he took me in and a smile twitched a corner of his lips and not being able to hold back anymore, I took a step closer to him and dug myself against his chest. His hands moved over to my shoulders and travelled along my forearms where he gripped them.

'Hassan,' I said but then I think it was Libby's voice I heard as I was bolted away from him and pushed to the table behind me.

'Touch me again you hoe, I'll tell that fucked up Uncle of yours to put you on a tighter leash.'

With wide and watery eyes, I stared back at Hassan. His whole face was twisted in a look of abhorrence at me.

'Why did you do that?' yelled Libby as she hurried over to help me up. 'Is that how you people treat women you barbarians?'

Her comment started up a round of abuse, where everybody in the class went on a rampage of debate and accusations.

And I sat there trying to breathe, staring at Hassan the whole time. He stared back, without emotion. No smirk, no sheepish grin, no anger, no hurt or mischief or anything. He stared back, exactly like the tall brick wall in our garden.

But my eyes, they wouldn't stop watering and my body wouldn't stop shaking and when Tony came into class and saw me, he asked for the college nurse to be called.

She came and Uncle was phoned. And I spent the rest of the week at home doing nothing apart from stare out of the window.

*****

It was back at college the following week when I saw Hassan again. I had come into class early to speak with Tony about the work I'd missed. He gave me some hand outs and I was already engrossed in them as the rest of the class began to appear. After the humiliation Hassan had put me through the other day, I didn't dare look up at anybody.

Something being flicked at my head did make me look up eventually. I brushed a hand over where I beginning to feel a sting. Another heavy pen bounced off of me and rattled on the table.

'Get off my chair.'

It was Hassan and seeing him, I couldn't help but smile. I hadn't seen him since the day he'd pushed me and said that horrid word. But it was okay, he'd been upset with my Uncle. Obviously he hadn't meant it.

I wasn't really a hoe. I loved him.

'Are you fucking deaf?' he shouted and this time I couldn't smile anymore. His eyes were dark and mean looking. He had a tight jaw and when he started picking up my work and throwing it across the floor, I got up.

Conscious of everybody looking, I began to collect my things as quick as I could manage in my dumbfounded state. Juggling my papers and stationary in my hands, I hurried over to sit on the only available seat, next to Ravi.

'You deserve so much better Samina,' said Ravi as Tony came back to begin the lesson.

189

I didn't. I deserved only Hassan.

*****

After class I followed Hassan to the courtyard. We needed to talk. He would have to talk. I couldn't understand his behaviour. I had to tell him about Fish boy and my Uncle's plans for this upcoming wedding. I had to tell him everything. I needed him to listen. He'd have to.

He was sat on the bench, with Wajid and Jatinder. Smoking.

'Can we talk for a sec?' I asked feeling afraid at the same time as hopeful.

Flicking the stub of his cigarette at me, he shook his head without looking my way. His friends stood up to leave, obviously understanding my need for some privacy with him. But Hassan pulled Wajid back and pushed him onto me. I stumbled and I took some steps back.

'I think she's gagging for a screw. Help her out will you?' said Hassan staring into my eyes. The look he was giving hurt. I was left speechless.

'She's dead cheap Waj,' he said roving his cold gaze up and down my body, making me shiver and feel exposed. 'Have a go. You'll enjoy it.'

'Shut up Hassan. You don't mean that,' said Wajid as he pointed at Hassan in threat.

'I do mean it. I've had her plenty. Seen enough of her filthy body. She's no good for me now.'

'Shut the fuck up Hassan.'

'Seriously, have her,' laughed Hassan as Wajid cursed. 'Okay then, Jatinder you have a go…'

Gripping my bag to my chest, I began to walk away as fast as I could, knowing I wouldn't be following Hassan ever again.

Chapter Thirty Seven

One final goodbye…

Autumn passed and December rolled in. The holiday season arrived and college was out. My wedding preparations were in full swing. Aunty Asma had been at ours for two weeks already and the rest were arriving soon. Including Habib.

My eighteenth birthday had passed.

I was spending my time researching something which scared the crap out of me. But I had to do it. The wedding celebrations were set to begin in a matter of days and a load of people were coming over from Pakistan. I wasn't happy. I didn't want this. No one could see this and despite my begging them, they didn't care.

Fish boy was here. He was supposed to have left for his shift already. And I was sitting in my usual corner on the sofa, engrossed in the dirt in my nails from having grown them so long and not tending to their needs.

I was dirty all over.

'You my dear need to smile more often,' said Fish boy as he plopped himself close to me.

'And you need to fuck off,' I hissed. I couldn't do polite anymore.

'Lately,' he grinned as he made himself even more comfortable and threw an arm over my shoulder, 'I have been noticing the delicate flower I once knew becoming too prickly. I may need to cut some of those thorns on you.'

Gripping both sides of my cheeks with his thumb and finger, he pinched me tightly.

I struggled in his hold.

'You're a bastard Fish boy,' I sneered making him angrier. 'A real fucking bastard and I wouldn't marry you if you were the last man on earth.'

'That you will do,' he said pressing the most disgusting kiss to my head as his fingers dug into my face tighter. 'And I will show you what a bastard is capable of on our wedding night. I will show you properly.'

I glared at him but this Fish boy was something else altogether. He leaned his face forward and was inches away from my lips when the doorbell rang disturbing him. I managed to push him away and struggle free as he laughed and went to open the door.

And before I could welcome my brother and his family back from Dubai, I went upstairs and locked myself in my room. I stayed there for the rest of the day ignoring Habib and his stupid pleas for me to open my door.

I became more determined.

I would be dead before I married that stinky Fish boy.

*****

'Come on Samina smile,' my cousin Farah chimed as she swayed her hips to the bhangra music which was on full blast. 'It's your mendhi tonight not your funeral.'

I ignored her. It's what I'd been doing all night. It was the night before my wedding. New Year's Eve, and they were all partying, not because the world would need a new calendar but because it was my mendhi. A dumb ceremony where my hands were coloured in stinky henna and my face rubbed with mucky turmeric and my hair greased in sticky oil, whilst the guests sang and danced and ate and enjoyed themselves, like pathetic twats.

I was ignoring it all. Counting the minutes until it all ended, and I could do what I'd been failing to do so already. It's not like I hadn't tried though. I had on three different occasions. But each time I popped the pill on my tongue, I spat it out. Cowardly. It was hard to swallow even one and my research had said I'd need to take at least twenty seven for them to do the deed. It was especially difficult because each time I had tried, the image of Hassan's smug face would appear behind my eyelids, taunting me.

'You weakling...'

He wouldn't even let me die in peace.

Why was he still tormenting me?

He wasn't even here anymore. He didn't live in my heart, did he? He lived there in that house I could see through the vinyl window of the marquee. And why had his light been switched on all evening? Why hadn't he gone away for the holidays, like he did each year with his parents?

Was he watching and laughing at my fate? I bet from his window he could see the evidence of this farce, of this sacrifice, which I was giving for having loved him, clearly.

'You're looking stunning,' said Habib. He had been sitting next to me the whole evening. His baby was asleep and his wife was dancing away happily.

'I'm sorry,' I whispered as I stared at my brother's hand. A tear rolled from my eye. I would do it tonight, for sure. And I needed him to forgive me and I needed to tell him I didn't hate him as much as I'd been saying I did lately. He was my brother after all. I had dishonoured him. I had kept a boyfriend and I had gone against his wishes and teachings.

I was the bad one. And before I went I had to tell him this.

'Come here,' said Habib pulling me against him.

'I love you Habib. I love you the most in the whole world,' I reassured him in case he felt otherwise. He kissed my forehead and his melodious laughter warmed my ears as Farah came and pulled him by his arm and forced him to dance with Maryam.

I watched him for a while. He would be okay. Maryam would take care of him.

'Ya Allah this music is too loud,' mumbled Aunty Bushra as she leaned on the floor to pick up a tray of sweetmeats. She was about to move away but I tugged at the hem of her green embroidered dress. She raised a brow and jutted her chin as to ask what I wanted. I stood up and flung my arms around her neck. She held me back and laughed.

'Samina come on let go now, I have a mountain of work to do.'

I released her and when she kissed my cheek, I managed a small smile too.

'You look beautiful. This dress is something special. The groom's family have great taste,' she said fixing my scarf over my head. 'Feesh cannot take his eyes off you tonight.'

I looked in the direction she was grinning at and instead of on Fish boy, my gaze landed on Uncle. And as Aunty made herself busy elsewhere, on slow but heavy feet, I approached Uncle.

Fish boy and a few others were sitting around him. All engrossed in talk of the state of Pakistan's corrupt politics. But I didn't care about them or the country with which I shared only my ethnicity and nothing else. I had to say goodbye to Uncle. He was Uncle at the end of the day. My Uncle. My father.

The one I had betrayed the most.

His gaze fell on me and with a whimper I also fell, at his feet. I stared at them. Once Uncle Dawood from the Mosque had said, 'Paradise lies at a mother's feet.' And Uncle was the only mother I knew. This was the last chance I'd get to relish the blessings of a paradise.

'Beti,' said Uncle as he lifted me up. I breathed in his familiar scent. The scent of the softest of Oudh's he always applied. 'What is this?'

Fish boy immediately made room for me by shifting a little but I didn't protest and sat in my Uncle's arms for almost an hour. When dinner arrived, I still hadn't moved and you know when some people said, 'a parent can sense what their child feels,' I thought this moment may have been one of them. Because I was so hungry. I hadn't eaten for days. I was living on crisps and fizzy drinks for weeks and when Uncle raised a spoonful of chicken and rice to my mouth, I leaned in and swallowed the food greedily. I ate and I ate and Uncle fed me and wiped my tears and fed me more.

I was glad to be having my last meal with him like this.

But he claimed he loved me. So why was I being forced to do this? He was my parent. He sensed my hunger. Why didn't he sense my unwillingness to marry?

'You okay my jaan?' asked Uncle as I shook my head to more food. 'You will be happy beti. Very happy. You have the family's blessings. Allah will make sure you are happy. This marriage is good for you.'

'I'm sorry,' I choked and I tried holding them in but they came out like the waves in a flood would.

'Your beti is getting emotional again,' laughed Tabrez Jee from behind me.

'My Samina is like that Tabrez Jee,' sighed Uncle patting my back. 'You do remember your promise to me don't you?'

'Rest assured Jawed, my family will keep her in good health and splendour. Our Feesh cares for her immensely,' replied the old man.

Kissing my Uncle one last time, I got up.

'Where are you going?' asked Fish boy.

'Bathroom,' I answered sombrely, having no energy to fight him anymore.

He laughed coyly and I left him to his emotions. Dodging past the guests, I hurried to my bedroom and cried into my Mummy's photo.

I was so sorry.

*****

Having calmed myself down, I kissed the photograph and slipped it under my pillow. With my back straight and breaths steadied, I went to my desk and took out the bottle of pills. I began to count them. I had to make sure all twenty seven were there.

A sudden bang in the air made me jump and looking out of the window, I saw evidence in the dark sky of the New Year. My day of doom had begun. But then my gaze rested on Hassan's window. His light was still on and for some reason he hadn't drawn the curtains.

I could see him.

His shadow was there.

My whole body began to sweat. His forehead was pressed on the glass and I could feel his eyes on me.

I had to say goodbye to him. I owed it to him. Despite his recent animosity, we had grown up together, hadn't we? I had to see him, one last time, afterwards I would come back to do this, for sure. This way his image wouldn't distract me because I'd have already seen him and said my goodbye.

Grabbing Aunty Bushra's long shawl, I wrapped it around myself and prayed I could do this without getting caught.

I was going to his house.

My heart was thumping and my legs were wobbly. Coming down the stairs felt a mission. Somehow I managed to open my front door without anyone seeing. Most of the people were outside in the fancy marquee anyway. And no one would have guessed the bride was leaving.

I stepped outside my house and shivered. It was a cold New Year's. There was slushy grey ice on the ground. And in the sky a colourful display of fireworks were showing off in the air.

I didn't stop to watch. Gripping onto the bottle of pills, I only stopped when I got to his front door.

Pressing the doorbell I rested my forehead on the glass of the door. My teeth chattered as the sounds of my doom reached my ears. The music from my mendhi party was loud. And the smell in the atmosphere, the mixture of spices and meat and firework dust made me close my eyes,

196

remembering the aroma of what Uncle had fed me only minutes earlier.

Sensing the vibrations of approaching footsteps coming from inside Hassan's house, I removed my forehead and took a small step back from his door. The vibrations stopped. The light in the hall came on. No one opened the door though.

I knew it was a late hour and many people around this end didn't dare open up to strangers at night. But this was me. He had to open up. I knocked again. I knocked on his window and I banged frantically on the door and held my finger on the bell continuously. The noise was deafening, I had to get him to open up.

'What the fuck?' yelled Hassan from inside and I was hopeful it was him and not one of his parents. I glanced at his drive and wiped a tear. Neither of their cars was there. Maybe they were in Manchester, as they always were.

The door opened and struggling a little, I forced my way inside.

'You mad woman get out,' shouted Hassan trying to reach for me but I ran up his stairs and turned into the landing towards his bedroom ignoring his fast approaching footsteps and extremely loud curses.

'I'm calling the police. Fucking get out you thief...'

'It's me,' I finally managed to voice amidst the chaos of the last few seconds. Flinging the huge material away from me revealing my face, I stomped up to him and shouted, 'It's me.'

He stumbled backwards and his jaw dropped.

'It's me,' I cried. He held his head and paced the room. I grabbed his arm making him stop in front of me. 'It's me.'

'I know it's you,' he shouted shrugging away from my touch and going over to the window. He opened his mouth to say something else but closed it again.

I was trembling pathetically as I choked, 'It's my wedding tomorrow.'

He looked away. However my helpless cries made him look at me again. He even took a few steps towards me but something made him stop.

'Look at me. Look how they've dressed me up,' I cried running my hands along my dress. 'Green and yellow. It's my mendhi.' I pointed at my garden with a shaky finger. 'They said these colours are meant to make me glow. And these bangles...' I jingled my wrists making him hear the melody of the glassed jewels as they clinked against each other. 'These are meant to symbolise happiness.' I pulled out the jewel from my hair which Fish boy's sisters had spent ages fixing into my hair. 'Look at this clip. It's made from roses, to make me smell nice. Look at me. I'm all ready to be a bride. Someone else's bride.'

'What are you doing here then?' he asked quietly as he turned his back to me. I threw the clip on the floor and took two steps closer to him. He was looking out of the window where my wedding could be seen and heard clearly. The lights, the marquee, the noise of the singing and music, and because his window was open, you could also smell the dinner.

'I had to see you,' I cried standing by his side and tilting my head to look at him. He turned his face to me with his brows creased. 'Hass I'm being forced.'

He looked away quickly, causing my already damaged heart to tear some more. 'Why don't you care anymore? What's happened to you? One day you're in love, the next you're ignoring me and calling me names and ...'

I hushed expecting him to say something but Hassan remained stoic and kept his stare on that window.

The digits on the small alarm clock on the window sill raced forward.

One minute. Two minutes. Three minutes...

*****

198

A whole painful fifteen minutes after standing there staring at both the clock and the side of his face, I wiped my tears. It was no use. He didn't care.

'I'm going Hassan,' I croaked with a dry voice. 'I only wanted to say goodbye to you before I went.'

'You know where the door is,' he whispered without looking. 'Remember to use the front door. You already know the back is blocked now.'

I closed my eyes for a second letting the sound of his voice absorb deep within the pores of my body. It was likely to be the last time I would hear him. Reaching his bedroom door, I gave him one last look. His back was to me and this was going to make this much easier to say, 'I came here to tell you I love only you Hassan, and I'm sorry for everything that's happened and will happen. Forgive me, okay.'

I opened his door and gripped the bottle of pills in my fist tightly, feeling the urgent need to taste them.

'Sorry for marrying somebody else when you love me, huh?'

Without turning to see him I replied, 'No. I'll be going somewhere else before it gets to that.'

'Where are you going?'

I shook my head as fresh tears made their way down my cheeks, 'I'm going really far Hassan.'

'On your own?'

'Yes, on my own,' I said.

'Oh they'll find you. Especially that fucked up brother of yours.'

'Not where I'm going he won't.'

'You don't have a passport,' yelled Hassan getting worked up. 'You've never been further than Blackpool. You freak out going to college for fucks sake.'

I laughed at the irony. 'You don't need a passport to where I'm planning to go. But once I'm gone...'

'Liar,' shouted Hassan after he had raced towards me and grabbed me by my shoulders flinging me around to face him. 'You're lying. You've always been a liar.'

'I'm not lying,' I screamed as he pushed me roughly and I landed face down on his bed. 'I'll die before letting another man touch me.'

'People who want to die just do it,' he said from somewhere near me. I felt the bed dip. 'They don't make a song and dance about it.'

Pulling me by my waist, Hassan sat me up against his headboard and I cried as he glared. He didn't look like my Hassan at all. I had never seen his eyes this colour before. They were as dark as the night outside and the vein which kept on throbbing along his neck had never been there either.

'Go home and play your dirty games with someone who actually cares. I saw your fiancé the other day. You two make a great couple,' he said through tightly clasped teeth. 'Go baby, go home.'

I watched how his sneer was replaced by a horrid laugh. A pretend laugh. Because had he been laughing for real that vein would have disappeared and his eyes would have twinkled, the way they always did.

But what was the use in trying to console myself? 'I'm going,' I choked and I shifted from his bed.

His laughter died down and I didn't look back at him. Instead I bent down to pick up Auntie's shawl. I draped it over my head and around my body. I reached for his doorknob and realising I didn't have the bottle of pills in my hand anymore, I panicked.

Crying out I turned and saw Hassan sat on his bed reading the small instructions I'd written and stuck to the bottle to remind me of what I needed to do and how. I ran to him and tried snatching it back. He grabbed hold of me and threw the bottle against the wall, smashing it, and making the pills scatter and some break.

'What is this?' he shouted as he shook me like I weighed nothing. 'What the fuck is all this about?'

'Let me go,' I cried as I looked at the pills desperate to pick them up.

'Samina…'

His voice had changed and he stopped shaking me, ending my struggle to get away from him. Looking at his face, I became lifeless as I watched something fall from his eye.

A tear.

I was numbed as he held both my hands tightly in his. I stared at the new tear drop forming in his other eye.

'You, you were going to...' His voice came out shaky and his words broken. 'You actually were going to... Samina...' Howling my name like a wolf fighting for his breaths, Hassan pulled me against him. His arms held me against his trembling body and feeling his lips touch the side of my face, I allowed every bit of me to cry its grievances to him.

And he listened to every cry, every breath, and every agony attentively and didn't loosen the hold he had of me against his body.

'Promise me, promise me on my life, and promise for every moment we've spent together that you won't ever consider this again. Never do this again. Fucking never. Promise me now.'

'I promise, but you promise me something too.'

'What?'

'That you'll never stop loving me.'

'I promise.'

Chapter Thirty Eight

Regret and dread…

In his arms I was safe. There were no loony people from Pakistan fussing over the colour of my skin or how my hair was too dry and needed regular oiling. There were no cousins performing mad dances and teasing me to reveal the story behind my sudden wedding. And there were no family members confusing the life out of me.

In Hassan's arms I was away from everybody and everything.

The minutes turned into hours. I had failed to acknowledge any pressure of the amounting dangers on Ilford Lane in that house where the music was still pumping. We continued to ignore the tick of the passing moments. I was absent from my own mendhi party yet I was oblivious of the consequences.

With Hassan, I always forgot everything.

*****

It was a little past three in the morning when the ringing of the doorbell brought some form of alertness. I woke up startled. Hassan woke up at the same time and immediately pulled me close, protectively.

'Open the door Iqmal. Open the fucking door.'

'It's Habib,' I gasped looking in the direction of his bedroom door.

'Relax,' whispered Hassan. 'Get up and hide all your stuff. Go up in the attic and I'll deal with this.'

'But Hass…'

'Trust me,' he said silencing me, as he combed my messy hair back. 'Do as I say. Go in the attic and stay there while I deal with this.'

I agreed. We both got out of the bed. Hassan helped pick up the pieces of roses from the remains of my jewels, and he gathered the broken glass from the bangles I'd been wearing. He threw them all behind his wardrobe as the bell carried on ringing and my brother's voice carried on looming.

'Remain quiet. Whatever happens, don't come down,' said Hassan as he quickly helped me up the attic stairs.

As he slid the small door close, a dark coldness enveloped me.

Hugging onto my knees against my chest, I tried making sense of the noises downstairs. Hassan was shouting he didn't know where I was and Habib and my cousin Faizaan were yelling abuse at him. I heard a shuffling noise and footsteps getting closer.

'Fucking get lost or I'm calling the police,' yelled Hassan and I bit on a bulky piece of my dress to stop myself from making any sounds.

'Samina,' shouted Habib making me close my eyes and rock back and forth. 'This isn't funny, get out wherever you are. Now!'

'Are you dumb? She's not here. Why would she be anyway?' replied Hassan in an equally menacing tone. 'She's getting married isn't she? Check the groom's house. Why are you here?'

I think my brother may have hit Hassan next because the painful cry which escaped his mouth and the sound of flesh being thrown against a wall were even visible in the dark I was hidden in.

'Come anywhere near my sister Iqmal, I swear I'll kill you.'

'Oh I'm really scared,' roared Hassan. His voice was out of breath but was laced with fury.

The loud bang of the door slamming told me they had gone.

*****

Moments later Hassan opened the attic door and I helped him pull the ladder down. Once on the landing, I recoiled at the blood trickling down one side of his face.

'He's a bastard,' screamed Hassan making me flinch and step back. 'Your brother is a bastard and he's going to get it real soon.'

I froze as he stormed towards the bathroom. My breathing wouldn't come out normally and I turned my head to stare at the front door downstairs. I tried whispering a name but I couldn't get it to come out.

When Hassan returned, I was still trying to choke up the name.

'What is it?' he scowled.

'Ha. Hab. Habib...'

'Yeah believe me the fucker's face is worse,' shouted Hassan as he pulled me inside his bedroom. And slammed the door shut behind us.

*****

His Parents were due back by midday and we needed to get out before they saw me or heard the news of my disappearance.

I was scared. The most scared I'd ever been.

All morning Hassan had been out and I was in his bedroom staring out of the window. The marquee was still up in my garden. The noises and the smells of the night had died down completely. The house looked dull and the silence around me was deathly. I couldn't see anything apart from the white of the tent and the greenish hue from the shadows of the balloons which decorated it's interior.

From where I was, the shadows resembled regret.

I hugged myself as the previous night's memory clouded my mind. The early morning confessions Hassan had relayed to me about his plans sent a shiver up my spine. I was about to do something which would destroy my family.

Further.

'Yo Sam...'

I flinched when Darren tapped my shoulder.

'Oye you, get off my girl,' laughed Hassan. I hadn't heard them coming in and momentarily I wondered how Hassan could even laugh. He had a black eye and his lip was cut and going by his boastful descriptions, my brother's eyes were probably black too. A lump lodged in my throat at the thought of my brother and I wiped at my eyes before the tears became visible.

'You been okay?' asked Hassan pulling me by my waist.

'Oh how mushy?' said Darren sticking two fingers in his mouth pretending to gag.

I moved away from Hassan, embarrassed.

'We'll be married in two hours,' said Hassan pulling me against him again. 'It's all set. Wajid and my mate Reyaan are bringing the Imam from the Mosque. I've nicked the keys to an empty flat my dad owns, and Jatinder and Harpreet are there sorting it out. Once we've had our Nikka, no dickhead will ever come near you again.'

'Apart from you,' laughed Darren.

I bit my lips.

'I can't wait to be your husband,' grinned Hassan as I gently moved out of his embrace. But he drew near again.

'Let me go,' I whispered.

'Yeah let her go, she's not your wife yet,' said Darren as he plopped himself onto Hassan's bed, the same bed Hassan had frightened me with a side of him I'd never seen before on. After his fight with Habib he had turned into somebody else entirely. He was forceful and terrifying. I hadn't liked it one bit. My body was sore from his roughness. My head was spinning, and I was finding it hard to even stand.

'What difference does that make?' said Hassan.

I stared at him blankly. His smirk and his cheerfulness, was annoying.

'Your fuck-eteers can't be trusted, so they're not invited. You can have Wajid and Reyaan as your witnesses and I've got a couple of guys coming to be mine. The Imam explained we need two witnesses each to sign our Nikka contract. And listen once the Imam asks if you agree, you have to say yes three times and like that we'll be husband and wife. We can have the civil one which we need to be married by British law later, yeah. What's important for now is the Muslim marriage. No one can take you away from me then, no one because by Islam you'll be mine. My wife.'

I listened to each word he said. He was right. In Islam the Nikka was the most important aspect of our marriage. It was the equivalent to our vows and once these were said, our relationship was halal. It wasn't a sin anymore. He would be my husband.

'Listen if Sam wants Parveen, Saira and the others present for her, why don't I send a text telling them to come?' frowned Darren.

'No way,' moaned Hassan. 'Not Parveen. No man, I don't want any of them there. Especially Saira. She's got a big gob and she'll tell her mum and then my mum will find out, and gossip travels faster than light in our families.'

'It's your big day Sam. If you want your mates there…'

'No Darren those girls can't be trusted. Samina agrees. Don't you babe?' said Hassan as he pulled me close again and attempted to slip his hand up my dress to touch me.

'Stop it,' I pleaded pushing him away.

'Okay so she's nagging me already,' chuckled Hassan waving his hands in the air. 'Anyway I need another shower before we go. All that running around organising this thing has made me sweat.'

As soon as Hassan left the room, I turned back to the window and waves of emotion filtered out from my eyes.

'I can take you back home Sam. I'm sure they'll be okay.'

'I can't go back Darren. My being there won't make any difference now,' I cried like an adult would, because my actions weren't ones of an innocent child anymore. They were bad and the worst type of bad any girl from my background could possibly inflict on her family. I had spent an entire night away from home and not on any normal night, which my family could've hidden and buried somewhere as a deep secret, but on a night where all my family and relatives were present. The shame my Uncle and brother must have gone through and were probably still going through was unimaginable.

Darren exhaled a long breath. 'Listen, I know Hassan loves you but if you're having second thoughts.'

I wiped at my tears and shrugged, 'I love him too and I love him for doing this for me. He's willing to marry me so my family can't force me to marry anybody else. He's willing to sacrifice so much for me.' I wiped at a tear roughly. 'But I'm stuck in between two sets of love. One for my family who make everything so difficult for me yet I still love them and I'm yearning to be with them already. And then there's Hassan…'

'Who's a complete idiot and you hate him and you can't stand him, right?'

'I hate him so much sometimes Darren,' I cried. 'He's been horrid to me recently. I love him despite everything. But I would rather be doing all this in a different way. With my family's blessing. I'm sure they would've understood if Hassan's father went and spoke to my Uncle, but Hassan wouldn't agree. He reckons us getting married without anyone knowing is right. I know it's wrong though. Oh Darren, I'm a mess. Nothing is making sense.'

'Why isn't it making sense?' said Hassan standing by the door with a towel in his hand. He looked annoyed.

'We're talking go away,' said Darren as he held a tissue box to me.

'No tell me. Do you want me to take you home?' said Hassan and I could see that vein bob in his neck.

'No,' I whimpered shaking my head.

'Well be a bit courageous for once and do this without any regrets.'

'Okay,' I said nodding my head and dabbing a tissue to my eyes. 'Okay.'

Chapter Thirty Nine

Wedding fever...

Dressed in the yellow outfit I'd been wearing in Fish boy's name, I was facing Uncle Dawood from our local Mosque, as he stared blankly at the wooden floor in front of us. Hassan had already told him what we'd done. About me eloping from my own mendhi and coming to him with the plan of suicide to get out from the forced marriage.

At the time Uncle Dawood hadn't known the desperate girl Hassan had been talking about was me and he had agreed to read our Nikka. However when he saw me the surprise on his white bearded face, made me muffle my cries into my scarf.

We were somewhere in Dagenham. In a cold flat. Jatinder said the heating wasn't working. And even though Harpreet had set up electric heaters everywhere, the flat was bitterly chilly. The snow falling outside made this a bigger problem. I had no cardigan or jumper, and the thin clothes I'd been wearing since the night before weren't doing much to hide the state I was in.

Or maybe I was afraid. Afraid of my actions and afraid of what the Imam was thinking.

'Listen beti Samina,' said the Imam, finally breaking out of his long thoughts. 'Forced marriages are not allowed in Islam and I cannot believe why normally liberal minded Jawed, would contemplate this. In our community there is a serious problem with parents thinking forcing their children to marry against their wishes is okay. Beti it is not okay. Our religion doesn't preach this. Our religion is one of love and one where forced marriages are haram. However it is also true and disheartening that in our community whenever a child of ours does something out of character or something beyond the boundaries of what our religion or culture dictates, parents decide the best thing to clear the mess is to get the child married and forcefully. Many find proposals here or around Britain and many simply take the child to Pakistan, India or Bangladesh, amongst other places, and get them forced to wed there. This is wrong. Marriages don't work like this and I hear you even made plans to end your life?'

I cried openly now.

'How could you forget the lessons in suicide I taught you at the Mosque? How can you think committing the biggest sin known to mankind will ease your suffering? Allah created you for a reason. He has already written your destiny before you were born, and beti you cannot alter the course of what he has ordained. And today I find myself conflicted on what to do about this Nikka. On the one hand under the rules of my job, I am required to conduct this to stop you youngsters living in sin or thinking of ignorant ways of ending your lives again. I don't want you committing any more haram. And on the other hand I have my loyalty to your Uncle. It will devastate him if he found out I read your Nikka and made you Hassan's wife without his consent. In Islam it is vital to have the blessing and the witness of one's parents to conduct a marriage or to make it valid.

'Uncle she has no parents,' said Hassan crossing his hands over his chest. 'She's an orphan.'

The Imam looked up and my eyes caught his. Before he looked away, he gave me a nod and left the room.

The next twenty minutes were the longest of my life. The Imam read our Nikka and I handed my life over to Hassan.

He was no longer my friend or my boyfriend.

He became my husband.

*****

I was trying to keep warm using Hassan's coat as my blanket when I heard his friends wishing him a good night

210

and leaving. I glanced at the four walls of the boxed room I was in but didn't see a clock. Looking out of the window, I assumed it was nearing nine or ten.

The small electric heater in the room wasn't sufficient. I had retired to this room earlier when sitting where Hassan's friends were busy eating takeaway pizza and fried chicken, got too much for me. I hadn't been able to keep my eyes open. Noticing my discomfort Hassan had asked me to go lie down on the only single bed the apartment had. I must have dozed off because when I woke up, I was snuggled with his coat over me.

His footsteps were approaching and I closed my eyes feeling embarrassed at how ugly I was looking for him on our wedding night. Despite this I was glad we were now alone.

'Is everybody gone?' I asked when he came and sat on the edge of the bed. He nodded. 'I really need some Paracetamol. I don't feel too good.'

'I'll go get some.'

'No don't go anywhere,' I said sitting up and grabbing his arm. 'I don't want to be alone. But why is it so cold?'

'This flat's been empty for months,' he said. 'I think the central heating is busted. I'll bring the other heaters in here as well.'

I let go of his arm and he left the room. Seconds later he emerged with two heaters. He set them up and instantly I felt warmer.

'Better?'

'A little.' I fell back into the bed but when Hassan took his coat away, I felt a chill touch me despite the heaters.

'I'll go home and see what Mum is up to. She's phoned seven times already.' Hassan stared into his phone as he pulled on the coat. 'I'll come back with some food in the morning okay.'

'What?' I panicked. 'No you can't go. Actually let's both go.'

'Are you mad?' he frowned. 'I can't take you. Your brother and that Uncle of yours will see you and take you home. I've got to talk with my parents tonight about this and see what they say.'

'What do you mean?'

'I need to go home or they'll know I'm with you,' he said.

'We're married now. Everybody can find out,' I said as I got off the bed and started straightening my hair out.

'I'll tell them tonight and I'll spend tomorrow with you okay,' he leaned in but before his lips could connect to mine, I nudged him away with my shoulder.

'Don't push me away Samina,' he warned coming back to assault my feverish lips. Once satisfied he said, 'I'll come back in the morning.'

'No…'

'Good night wife,' he whistled as he left me.

Completely dumbfounded.

Chapter Forty

A jab through the heart…

A warm hand touching my forehead forced me to flutter open my eyes.

'Smile for the camera,' he said and my eyes closed again. 'Oh don't be like that. Is this any way to welcome your husband after being away from him for two nights? Come give me a kiss.'

Clumsily I shifted further away and curled myself against the pillows I'd ripped to wrap around me in order to keep a little warm in his absence. But right now I wished he would go back. I had no desire to see him.

He hadn't come for me sooner. I'd been waiting alone and cold and afraid and hungry and he hadn't cared. He hadn't cared at all.

He pulled my upper body up. Gripping my face, he squeezed my cheeks together a little too harshly.

'On second thoughts forget the kiss. You stink and look terrible.'

As my head hit the mattress my suspicions were confirmed. Hassan didn't know what our Nikka meant. He had no idea what a wife was to a husband. Why else would he forget about me and leave me locked up in an empty flat with only a bed? No curtains. No blanket. No kettle. No food. No drink. No light. Nothing apart from a bed, two pillows and three electric heaters which wouldn't work.

He was wearing a new coat. A new scent. And a new haircut. I wiped my eyes out of habit but realised I had no tears anymore. I may have cried them all.

'Why is it so cold in here?' He got up and frowned when he turned the heaters on and nothing happened. Going over to the light switch, he pressed it on and off staring at the light bulb dangling from a cord from the broken tiled ceiling.

'Fucking Harpreet,' he muttered leaving the room and returning with some sort of card in his hand. 'He only went and forgot to charge the key for the electricity.'

Sitting down on the bed he reached for my head and pressed a palm to my forehead. 'You still have a temperature,' he said. 'Was it really cold and dark?'

I ignored his question. The electricity had run out an hour or so after he'd left that night. He had no idea of how afraid I'd been.

'Answer me,' he asked. 'Was it really dark?'

I pursed my lips and looked the other way.

'Look here a sec.' Pulling me by my face, Hassan smiled as he snapped a picture of us on his phone. Releasing me, he began texting someone. I fell back on the bed and watched him grin when he received a call. He didn't answer it though.

It must have been only minutes later when somebody started banging on the front door. Finding myself disillusioned, I grabbed hold of his hand and he helped me sit up.

'Who's that?' I asked with uncertainty and fear.

For a moment Hassan didn't say anything. He just stared at me.

'What is it?' I said. 'Who's at the door?'

'Whatever happens next remember one thing,' he said as he hugged my head to his shoulder. 'I did love you once.'

Before I could understand what he said, he'd already left the room.

Did love me once?

'Fucking Iqmal, where is she?'

Habib had found me. A sense of belonging gave me the strength to get off the bed and run outside to him. And when Habib enveloped me in his arms and kissed my head and my face regardless of how stinky I was or how ugly I looked, those dried up tear ducts moistened again.

Uncle's voice also reached me. His firm hands pulled me away from Habib and held me into his own chest.

But I was extremely weak. I lost the ability to control my limbs and slipped down his body.

'Beti,' cried Uncle catching me in his arms.

'What have you done to my sister?' spat Habib.

'Beti open your eyes,' urged my Uncle patting the sides of my face. 'Look we are here to take you home. My jaan you are not in any trouble. Just open your eyes and look at us.'

'Uncle,' I murmured as his face came back into focus.

'Yes my jaan,' said Uncle wiping the water around his eyes with the back of his palm. With Habib's help Uncle sat me up on the carpeted floor and I sobbed as both covered me in hugs and words of love and relief at finding me.

'Sorry,' I cried holding onto both their hands, afraid of them leaving me here alone.

'Baby it's all right. So long as you're safe, it's okay,' whispered Habib as he ran a hand over my body checking for any signs of mistreatment.

I began to cough. And as I coughed my whole body convulsed violently. I'd been doing this a lot since being stuck in the flat. Uncle began patting my back. 'Get water.'

'She's burning up. And why is it so cold in here Iqmal?' shouted Habib. 'Turn the fucking heating on you miser. And get my sister some water.'

Instead of rushing to fetch me the liquid, Hassan stood with his arms crossed over his chest. I caught his gaze in my fit and what I saw shouldn't have startled me. But it did.

He was smirking.

Instead Uncle left my side and began looking around the apartment for the water. I think he used the freezing tap water in a small beaker by the bathroom sink in the end.

As I drank the water thirstily, Habib said, 'Uncle what's wrong with her?'

'She has a high temperature and she's shivering. It's not a good sign. We need to take her to the hospital. Help me carry her. She won't be able to walk down those stairs,' said Uncle gathering me up.

Hassan chose the moment to remind us of his presence by sauntering over and moving Uncle's hand out of mine. 'Sorry to break up this happy reunion,' he sneered. 'Stop fussing over my wife. She's fine.'

Uncle's already pale face lost any trace of colour as he choked, 'Wife?' He looked at Habib hoping he had heard wrong.

I closed my eyes in regret.

'And excuse us please,' said Hassan. 'My wife's not too good to be entertaining guests today. I just wanted to act like a responsible son in law so told you where she is. But you can bugger off now.'

'Why is he calling you wife?' said Habib raising his voice and I dug my face in my own hands. I couldn't look at either of them.

'Don't you know dear brother in law,' grinned Hassan. 'Samina and I had our Nikka on Friday, right after Friday prayers. We're currently on our honeymoon. And you're intruding.'

Immediately Uncle shifted me onto Habib's hold and stood up. Habib frowned at him but supported my weight nonetheless. I removed my hands from my face. Was he leaving me here?

'I'll be waiting in the car,' said Uncle. His voice was lowered and I had broken it.

'Uncle she needs a doctor,' sighed Habib and I could clearly feel disappointment in his voice too.

'Ask her what she wants. After all she's old enough to make her own decisions,' said Uncle in an equally low whisper as he turned his back and headed out.

There followed a few minutes of silence next. All of us consumed in our own thoughts and as I glanced at Hassan,

216

what I saw made me grip onto Habib tighter. His face was red and his fists were curled and his jaw taut. And that vein, the one I'd only recently discovered was the largest it had ever been.

'It's alright I'll take you home,' said Habib brushing my hair out of my face. 'It doesn't matter you married him. So long as you're happy, you have my blessing alright. It's fine. I'll go to his parents and sort this mess out. But first I'll take you to see a doctor. You're not well Baby.'

As Habib started helping me up, Hassan charged at us and with a firm grip pulled me behind him and then pushed Habib away, startling us both.

'I can't believe this,' he yelled making me scream and fight to loosen his hold on me. 'I can't fucking believe this.'

'Iqmal,' grunted Habib pointing a finger at Hassan. 'Drop her hand and lower that voice. You're frightening my sister.'

'Fuck you, she's my wife. I'll do what I want with her.'

'Don't provoke me kid,' my brother hissed and I knew he was trying his best to keep himself restrained. I could see it in his eyes clearly. 'That's my Baby you're talking about.'

Hassan laughed as he swung me in front of him and pressed my back against his body. A low whimper escaped my mouth as the action made my head hurt. I began to feel dizzy.

'She isn't a baby, she's my wife. My bed partner, my fuck…'

Habib didn't let Hassan say whatever revolting name he wanted to give me because after pulling me away from Hassan like I was a rag doll, he punched him, not once, but again and again on his face making him spit blood.

When Habib was done, Hassan staggered on his feet as he wobbled and kept a hand to his jaw. I cupped my head in both my hands when I saw the extent of blood coming out of his mouth and his nose.

He also had tears in his eyes.

I promise they were tears because his chest was moving up and down too fast and his eyes were closing and opening, like he was in trouble. Not physical trouble but his emotional state wasn't the best. He was crying. I promise it was real tears and not the impact of my brother's punches.

'Touch her again,' yelled Habib, 'I'll kill you because I may tolerate a lot but I won't tolerate you hurting her like that. Learn some respect and when you have, you know where to find her.'

Hassan was still cupping his bleeding mouth when Habib took hold of my arm and yanked me towards the door. But looking back at Hassan seeing that he was still wiping the water from his eyes, I forced myself to stop and once again I betrayed my own brother and ran towards him. Taking the hem of my long dress, I began wiping at the blood on him.

I didn't dare look back though. I was trembling with the fear of what Habib's expression would be like.

'What is wrong with you?' I cried despite my own troubles as I wiped his hurt. 'Why are you behaving this way?'

Moving his glare from my brother to me, Hassan's whole body stiffened. His stare was as cold as ice, yet his whole face was red with both blood and rage. His breaths were so heavy.

'Why are you doing this?' I asked completely ignoring my brother's instructions to leave Hassan and to go home with him. But I knew Hassan. I knew every bit of him. He was just mad at something that was all. He'd be okay once he had calmed down.

And as Hassan's breathing eased, he cupped the back of my head and stared deeply into my eyes.

'It's alright,' I reassured him. 'Everything's going to be better now. My Uncle knows about us. My brother loves me a lot. I promise he's real lovely and will understand why we did what we did. He'll love you too. I promise you he will. And I'm sorry he hit you but that's only because…'

'Because why?' Hassan snarled gripping my head tighter and shaking me. 'Tell me why Samina? Tell me why your precious brother is real lovely?'

Habib sighed loudly and rubbing his face in his hands, he said, 'Quit the games. She needs a doctor. Both of you come. I'll take you kids home and have a word with your parents.'

'No you quit the games,' shouted Hassan. 'My parents hate you. You're the reason why all this shit has happened in the first place. Do you remember my sister?'

My eyes shot up and my lungs sucked in all the oxygen I had left. Noticing this, Hassan wrapped his arm around my waist holding me up.

'Yes I remember her very well,' said Habib.

'Good to hear that,' said Hassan shaking his head up and down.

'Hassan…' I whispered.

'Let me say what's on my mind Samina. It needs to be said,' Hassan whispered. My head throbbed but I kept strong even though my body was dying to drop. I was cold, freezing cold.

'Say it then,' said Habib from somewhere in the room.

Ignoring my brother for the second, Hassan touched my forehead, 'Your temperature is rising. Your teeth are chattering, go and sit down.'

'No I want to be with you.'

'People don't always get what they want.'

'What do you mean?' I asked as his expression changed and a fresh tear rolled down his cheek.

'Listen, come take hold of her. She'll fall if you don't because I'm about to let go of her...'

I screamed as he did let go. Not only did he let go, he swung me by my arm and pushed me onto Habib.

'Are you mental?' roared Habib catching me.

'Yes I am. I've been mental since your fucktard Uncle told me it was you who took my sister's life!'

'What are you talking about?' shouted Habib.

'Yasmin was pregnant with your baby when she died. The baby died with her. You took two lives not one. You're a murderer Habib.'

'It's not true,' I said. He had it all wrong. 'Habib tell him she wasn't having a baby. Tell him you loved her. Tell him you were planning on getting married to her. Tell him.'

'Stop pretending Samina,' shouted Hassan as he took a step towards us but then stopped. Pointing his shaking finger at me he said, 'You've known this all along. You've been pretending you actually cared for me, when you've spent all these fucking years hiding the fact that your very own brother was responsible for my sister's death.'

I shook my head, 'No…'

'She died in a fire,' spoke Habib tightening his hold on me.

'Yasmin survived the fire you bastard,' yelled Hassan holding the back of his head. 'She died because you betrayed her.'

I moved away from my brother and went to sit down on the floor in the corner, away from both of them. Hugging my knees, I rested my face on top and cried.

'My sister was heartbroken. At the hospital before she died she told my mum and dad she wanted to live because of her unborn baby. She didn't want to die.' Hassan's voice was shaky now and his vulnerability matched mine when he too slid onto the floor and sat down.

'She would have lived,' he continued as his tears flowed freely. 'The doctors said her burns weren't all that bad. They said she would make it. But my mum and dad weren't happy. They rather she died. She was pregnant that's why. She had ruined our family's honour. She had brought shame on my parents. They wouldn't be able to show their faces to any of our relatives. She couldn't marry that guy in Manchester they were fixing her up with anymore. How would they tell his family she already had a boyfriend and was expecting his child? Fuck Habib they told my sister of all this. My mum cursed her. My dad said she could go to hell, whilst she, my only sibling lay on that hospital bed covered in burns...'

'I had no idea,' said Habib, and his voice was equally shaky. 'I had no idea she was fine. I was at the hospital that night trying to get in to see her. The nurses wouldn't let anyone in who wasn't her immediate family. Believe me, I was there. I didn't betray her. Before the fire I was with her the whole day trying to fix things.'

'Shut up with your excuses,' said Hassan wiping yet another tear from his cheek. 'My sister died of a broken heart.'

'It wasn't like that,' said Habib as he looked at me.

'What was it like then?' asked Hassan. 'I remember her crying when my mum and dad left the hospital room to absorb the stuff she'd been rambling on about; the baby, the mysterious boyfriend and how much she fucking loved him. She held my hands as she cried this. And for fuck sake I was there when those fucked up machines began to beep and she went still. She died with her hands in mine,' shouted Hassan. 'And fuck you bastard, she did die of a broken heart because you didn't do the decent thing and marry her when she asked you too.'

'Calm down,' Habib shouted back. 'It was the fire which killed her.'

'No,' screamed Hassan as he got off the floor and charged at Habib like a bull does at a matador and cornered him against the wall.

I sat watching.

'Yasmin died from a heart attack which you caused. It wasn't the fire. My parents feel responsible for her death till this day. They regret saying what they said to her. My mum's been taking pills to sleep for years and my dad has nightmares when he eventually does manage some sleep.'

'I'm sorry. I really am. But this is no one's fault. It's unfortunate,' said Habib holding Hassan back at arm's length.

'It was unfortunate,' hissed Hassan. 'Until the day your Uncle revealed all. I had no idea you were the bastard who betrayed my sister.'

For a few seconds both just stared into each other's eyes and I watched as Uncle stepped back inside the apartment. Maybe he had been outside the whole time.

'Oh Uncle Jee, I owe you a big thanks,' said Hassan as he pushed Habib into the wall and took a few steps back. 'If you hadn't told us I was exactly like my sister; dirty, bad, filthy and lacking in any morals that night when you caught me trying to get off with your niece in your own back garden, I wouldn't have known any of this.'

Habib dropped his hands to the side. He also dropped his shoulders and when I looked up at him, I could see him looking right back at me.

'Why are you saying this now?' said Habib not taking his eyes off me. 'This marriage to my sister, is this…?'

'No mate,' said Hassan. 'I'm not a complete dog like you. I genuinely did care for her. Didn't I, Baby?'

My head dropped.

'However once Uncle Jee revealed all, I couldn't get myself to see her again. I felt hatred for her brother and her family and I was beginning to hate her too. So I listened to your Uncle and kept my distance. Until now that is…' Hassan began to laugh and his laughter was pressing sharp blades into my heart. He was killing me. This was his plan. This was all a ploy to get back at Habib for something which wasn't his fault. I knew because I was witness to it. My brother did not kill her. She died in a fire.

'You're not going to do this to her,' said Uncle as he wiped at his eyes. 'You actually did this to my innocent beti on purpose. This is all you're doing. Is this your revenge? Did you plan to ruin her?'

'No she ruined herself Uncle Jee. She came to me herself. She hadn't even washed the henna from her hands when she came. She's not as innocent as she makes out though. Imagine, all these years and not once did she tell me her precious brother killed my sister. And I thought she was my best friend. My soul mate. Anyway yep, she came to me herself but I must say it was a fun night…'

'Enough of this now,' cried Habib as he charged to launch a punch at Hassan, but my Uncle stopped him.

It didn't stop Hassan though. Reaching me he pulled me up by my arm and pushed me to my Uncle shouting, 'Get out of my house the lot of you and take my bitch with you. I've used her enough. She's no good to me anymore.'

'Don't you dare Iqmal,' my brother cried shaking his head. 'Don't do this.'

'I already have. But be careful, you might want to keep medicines and knives and ropes and things like that out of her reach. She might try topping herself again,' Hassan said as he laughed. 'Remember the promise you made, Baby,' he teased. 'You promised on my life remember. So don't try the suicide stunt again.'

I looked the other way.

'She's your wife Hassan,' said Habib putting both his hands together. He was begging him. His face was full of tears. 'You've married her. Come on mate. I'm sorry. I'll do whatever you want. Just don't ruin her like this. I swear I'll give up everything I own to you but don't ruin my Baby like this.'

'Oh fuck off will you,' snarled Hassan. 'I've got somewhere else to be. So if you could all piss off out of my dad's flat, that'll be jolly good.'

'Leave this instant,' shouted Uncle with a menace as high and dangerous as Hassan's. He grabbed my arm and forcefully dragged me out of the room.

And I cried out as he succeeded in taking me away from Hassan, my husband.

Chapter Forty One

A hope for the broken heart….

Doctor Patel said, 'She needs therapy.' Apparently, talking about anxieties helped overcome them. He also prescribed some pills to make me sleep properly and forget about everything, which I refused to take. Because even after so much advancement in medical sciences and technology, these clueless doctors had failed to understand a broken heart couldn't be fixed with pills or therapy.

A broken heart was going to stay broken for ever. Especially mine.

It's pieces were too many to fix.

I often wondered why Aunty Bushra kept the pills locked away with all the other pills and poisonous household substances, including the knives and scissors. They needn't worry. I wasn't going to consider suicide. Those days were long gone.

I was just drifting. Each day, each hour, each minute just passed. My mind had become a hollow ball of nothingness. Empty. Completely void of emotion and stuff known as feelings.

Aunty Bushra had taken me to the doctor's again. I'd been here three times since returning home. The results from the blood and urine samples I'd given the previous week were back from the hospital.

We were waiting in the reception area for our turn to see Dr Patel. Sheetal, the woman from the beautician's down the road, walked into the surgery and Aunty Bushra released a strained breath. Without even queuing up to sign her name in, Sheetal found it more necessary to come by and say hello to us.

Aunty tried to smile back, 'Oh Sheetal what are you doing here?'

Sheetal's gaze briefly wavered from my direction to greet Aunty and to tell her she had a cold. Then her eyes resumed her scrutiny of me again.

'Samina isn't well,' said Aunty patting the chair next to her.

'Yes I heard,' said Sheetal as she plopped her overweight rear on the tub chair. 'How unfortunate her fiancé wasn't who he seemed. You should count yourself lucky you were saved before the marriage actually went ahead. These foreign boys without proper visas cannot be trusted ...'

As Sheetal went on speaking about her take on the events of the wedding which almost happened, I stared at Annie who was fast asleep in her pushchair, tucked in between her cosy fleece. It was Aunty Asma's suggestion we told curious people Fish boy wasn't who we'd initially thought he was.

'Tell them he already has a wife in Pakistan. Tell them he was only after our Samina for the visa to stay in the country indefinitely,' she had said. She reckoned it was easier putting the blame on the groom's side, rather than telling people I had eloped with my lover and then married him, only to be dumped the way I was.

Everybody agreed.

Uncle was furious when we had reached home that day. He was mad at Habib. He said I had only done what he'd already done by taking off and getting married without anybody knowing. I simply followed in his footsteps. I had seen him as a young man flirting with girls and having relationships with them, which is why I behaved the way I did with the first local boy who took an interest in me.

Uncle was mad at everybody.

He was mad at Aunty Bushra for not keeping a closer eye on me. He accused her of neglecting me and never being the mother figure he'd wanted her to be. He was also mad at Maryam for not being a good sister in law to me and not knowing me well enough to have sussed out my plans earlier. Maryam as always had taken offence to this and on top of the revelations of Habib's past, she returned to Dubai days later with only Salman. Habib was forced to follow her the next day.

But most of all, Uncle was mad at himself for planning my wedding when I was against it. He was mad at himself for revealing to the Iqmal's it was Habib who Yasmin had loved. He was so mad he didn't eat or drink for days. He didn't even go to the Cabbie for days. It was only when Tabrez Jee came over and accepted his apology for having him humiliated in front of his whole family and relatives, did Uncle begin to show signs of some life again.

But Fish boy, he was still here. In the flat above our Cabbie. And he was still working his shifts there because it was the least my Uncle could do for the poor man. Offer him a home and a job. It was compensation to Tabrez Jee. He could remain here and be treated as a son despite what I'd put him through. Because family mattered, and Aunty Asma's husband had threatened to cut off all ties with Uncle if he didn't.

Understandably, Uncle was mad at me. He didn't talk to me anymore. In fact he didn't even look at me. He had told Aunty to tell me to stay out of his sight when he was home. So as soon as he would come home, Aunty would remind me to go upstairs and lock myself in my room.

It was okay to be kept out of his sight though. I did take his honour away. I had destroyed him and I had destroyed our little family. I had ruined everything and everyone I knew. So being locked away in my room was fine.

'Only Mandeepa, you know our Ranjita's mother,' continued Sheetal, making me look up, 'Came to the parlour last week and said something about Samina being married to that boy, you know Sheila's son, what's his name again, Haroon, no, Hassan?'

'Its rubbish,' said Aunty in a clipped tone. 'My Samina is having a hard time dealing with the shock of Feesh's deceit than to deal with such malicious gossip. Please

Sheetal do not repeat this nonsense again. Mandeepa doesn't know what she is saying.'

Sheetal shook her head as she eyed me curiously, 'Why is Feesh still living above your office? My husband said Jawed is planning to retire soon and let him take over.'

Auntie's face paled. How was she supposed to answer this? Surely if Fish boy was a fraud, Uncle wouldn't have kept him on at the Cabbie.

'Sheetal you know what it's like with our elders. Once they make a decision we have no choice but to accept. Feesh is my sister in law's husband's nephew and he threatened to cut off ties and divorce her if we didn't let Feesh keep his job. But rest assured he is not allowed at our home. That we made sure. He has to keep his distance from our Samina.'

'Oh,' Sheetal mused as her fingers twitched over the keys of her expensive looking mobile phone. She probably couldn't wait to send what she had learnt to the next batch of eager listeners. Gossip travelled faster than rats around here. A morsel of food could only be swallowed with a drop of gossip. It was more vital than plain water.

'Samina Ismail,' the receptionist called. 'The Doctor is ready to see you.'

Aunty released a heavy breath and gestured for me to stand, 'Come Samina it's your turn,' she said taking control of the pram.

And as I passed Sheetal, she gave me an odd smirk. Everybody looked at me like that now.

*****

'No no. There must be a mistake,' cried Aunty as I stared out of the window without revealing the turmoil I was hiding behind my blank disguise.

I was pregnant. Both the urine and blood tests had confirmed this.

'Doctor, please check again. It's not possible,' said Aunty wiping at her tears.

227

For some reason the past six weeks had aged her immensely. The bags under her eyes didn't suit her normally polished face and the faded colour of her hair was unusually dull.

'Listen, Mrs Ismail these things happen,' said Doctor Patel. 'Please try to be supportive. Samina is fragile as it is and the baby will be demanding on her body furthermore. I will prescribe some baby friendlier medicine and some vitamins to help.'

Doctor Patel looked at me with a weak smile, 'It's important you look at this positively. There is help available. You have options. It's not a bad thing.'

'It's not bad thing?' Aunty scowled as she cried. 'She's pregnant. She's having a baby without being with a husband. What will I do? How will I tell her Uncle this?'

Dropping to the chair next to me, Aunty gripped my arm and tugged at it, 'How could you? After everything he did for you. This will kill him.'

'Mrs Ismail please calm down,' said Doctor Patel sternly.

Aunty released my arm. 'Sorry,' she cried. 'Lekin Doctor Saab, what should I do?'

'Bhein Jee please try to stay calm. Samina needs your support. I also think you need some help too. Can you come to see me later on in the week?'

I had destroyed everybody in my family.

*****

The same night whilst I was trying to get myself to sleep, Uncle came barging into my room and because I hadn't seen him in weeks, a heavy breath of longing escaped from deep within me. But everything happened too fast and I began gasping out of fear, struggling to keep on my feet as he forced me out of my bed. Pulling me down the stairs, he opened the front door. And despite I was only wearing a thin tee shirt and leggings, and my feet were bare, he pushed me outside exposing me to the heavy rain falling and he closed the door behind me, leaving me there.

I may have been there for several minutes. Soaked and freezing. It was Aunty Bushra who eventually came and pulled me inside the house. She towel dried my hair and forced me out of the wet clothes. She helped me into a warm jumper and fleece jogging bottoms. Then she embraced me in her arms.

'He's angry about the baby. He's told Habib and he's equally angry. I don't know what will happen now? Ya Allah help me to deal with this,' she cried.

Later, I drank my hot chocolate as I stood by the window in the kitchen staring at the brick wall as it glared back at me.

*****

The next morning Uncle stayed at home and I was remained put in my bedroom.

Downstairs I could hear voices. Rahese, Hassan's father and Uncle Dawood were there. Uncle shouted abuse at the Imam. He accused him of corrupting youngsters in the community by conducting marriages without telling their parents, and as the Imam tried to explain the rights in Islam, Uncle shouted for him to get out of his house.

Uncle went on to tell Rahese about the baby. But Rahese sounded as smug as Uncle had sounded in the garden the day he had punched me and accused Yasmin of all sorts.

'How can you be sure the baby is Hassan's and not your dirty niece trying to trick him into accepting her as his wife?' said Rahese.

'They are husband and wife. We can't deny this. We have to deal with this now, in time to save our remaining honour. Let's make the marriage public, take her home. She's your daughter now.'

Rahese laughed, 'Your daughter tarnished your name and your honour the night she crept into my house and threw herself in my stupid boy's bed. You have no honour. Jawed, your daughter, your niece or whoever the filthy orphan is will never be the daughter of my house. And the baby, how can I be certain it shares my blood? We all know Samina's reputation isn't one to be trusted. Who knows how many Hassan's she's been with?'

Hearing this, I began to shake. And what Uncle said next triggered something inside me. Seriously I hadn't felt anything in days and I hadn't cried once since returning home after Hassan's betrayal. But my tears wouldn't stop now because I didn't like what Uncle was saying.

'You can leave my house too. It was my mistake thinking you could be civil and talk about this sensibly but I've realised I don't need you or your son to look after my niece or her child. I raised her and now I will raise her bastard child too. And believe me a day won't pass without me reminding the bastard what a dirty little sin he is and what type of people he shares his blood with. And as for the mother, she's been living under my mercy since she was six and I don't need to beg the likes of you to take her off my hands. I'll send the divorce papers soon. Get your son to sign them as soon as possible...'

I didn't like what he said one bit and looking in the mirror as I cried, I wanted Baby out. I didn't want him inside me because this world was mean and horrible.

It was better for Baby to simply disappear.

*****

The following day without telling anybody, I left home and took the bus towards the only hospital I knew, 'Newham General' in Plaistow, right opposite my college. I had to see a Doctor there and ask them to take Baby away from me.

But believe me I didn't want to hurt Baby. Promise, I was already in love with him. I just wanted to keep him safe from fake people and fake relationships. I wouldn't be able to tolerate anybody calling Baby a bastard and abusing him.

Four hours later and having spoken to three different nurses and one doctor, I was being wheeled into the ultrasound department for pregnant women. The doctor felt I wasn't in the right state of mind because when he asked if I wanted an abortion, I had said no.

I just wanted Baby out of me and kept safe.

And I couldn't stop crying as I requested this. I was all over the place. I swear I was.

Doctors and nurses, it wasn't their job to listen to emotional wrecks and broken people. They had far important jobs to do like to save lives. It's understandable then they didn't want to hurt Baby either and took me for an ultrasound to check on his health.

Soon enough I was laying on a narrow bed with my top rolled up over my stomach. A cold cream was applied to my lower abdomen and despite them telling me to relax and stop crying, I couldn't.

I was so scared.

A gadget rolled over the area where the cream was and …

Chook. Chook. Chook. Chook. Chook. Chook…

'Your baby's heartbeat is perfect,' beamed the lady controlling the gadget and studying the monitor.

I wiped at my tears and as my breaths hitched I turned to look at the monitor.

'See there, that's the heartbeat. It's sometimes possible to see it at six weeks.'

I stared at the tiny white dot which kept flashing. It wasn't a flashing though, it was Baby's heartbeat.

Chook. Chook. Chook. Chook. Chook. Chook…

Baby's beating heart.

'You're about six weeks gone. And stop worrying so much,' said the lady pressing my hand between hers ever so gently. 'Your baby is absolutely fine.'

She turned the machine off and the sounds of the heart beating inside of me vanished.

'Please again.' The plea from my broken soul touched the lady and she turned the machine on again. I closed my eyes and listened.

Chook. Chook...

'It's beautiful isn't it?'

'Beautiful,' I replied in full agreement as something magical occurred.

I smiled. I actually smiled.

Chapter Forty Two

The blue eyed monster…

I was kept at the hospital overnight. They had phoned my Aunty after I'd started panicking about getting in trouble again. But I wasn't worried anymore. The night away from the confines of my bedroom was welcomed. I was feeling better. I was smiling.

I kept thinking of Baby. How cute he would be? How tiny he would be? What colour eyes he'd have? I was so excited to the extent that my heart had memorised the sounds of his heartbeats. I kept hearing his cute heart beating over and over again.

I would never allow anyone to call him a bastard again. I may have tolerated a lot of crap in my life but no way was I going to let anybody hurt my child. I had vowed this and I had promised the doctor this as well. And with a pleasant smile, the doctor had said I could go home the next morning.

Thankfully I had enough money for the fare by bus, and decided to go home by myself. I needed the fresh air and I had to learn to do things for myself now. I was going to be a mother after all.

A single mother.

But as I was walking towards the bus stop which was right outside the college, I wondered whether Hassan's father had told him about Baby yet. I knew from the past Hassan was a complete softy when it came to babies. When Ayaan had been tiny, he would spend ages playing with him and sometimes when the chance arose, he also adored little Annie.

Maybe if I told him about Baby he'd find it in his heart to forget the past and start afresh. He would want the best for our Baby. And I couldn't wait to see his eyes light up as I told him he was going to be a dad soon.

Stopping at the bus stop, I wondered whether he was in college. It was a Tuesday. He'd be in Chemistry. Thinking about it again, I turned towards the college gates and stepped inside the building.

However a nostalgia gripped me and forced me to take a step back outside. I'd see too many faces I knew. I was sure Wajid, Reyaan and Jatinder had told everybody about what I'd done by now. Everyone would've judged me already. And Ravi, he already thought I was a hypocrite, always pretending to be something I wasn't. Muslims girls didn't do what I did full stop. He would make sure to remind me this.

Like my other friends. Parveen, Ranjita and Saira. They'd come to see me a few weeks earlier. Aunty had invited them to cheer me up. At first they were all, 'Oh, we're so sorry for what happened. How could he hurt you like that?'

But the pity soon turned to something else altogether.

They were hurt I hadn't told them anything about my plans to run off with my ex-boyfriend. An ex-boyfriend, they'd warned against a lot of times. They were offended they weren't given the privilege to witness my Nikka. They were sad I hadn't invited them to my mendhi either. If they were there, they could've stopped me from going over to Hassan's and the whole affair would never have happened.

Never mind the forced marriage though…

They were frustrated because their own parents had started looking at them suspiciously too. And they couldn't believe I was actually brave enough to have done what I did. Their own parents would've killed them if they had done the same. They said I was lucky I was an orphan because if my parents were alive, they would've died of shame by now.

These were my friends.

I told you relationships were false.

But there was one I still believed in so bad. I had to see him. Six weeks was a long time for him to have relaxed. I was as sure as the sun which always came out, albeit in different moods for different seasons, Hassan would be pleased with the news.

I rushed back inside the college.

*****

Wajid saw me first.

I couldn't look him in the eyes. I felt exposed. I didn't like it. I felt I didn't belong anywhere anymore.

'He's in the common room.'

Without a word, I walked away.

*****

I entered the large common room and scanned through the groups of students gathered around. It was noisy, as it always was. Slowly I walked further inside the room and stopped when I saw him staring back at me.

With a deep breath in, I made myself go and sit on the empty chair next to him. I pretended not to notice how he shifted a little away. Releasing the breath, I allowed my trembling hand to cup his one over his knee.

'Samina,' he whispered tilting his face to look at me.

'It's me alright,' I managed to reply with a sombre chuckle.

He looked away after removing my hand. Ignoring the rejection which I'd become quite an expert in, I absorbed the sound of my name on his tongue and hoped Baby liked it, as much as I did.

'We need to talk,' I said.

'I have Maths now,' he stated as he got up.

'It's important,' I replied trying to keep some level of dignity when in actuality I was prepared to drop to his feet and ask for all sorts of forgiveness for whatever it was I was supposed to have done to him.

'Not as important as my education,' he said blankly as he began to walk away.

'It's far more important,' I said grabbing hold of his firm arm as I too got up.

For a few short seconds he looked at me before he shrugged out of my touch. 'Like I said it can't be that important.'

'Hear me out first and then decide,' I said looking into those same eyes in which I could see my whole world once.

They were still beautiful.

'Be gentle…' I gasped as my body was pushed back onto the chair completely taking me off guard. I winced as my elbow hit the wooden arm rest and I was still reeling in shock when Hassan glared at me like he was about to commit third degree murder on me.

'I don't want to hear anything from you,' he hissed pointing a finger at me. 'I don't want you anywhere near me. You and I are not friends. We are not anything.'

'You're my husband,' I shouted as a crowd gathered around us. 'We're married,' I reminded him. My demeanour was no longer calm. I'd had it. Standing up from the chair, I pushed him back with all the energy I had. 'Don't tell me we are not anything,' I said and I didn't care the whole common room silenced around us. 'You married me Hassan. I'm your wife and I'm having your baby. Don't you dare say I'm nothing to you…'

Hassan's jaw twitched tightly as he came close to me and the vein in his neck looked bright green. He forcefully grabbed me by my elbow and in the matter of a second I was being pulled out of the common room. A few warnings followed behind us and I heard a male voice say, 'Leave her alone.'

But Hassan wasn't listening.

And I was afraid. His grip was hard and I was struggling to keep up with his huge strides.

'Let me go, you're hurting me,' I pleaded. I tried punching him but he was unrelenting and far too strong. Fears so frightening played in my mind and travelled to my heart causing me to beg him to let me go. Baby could get hurt. The nurses at the hospital had told me to be extra careful. The first three months of a baby's growth were critical and here was Baby's father pulling me like a sack of potatoes through the corridors of my college, as everyone stared.

No one stopped him. It was like I was being abducted by a member of a dangerous terrorist group where no one dared to help a hostage like me in fear of getting blown up. But I needed him to stop for the sake of Baby. His grip was hard and his strides too big and too fast. I was struggling in the worst and most defenceless way to keep myself from falling on my knees and being dragged on my belly. Baby would have no chance then and there was no way in the world I would let anyone harm my only relation which actually meant anything anymore.

Pushing open a door to a dark room, Hassan hurled me inside and let the door slam behind us. He threw me out of his hold and fearing I would fall, I grabbed hold of a table's edge and huffed for breath leaning against it.

'Don't touch me again,' I yelled after a few breaths and relief I wasn't hurt. 'Don't come near me again.'

Pushing his head back, he began to laugh.

'I hate you,' I cried as I shouted. 'I fucking hate you for what you've done to me.'

'I hate you too,' he shouted back. 'And I don't care you're my wife. I fucking don't care about you. I never did and never will so don't show me your face again and what the fuck was that? I am no fucking father to a baby. And if I am, tell me what it costs to get rid of it.'

My rage at his heartless words forced out a monster in me. Years of tolerating my Auntie's physical abuse had taught me violence and raising the hand on someone was inhumane and I had vowed to never do it. Yet I ran towards him and connected my palm with his cheek slapping him across his face. Not once but twice, on both sides. And when I was done, I fell on a chair letting my brain come to terms with I had become.

I had raised my hand on someone. My own husband.

The whole thing made me cry helplessly.

Hassan was someone else entirely. A bigger, evil monster who I'd failed to recognise properly, a monster of the worst kind who found a woman's vulnerability pleasing.

'Here's a hundred pounds,' he said. 'I'll have more for you later seeing what a poor cow you arc. Use this to get rid of the ugly duckling.'

'The only ugly thing I know is you Iqmal,' I said taking my hands away from my face so he could see what he had rendered me. However his grin made me look away. The money caught my attention and I picked up the notes and ripped each one into pieces and threw them at his face.

'That's your claim to my Baby,' I cried. 'Come anywhere near me again and I'm reporting you to the police. Touch me again, I'll kill you. Something I should have allowed Habib to do already.'

'Bitch,' he yelled taking a step forward. But I'd had enough.

'Fuck off,' I swore as he came near and stood over me like a menacing murderer. 'I'm not scared of you. I'm not,' I shouted smacking him again, this time leaving a dense red fingerprint above his jaw. 'I never want to see you again. You're a bastard and I'll never forgive you.'

'I'll never forgive you…'

I must have shouted it a hundred times as he stood watching me until I had no energy and fell back on the chair resting my spinning head on the cold table.

The slam of the door told me he was gone.

Chapter Forty Three

My malady...

Tears are formed when sadness and sorrow mix with heartbreak. No matter how hard you try hiding your feelings from the world, the moment the first tear leaves the eye, you've been exposed. You're suffering. You're in severe pain. And believe me there's no such thing as crocodile tears because people who shed tears simply have no control over them.

Tears travel from the heart. They are a result of pain and can never be forced.

My pain was severe. My never ending tears were proof of this.

Libby had found me. Worried by my despondency, she called a teacher. Soon I was with the Principle in his office and he was sorting a place out for me to study at the nearby Adult College in Barking. He wasn't willing to let me quit. My application to Oxford University had already been accepted and I had a conditional place waiting for me for the coming October.

As Sir spoke to them over the telephone, I stared at the bruises on both my wrists. Bruises Hassan had given as he violated me in front of the entire college like a piece of trash. I'd seen the stares and I'd heard the whispers I was receiving as Libby tried consoling me. I'd seen how the tutors stood making guesses as to what was wrong with me. And I'd seen the likes of Wajid, Jatinder and Ravi staring at me, like I was a species from a new race of aliens and not the Samina they knew.

Hassan had branded me a crazy woman. A dirty, fallen woman. And I wasn't strong enough to face this on a daily basis.

It was all set. I would be going to a different college and what Uncle or Aunty thought about this didn't bother me. I would do it anyway. I needed to get those grades and get out of here.

Oxford would mark a new beginning for Baby and me.

*****

The days turned into weeks and the weeks into months and I was surviving.

Surviving the aloofness of my family.

Uncle still hadn't spoken to me. I vanished whenever he came home. Habib hardly phoned and when he did, he'd ask how I was and satisfied with my short answers he'd hang up.

Fish boy was coming over all the time now. He stayed for hours talking with Aunty Bushra, playing with the children, cooking sometimes, cleaning other times, always sucking up to her. He had even commented on how I was putting on weight. But like I'd learnt to keep my head down and ignore most comments and most people, I'd learnt to ignore him the best.

The Adult College brought a breath of fresh air. The building was light and airy without the hustle and bustle of rowdy teenagers and blue eyed monsters. It was good. I could be myself and do my work without judgements. The tutors were supportive and I was working my backside off to make those grades. I'd missed a lot of lessons and had loads to catch up on. But I was doing well. I did have heaps of spare time locked up in my bedroom, and all of it was spent buried inside the covers of Science and Maths books.

My pregnancy was going well. My bump was huge already. And seriously I couldn't wait to hold my tiny Baby. It was a boy. The lady at the hospital had told me at the last scan.

My own little boy. I couldn't wait.

I tried not to think much about Baby's father. This was hard, but it made me determined to be a great mother and do well at college. I didn't need Uncle, or Hassan's family to support me. I would show everybody.

Most people didn't know about my pregnancy anyway. I never went anywhere that's why. The only place I went was college and Aunty would drop me and three hours later she'd always come to pick me up. The only other place I went was the hospital and even then Aunty would usher me inside the car as fast as I could move. She didn't want anyone seeing me. No one was to know I was pregnant. This was Uncle's order.

Fish boy had been warned not to tell anybody in the family too. The dishonour growing inside me was evidence of my deeds to the community, and for Uncle his honour was everything.

The Baby had to be kept a secret.

*****

June arrived as did my final exams. I skipped through them and only relaxed when the last one was completed. I had crossed a new milestone. End of college. Now I had to pray I had done well so I could go to Oxford and study the degree in Medicine I wanted.

And as for Baby. He would arrive by the end of September. University didn't start until the end of October. If everything went as planned, I could register him at a crèche when I went for my classes. I had it all sorted and my tutor at the Adult College had assured me there was always help available and told me not to worry if I couldn't manage. I could always wait and apply again the following year.

I didn't mind deferring a year either because Baby's arrival was something I was waiting eagerly for.

He was my hope.

*****

The day of the results arrived. I got top marks. My joy was immense. I had made it. I had done it against all odds. My perseverance paid off in the end. I was delighted and I couldn't wait to tell Uncle.

Uncle…

I stopped and held a hand over my bump on my way to the car park. No I couldn't tell Uncle. He was mad at me. I hadn't seen his face despite living under the same roof for months. Seven and a half months and he still refused to look at me.

Wiping a stray tear from my eye, I waddled towards Auntie's waiting car and got in.

'I got three A stars in…' I paused as an unwelcomed sensation travelled up my spine and made me put a hand over Baby protectively.

'Congratulations, my dear. This is wonderful news,' said Fish boy as I attempted to get out of the car. What was he doing here?

'Hey Simmi relax,' he grinned as he grabbed my wrist stopping me from leaving. 'I won't bite.'

Nervously I stayed put and took heavy breaths to compose myself. Lately I was feeling too tired and my feet were swollen, and my head ached due to lack of sleep. The nurses said this was normal during the last trimester of pregnancy and I had nothing to worry about. However on my last check up, I'd had a higher blood pressure than usual. Having high blood pressure during pregnancy although common wasn't something to ignore.

'Relax. Relax,' Fish boy slurred as he began to drive. I fastened my seat belt. 'I must admit you do look radiant these days. Pregnancy has made you blossom like a flower.'

I ignored him.

'You must be wondering what I'm doing here so let me tell you that your Uncle has sent me to talk to you about something very important.'

I faked not being interested. My Baby moved and I looked down at my bump and hid the movement behind my bag. Lately I'd been feeling tightening sensations. At times they scared the life out of me. Baby's head would poke through my skin and although it was nothing less than a miracle and I'd marvel at the sight, it was uncomfortable and would have me holding my breath.

'Are you okay?' asked Fish boy stopping the car along Longbridge Road. I wondered why he was going down this road. Aunty never took this route.

'I'm okay. Please take me home,' I croaked.

'Why are you so afraid of me?' said Fish boy as he brushed a finger along my cheek. 'I thought we could celebrate your results and have a nice meal together first.'

'Please take me home,' I requested holding back my tears as Baby moved some more.

'I will,' he grinned moving his touch away and pointing outside. 'But first we will eat at that new restaurant.' I looked out at the tiny parade of shops lining the road he pointed to. 'We will celebrate together because I care for you. You can clearly see how devoted I am to you. Take my misery away and marry me Simmi. Sign those divorce papers. Let me give your baby my name.'

I shook my head as he moved closer and stared at me.

'Why haven't you signed those papers yet? Once you will, that bastard will also have to sign them.'

It was true, neither me nor Hassan had signed the papers which Uncle had drawn up by the Shariah Council. We needed a divorce from them because we hadn't registered our marriage under British law yet. We were husband and wife only under the laws of Islam.

'Sign them. Marry me.'

'I can't,' I whispered. I didn't like him. He had always repulsed me. And because of how his hand had rested where Baby was moving, I felt terrified of him.

'Why?' he said pressing his hand over my belly as he peered into my eyes.

'Please move your hand. I can't marry you Fish.'

'It's Feesh, not Fish,' he groaned as I tried moving his hand off me. 'You've got the children calling me Fish as well now. Anyway, Uncle Jawed said he is willing to forgive you for your disgrace if you agree to be my wife and sign the divorce.'

I shook my head. And he pressed harder. I was scared. I didn't trust him one bit.

But then glancing outside, looking at that same restaurant he wanted to take me to, I saw Darren and Ola sitting at a table by the windows. I swear I didn't know what came over me to do what I did next because I pushed Fish boy's hands away, unfastened my seatbelt and shifted my heavy body outside of the car and ignoring his surprise, I hurried into the restaurant as fast as I could.

Darren saw me first and stood up from his chair. I pointed behind me.

'Sam what is it?' I noticed concern on his features as he took me and my heavily pregnant and panicked state in. I was out of breath and the tightening in my stomach was extremely uncomfortable. I began to hyperventilate and as I spotted somebody else, who I promise I hadn't seen earlier, rising from his seat and rushing to me, my vision blurred and I fell against him.

'Sweetheart,' was the last word I heard.

Chapter Forty Four

Shadows and demons...

Silent. He was silent. Completely silent.

And I was tired. Extremely tired.

A monitor was attached over my bump keeping a record of Baby's heartbeat. Baby had been in distress earlier. My blood pressure was sky high but I promise I had been happy before. It was only when I'd seen Fish boy.

And now I was afraid.

Afraid of what waited for me when I got home. It was obvious Fish boy would have told Uncle he'd seen me in Hassan's arms. It was inevitable. Little did he know as soon as my consciousness had returned, I had pushed Hassan away and allowed the paramedics to tend to me instead.

The Baby was my concern. Not Hassan. I had run into the restaurant because I'd seen familiar faces who I knew would help me. Darren and Ola. It was Ola who had sat in the ambulance as they brought me to the hospital. Not Hassan. And I didn't know why he was still around.

My concern was for Baby.

A while later, a nurse came through the curtains and checked my vitals again.

'Your blood pressure is stable now and your baby is absolutely fine,' said the nurse. 'You can go home.'

'How can you say that?' said Hassan as he stood up. 'She's not well. She couldn't breathe. Her belly is massive. Look at her feet, they're like balloons. She fainted today and almost fell down and you're saying she can go home.'

I looked away closing my eyes.

'She's okay now. The doctor wouldn't have discharged her if she wasn't,' said the nurse. 'High blood pressure sometimes causes dizziness. She panicked when she felt the Braxton Hicks contractions. She'll be getting far more of those now. But stay prepared. The baby's head has fallen.'

'What, how has my baby's head fallen?'

I laughed. I couldn't help it. He was clueless. He hadn't seen me so heavily pregnant before. I guess it was a shock to him. But opening my eyes and seeing the way he was looking from me to the nurse, made me stop laughing.

'It hasn't fallen anywhere,' grinned the nurse as she wrote down a number on my record. 'It just means your baby is in the right position to be born soon.'

'So why are you discharging her? This means she can give birth any minute. So what'll happen if the baby comes and I'm not there?'

Covering my face with the blanket I wore, I broke into sobs. I couldn't help it.

And when he came near me, I shrugged him away.

What more could I do?

*****

It was nearing ten in the night when I was finally allowed to go home. I was given a bag of medicine and a booklet explaining the signs of labour. Stuff I'd already read heaps about. But the slightest of Baby's movement was making me anxious. I had to relax. I still had six weeks until the due date.

Hassan was driving me home. Again a silence between us kept us both in our thoughts. Perhaps of where fate had brought us.

The car soon pulled over into my driveway and as I shifted to leave the car and face the music which was bound to be waiting for me inside, Hassan's hand cupped mine.

'Look after yourself…'

246

Closing my eyes, I stilled as his gentle touch sent a longing through me. But as quickly as he had touched me, that is how quickly he moved his hand away. The warmness seeping through me stopped and instead a dread filled me. Opening my eyes I saw my family standing outside my front door.

Reluctantly but without any other choice, I got out of Hassan's car.

'See I told you she's with him,' screamed Fish boy making me flinch and look into Uncle's eyes. I hadn't seen his face in months. He looked older but much smaller. His shoulders were sagging and his face had shrunk. He had lost weight.

'Uncle,' I choked finding the word weird on my tongue not having said it for so long. I fidgeted with my bag and pulled out my results sheet and taking the few steps towards him, I said, 'Uncle I got three A stars' in my A levels. It's the best I could've got.'

His tight lips didn't tilt upwards and neither did he embrace me or twirl me around in his arms as he had done when I told him my GCSE results. Instead he stared right past me. At Hassan's car.

'I told you she tricked me into taking her along Longbridge Road, and then she made me stop the car and he appeared out of nowhere and took her away. She's been seeing him all this time...'

I turned to Fish boy and shook my head. 'Why are you lying?' I asked as my tears appeared. 'I was at the hospital.'

'Come in now Samina,' said Aunty Bushra grabbing my arm and proceeding to lead me inside the house.

'Stop right there,' said Uncle through tight teeth still staring into Hassan's car. 'Tell her to leave right away. Tell her to go back inside that boy's car and leave this instant.'

My breaths stopped and I felt a weird sensation inside my fingernails and it quickly began to spread along the rest of my fingers and hands.

'What are you saying?' Aunty stammered nervously. 'She looks terribly tired. She needs to rest.'

'Get out of my house!' yelled Uncle and a scream travelled from my lungs when he grabbed me and began forcing me out of Auntie's hold.

In a matter of seconds, I was hiding behind Hassan's back as Uncle shouted words which made no sense to me. They were dirty words. Words used to describe women who sold their bodies and stood on street corners after hours. He said these words in Urdu, and Panjabi and Hindi and I listened to them all.

But when Uncle began cursing my unborn child, I couldn't bear it anymore. I screamed into Hassan's shirt unable to hold on any longer.

How could anybody wish death for my innocent Baby?

On shaky legs forcing myself out of Hassan's way, I went over to Uncle and I swear every inch of me trembled as I looked up at him. His eyes were hugely wide and his fists were ready to attack me again but I needed to say this and I would because it was what I felt, 'You are not my father.'

He smacked me as his reply making my eyes sting and my head drop to one side of my shoulder. Immediately he yelled at Aunty and Fish boy to come inside the house.

And I stood there watching the front door slam in front of me, my palm over the stinging on my cheek and one hand over my Baby. The pins and needles had spread to my toes.

Slowly I looked over at my husband. He was stood by his car with his back to me.

And for some silly reason, I actually waited for him to come over to me and take all my hurt away.

He didn't come. He stayed there.

He stayed there until all the curious neighbours had gone back inside their houses and Aunty had come back out to take me inside.

Like an abandoned pet, I kept my watery eyes fixed on my husband who stood with his back to me as Aunty pulled me by my arm and took me inside the house.

And he didn't do anything about this, at all.

*****

Once inside my bedroom I went over to the window and the shadow I'd wait to appear every night, did appear. Not only did his silhouette remain there, it held two palms against the glass of the barriers between us.

Despite everything that had occurred, I found myself doing the same. And as Baby moved inside me, I wiped at my tears trying my hardest to get them to stop falling.

'You met your daddy today,' I cried taking my hand away from the window and placing it over my bump where I could feel him playing. He always played at this time and he'd keep me up for hours as he somersaulted inside me.

Unfortunately my precious moment talking with my Baby didn't last long. Fish boy came into my bedroom and sat on the bed.

I pointed at my door. 'Please get out of my room,' I said feeling my head spin at the sight of him. His rubber lips were tilted upwards and he picked up Baby's teddy bear which my tutor had gifted for him when I'd left college.

'Don't touch that,' I warned staying put by the window not being brave enough to go near him to snatch it back.

'Or else?'

'Aunty,' I called hoping she would come and take him away. I was tired and wanted to lie down and try getting some sleep. I'd had a long day and my cheek where Uncle had hit me was still throbbing, as was my head.

'Aunty,' I called again but on my third attempt Fish boy got up and captured my neck in between his arms and he held a hand over my mouth muffling any sounds I could make.

249

In my panic, I punched at him and tried calling out for Aunty but it was no use. He held me too tight. I began gasping for breath and I think he realised I was in trouble because as fast as he had grabbed me, it was that swiftly, he released me.

'You are a hard one,' he spat. 'Let me tell you, I will get my hands on you really soon. That bastard husband of yours will watch how I make you mine. You have humiliated me enough. I won't stand it again. I don't want you anywhere near him, do you understand, dearest Simmi?'

I didn't reply. Couldn't. I was beginning to feel dizzy and I was out of breath. I held onto the panel below the window and tried taking deep breaths.

'Do you understand me Simmi?' he slurred behind my ear.

Still gasping for breaths I said, 'Why can't you just leave me alone?'

'Should I show you why?' he drooled into my ear as he turned my body around. I cried at the look in his eyes. It was disgusting and when he took my hand and rubbed it over the fly of his trousers I had no control over my reaction and threw up all over his shirt.

The vomiting was severe and as I gagged, I felt dizzy and weak and amidst the panic and the sickness I was going through, I glanced out of the window and Hassan was gone. But that didn't make me stop shouting out for him because his Baby and I were in danger. I could feel it.

'Hassan…'

'Shut up,' snapped Fish boy as he scowled at the mess on him and as he left my room, I took my chance and hurried towards Uncle's bedroom and freaked out even more when neither him or Aunty were in it.

The doorbell began to ring downstairs and realising Fish boy was standing by the wash basin trying to get the sick off his clothes, I hurried past the bathroom. The doorbell kept ringing and I began climbing down the stairs.

'Aunty,' I cried as a tightening like the one I had experienced during the day gripped me and made me halt on the step I was on. I held onto the banister with one hand and with the other I held Baby's movements, trying to reassure him I was okay and him safe.

He needn't worry.

I tried closing my eyes and forcing myself to relax as the doctors at the hospital had said but the constant ringing of the doorbell wouldn't let me concentrate on my breaths. And then I smelled Fish behind me and when I placed my foot on the next step down, he grabbed my pony tail and tugged me backwards.

'Fish please,' I gasped as another of Baby's movements made me feel like I was about to lose my vision. 'My Baby…'

'What is going on…?'

My Aunty never did find out what was going on because a heavy hand connected to my back and made me lose my balance.

And when the front door flew open and Hassan's voice filled my remaining senses, it was no use.

I was already tumbling down the stairs.

Chapter Forty Five

Losing hope…

There comes a moment in your life when you are rendered deaf even though medically it can't be possible. Because you're capable of hearing, you're ears are not disabled yet you can't hear a thing.

The nurse wheeled me into a different section of the hospital. I'd passed through the maternity wards. I'd seen women with swollen bellies. I'd seen women with bundles wrapped in shawls. I'd seen happy faces, tired faces and rejoicing faces. Women with their partners and families, tenderly stroking the soft skins of their new-born.

I could see them, though I couldn't hear a word they were saying. I couldn't hear the cries of tiny boys and girls wanting their first feeds, or wanting a change of their soiled nappies. I couldn't hear the nurses congratulating and instructing on how to do what. I couldn't hear blissful fathers cuddling and posing with their new additions because I was in a state where all I could sense was the stench of my own dysphoria.

Because I was being wheeled to the room near the mortuary where people like me went to see their dead baby.

'I can call somebody from home,' said the nurse as she pulled the wheelchair to a stop. 'You don't have to do this on your own.'

Her words reached a corner of my brain somewhere but I'd lost the ability to respond. I wanted to say, 'Yes, please get somebody. Get my Mummy.' I wanted Mummy to do this with me.

I was the most painful, the most helpless I'd ever been. I needed her.

But where was she?

We went through the doors when I failed to provide the nurse with my request.

I simply swallowed my yearning.

The room was bright, creamy and airy. Everything was in its place and there was a distinct smell. Or was it the smell of my own grief?

How was I going to say goodbye to my Baby, to my hope?

Without hope, what is left of a person?

I looked down at my cast, at the catheter pricked on my hand and the fluid bottle following me on the stand I was holding onto. I looked down at my bare legs and trailed my eyes to my mid-section where I had been cut. My hospital gown was still stained with the evidence of what I'd been through.

The bone in my right arm below my elbow had fractured. The right side of my body was badly scraped and my ankle was sprained. My forehead had a huge bump and the top of my nose was grazed.

This was my damage.

But Baby, he wasn't so lucky. He died inside me. He was dead before I had even reached the hospital.

They had to perform a caesarean on me, by force. Apparently both my emotional and physical conditions weren't strong enough to allow me to go through the stresses of an induced labour. A section was the best option.

But I wanted to keep him. I wanted to keep him inside me forever. I could deal with it, I promise I could. It wouldn't have mattered if my belly would remain huge. It wouldn't matter if I'd have back pains and insomnia and cramps and swollen feet forever. I swear none of these things would have mattered. Because I wanted to feel him kicking me. I wanted to see the outline of his tiny feet rubbing against the wall of my abdomen. I wanted to feed him all the foods he had grown inside me loving. I wanted him to stay inside me where I could feel him.

Even if he hadn't moved for many hours.

They didn't listen though. No one listened and they took him out. Left me barren, empty and more broken than I already was.

Promise my ache was severe. My never ending tears were proof of this.

I couldn't even bear to see a cut on my knees as a child. What transformations a person goes through as life prolongs, huh?

How one automatically learns to bear pain?

The physical pains are like that, I suppose. They are easy to bear because they heal. The nurse said the section would take a couple of weeks. The catheter will be out in a day or two and I would have no hole left on my hand where the needle was pricked. And my cast would be out by a month or two, and I'd be healed. Completely.

What of the emotional pains? The pains of the worst kind. The pain of seeing my Baby for the first time and dead. How would I bear this?

'Are you ready Samina?' the nurse asked as she leaned against my knees on the floor. I looked into her eyes and wondered why hers were watery. Surely she had come into this room with a battered eighteen year old waiting to be introduced to her dead baby before.

'Samina, are you sure you want to do this?' She took my hand in hers and squeezed it as another nurse dressed in a different coloured uniform to hers popped her head in.

'Are you ready?' she said.

'Samina?'

'Yes. I want to see my little boy...' I choked.

'Mandy she's ready.'

Mandy disappeared and my nurse stood up. 'I'll be outside if you need me.'

I was left to feed on my tears as they dribbled into my mouth.

Minutes later Mandy came inside carrying my child wrapped up in a white shawl. My heart stopped craving on the salt from the tears and began hammering violently against my ribs. It wanted to escape. It wanted to run away and never come back inside my body.

My body was rubbish, that's why. It never had any happiness. For years it had been deprived from the essence of truthful love and now for once when it saw some hope, a chance to love again, it was let down.

A heart could only take so much. It was only a vessel after all. It needed some escape sometime.

'Oh sweet angel. Go to mummy. Bask in her arms for a while before you have to enter the gardens of Heaven,' said Mandy as she rocked my Baby like he was the most precious thing she'd ever held.

My heart stopped running away.

'Do you want to hold him?' said Mandy as she held him towards me.

I looked at the pattern on the white shawl draping over her arms and slowly but eventually my heart started beating again and my good arm reached out begging Mandy to give him to me.

And as soon as he was in it, I held him as close as I could.

I kissed him as if he was alive. I kissed him again and again. He was my Baby. He was beautiful. His skin was pale and soft and his fragrance was one I would never forget. He was light, yet he filled my hands with the best weight possible. A weight I could forever hold.

I rubbed my face on his face, his cheeks, his nose, his lips, his forehead. I nuzzled against his neck and kissed along his tiny features. He was perfect. My son was absolutely perfect.

His fingers were long and his hands were little. His small feet were so cute. I kissed each and every finger, each and every toe. I unwrapped his shawl and inspected every inch of him and admired how well formed he was. His hair was black like mine and I brushed my hands through it repeatedly as I began to sing verses of the Quran to him.

Verses my Mummy once sang before lulling me to sleep.

'Do you want to dress him in your own clothes?' asked Mandy.

'Clothes…?'

'I understand,' whispered Mandy as she sucked in her lips.

I began to cry desperately. What type of mother was I? I hadn't even prepared an outfit for him. My tears, big fat ones, the chunkiest ones ever, fell onto his chubby cheeks as I held him close and apologised.

I was sorry. I was so so sorry.

My tears fell to his lips, and as I cried I wondered if he could taste me. Could he taste my yearning? Could he open up his small mouth and perhaps even smile at me or cry with me? My bust was heavy and it hurt on top of all the other agony I was feeling. The nurse said it was due to my milk coming through, now that I'd given birth

'Wake up Baby,' I cried wanting him to latch onto me and take what was his. I tapped his lips with my finger tip gently.

'Look at Mummy, look at me Baby…'

Mandy was fast to come over and place a hand on my shoulder.

'Why does he not open his eyes?' I asked.

'Your angel is asleep that's why.'

'Why did I wake up?' I cried. 'How come I didn't fall asleep with him?'

Stroking Baby's cheek with a thumb, Mandy said, 'If these things were simple to explain, we would be too advanced in our knowledge. Some things can only be explained by the Lord.'

'Are you Muslim?' I asked. Her words were something like Uncle Dawood would say.

'No,' Mandy smiled. 'But all faiths have phenomenon which cannot be explained. It was God's will. He loves your baby too dearly thus he took him from this world to

256

put him in a much better place. But my darling, you still have hope. Never give up on hope.'

'Hope.' I kissed Baby. He was my hope. I should've died too. There was nothing for me without him anymore.

'Time will heal. For now spend these precious moments with him. Talk to him, sing to him, tell him a bedtime story, it's the only chance you'll have.'

I cuddled Baby closer.

*****

Minutes or hours later I was so consumed in my silent Baby I failed to notice the talking outside the room.

Mandy was standing by the open door. 'Is it okay?' she said. 'They want to see him.'

In my poor state, I jutted my chin and Mandy took this as my consent.

I held onto my son tightly as a fear engulfed me. Hassan's parents had arrived.

'Oh Samina,' Sheila said as she ran towards me.

'No,' I cried when she took Baby from my lap and swirled as she held him to her chest.

Rahese stroked my head lightly. I tried moving him out of the way to see Baby but Rahese decided to pull my head into his bulky midriff. However when I heard a new voice, a voice I could never forget, I had to close my eyes for a second.

'Come Hassan look at your son.'

'Oh Mum ...'

Rahese released me when he heard his own son's pain. In an instant he was sitting across from me next to Hassan who had Baby in his arms. Hassan was crying. His body shaking. His eyes downcast. And his face fallen. His parents were comforting him. His mum rubbing his back and his dad helping him hold Baby properly.

I tilted my head to the side trying to see Hassan's face properly but I couldn't see it. I could see his nose, his shaking lips, trembling jaw. But his eyes, I wanted them to look at me, once. So he could see his revenge had paid off.

His sister's soul would finally be dancing. A baby for a baby.

Little did Hassan know Yasmin was the lucky one. She actually got to go with her baby. Her baby was still inside her when she went. My pain was bigger. My Baby was going and I was staying. Staying to live amongst people like him.

I wondered why he was crying though. I mean what did he share with my Baby anyway? He fathered him through a ploy of revenge. He hadn't cared when I told him about him. He threw money at me and told me to go kill him, so why was he crying like he'd lost the most valuable thing of his?

He didn't care!

When I was nurturing him in my womb for months, he hadn't been in touch once. He hadn't stood by the window even though each night I would stand there like an idiot waiting for him to appear. He had only appeared the night Baby was killed.

So what gave Hassan and his parents the right to hold Baby like he was theirs? He wasn't theirs. He was mine and only mine.

'He's beautiful,' said Sheila sniffing back her tears. I watched her pick up a bag from the floor. Taking out a pale blue outfit from it, she began unfastening the buttons and Rahese helped her change Baby into it.

That was my Baby...

They took pictures of him. They rocked him up and down and I couldn't endure it anymore because he could have easily fallen. A baby needed to be held delicately. They were fragile and my Baby was the most fragile of them all. He was departing.

He was leaving his Mummy.

'Give me Baby,' I cried helplessly holding out my good arm. 'Give him back to me.'

Everybody but Hassan looked up and I was glad when Mandy finally requested Hassan's parents to try to understand how difficult this was for me. They gave Baby to her and she gave him back to me. I cuddled him against me.

I told Baby not to worry. I had him now. He didn't need to feel afraid. I kissed him over and over. He had to be reassured he was safe.

*****

They soon left after that. Rahese had a funeral to arrange. My Uncle wouldn't arrange it. He hadn't even come to see me. Neither had Aunty. No one had come. And my Baby was going to be buried the following morning and I couldn't do anything about it.

Kareem. Kareem Iqmal.

Hassan chose his name. I didn't give him the right to choose it but it was okay, the name he chose.

Kareem was my father's name. Hassan named my son after my dad. That was okay. I liked the name. It suited Baby. It suited him a lot.

Why hadn't Hassan gone home with his parents though? Why was he here?

'It's time,' said Mandy in a whisper. 'The vehicle from the Mosque has arrived. You need to say your final goodbyes.'

I shook my head and held Kareem closer to my chest. I'd held him for nearly four hours and hadn't tired. I could've gone on holding him forever.

'Samina let him go. I'll be with him. He won't be on his own. I promise.'

Hassan was kneeling on the floor. He had finally mustered the courage to look at me. The monster had fainted at the sight of me. Coming through, he'd even had the audacity to pull my head against his chest and cry his pathetic apologies.

It was all fake. His *'sorry'* meant nothing to me.

259

What would I do with it anyway? They were useless.

Sorry, what a word huh? First hurt people, make them cry, render them helpless and alone, and then say sorry. What a fucked up concept?

His hand was holding Kareem's and the other was cupping my knee. His eyes were dropping tears as chunky as mine. Yet his words held no credibility. I didn't believe he could keep my Kareem safe at the Mosque until he was taken to the graveyard and buried under soil and mud.

'You never keep your promises,' I cried into Kareem's soft head. 'If you did my Kareem would be opening his eyes and looking at me.'

Hassan dropped Baby's hand and as his head fell on my lap an excruciating pain from my cut reminded me of the ordeal I'd been through in the operating theatre. His head jerked up and Mandy came to my aid.

'She's had an operation. Be careful. Are you alright?'

'It hurts too much,' I said finding even crying agony. Every breath, every cry of mine was reminding me I was as broken on the surface as I was deep inside my bruised and cracked skin.

'I'm sorry. I'm sorry Samina. I'm so sorry,' said Hassan as he held his head in both his hands. 'I'm sorry. I'm so sorry.'

I cried, 'I won't forgive you. You can be sorry all you like. I won't forgive you ever…'

Hassan cried louder. And as he cried, I cried too. But it wasn't long when I realised what I doing. Holding Baby to my chest, I began apologising for fighting with his dad. Because at the end of the day, Hassan was his dad.

And Baby deserved to witness some peace. At least now when he was going.

'Hold Baby,' I said. 'Let's say goodbye to our son together.'

He was at my knees instantly and taking Baby from me, he whispered, 'Sorry,' and kissed him fervently. And my fingers, the ones from the good hand which still moved, began brushing through Hassan's hair.

A man knocked on the door and my eyes widened as he brought in a wooden casket on a wheeled trolley. I gripped onto Hassan's hair tightly. He looked up at me. His eyes were swollen and bloodshot and wet. Slowly my fingers untangled themselves from his hair and took Kareem from him. I held him protectively. I wasn't going to let them put him in that casket. I had dreamt of a frilly broderie Moses basket for Baby to rest in, not that. That was for grownups, old people, ill people, not for tiny little babies like my Kareem.

'He really needs to go now. You've been real brave Samina. But the nurses want you back in the ward. Your medication is due,' said Mandy as she began wheeling my chair next to that box.

Hassan took Kareem from me and helplessly I watched him recite verses from the Quran in his ears. I heard him whisper, 'Sorry,' again. I watched him kiss him over and over and when he held out Baby to me again, I simply didn't know how and what I was supposed to do anymore.

How does a mother say goodbye? How does a mother place her new born baby in a casket? How?

'Kiss him goodbye.'

I kissed him goodbye.

Chapter Forty Six

Settling the score…

The next morning an aching body, a fever, and dangerously high blood pressure meant I couldn't leave the hospital to attend the funeral. Darren had come to take me but the doctors didn't allow it, despite his pleas of returning me safely.

'It's okay,' I had told him. 'I've already said my goodbye.'

He had watched me for a few minutes, and then he left. Obviously in a hurry to witness his best friend's son being buried.

He had however promised to take photographs for me.

'Hmm,' was all I had murmured.

My calm surprised me. I wasn't numb though. Not this time.

This time I could feel everything.

*****

Later the same day both Aunty Asma and Aunty Bushra were sitting by my bed, openly conversing about my fate, thinking I couldn't hear them. Little did they know I was awake and my mind refusing to open my eyes and acknowledge them. I had no desire to see anybody anymore.

'Oh sister Asma,' said Aunty Bushra. 'I tried my best. There is no use now.'

'You didn't try hard enough,' the other Aunty snapped. 'You failed in gaining her trust. A simple task and you couldn't do it. You do know Murad is Feesh's uncle and unlike you and me, he has a big mouth. He's already blabbed openly to everybody in Pakistan. Tabrez

Jee has been on the phone non-stop since his stupid boy pushed her.'

'He didn't push her. He would never do that,' retorted Aunty Bushra. I curled the bedding in my fists, trying my hardest not to open my eyes.

'Why is he in custody then? Those Iqmal's are dead set on sending him to prison for this?' said Aunty Asma. 'I'm surprised they let her shameless husband off so easily when he almost killed him last night. Did you see how he punched and kicked poor Feesh? Murad and I were by his bedside all night but the police just took him and locked him up as soon as he awoke. Tabrez Jee and his family are going berserk in Pakistan. They've already threatened my Murad's family in the village. And I wouldn't be surprised if those threats are real, considering the thugs they acquaint themselves with. We need to make the girl give a statement in Feesh's favour as soon as she can.'

Aunty Bushra began to cry. 'I tried to make her like me. You know how she was. She never accepted me as her mother. When she returned home after eloping, I did try to make her feel I was there for her. I also reassured Feesh she would eventually take a shine to him. He agreed to stay away from her. But when he found out she was having the boy's baby, he wasn't happy. Oh you know how hard it was to appease him to keep this all a secret.'

'Yes,' said Aunty Asma. 'Her actions have destroyed us all. So now what? I'm sure Feesh will not marry her after this. Tabrez Jee wasn't happy when we planned to get her divorced from her lover and remarried to his son in the first place. It was only when I reminded him the house was still on her name that he agreed.'

'Which is why she is still living with us… If Jawed had his own way, he'd have thrown her out onto the streets the day she returned. Habib had taken his bulk of his hefty inheritance from the commercial property already. Thank God, Jawed was lucky to get a mortgage and pay the arrogant monkey. But he could never afford to pay Samina out. The house is hers. We had to keep her with us despite everything. Oh how I wanted to poison her months ago. How shamelessly she walked with her big belly in front of everybody?'

'Well,' said Aunty Asma, 'I suppose it is a good thing she's no longer with the child. And from what you tell me I doubt Hassan wants to be with her anyway. Get her to divorce him and make Feesh grovel to gain her affection again.'

'How will he if he is behind bars for causing the loss of the child?' groaned Aunty Bushra.

'Don't worry about Feesh. Murad and Jawed are doing their best to have him bailed. Once the doctor has given the report confirming she fell due to high blood pressure and not a push, he'll be released. In fact Murad is there right now. Perhaps he's even got the reports.'

'It's fortunate she was at the hospital during the day then. Her blood pressure was very high,' whispered Aunty Bushra. I felt her coming near. The stench from her perfume was choking me. I felt a hand on my forehead. 'Sister Asma her fever is high. Should I call the nurse?'

'It would have been easier if she died along with the baby. The house would have gone to Jawed and I. The house is worth more than half a million. But now we will have to stick to our original plan, with Feesh as our only hope in getting our hands on some of the funds. Tabrez Jee has already said you and I will get a generous share once Samina hands it all over to his son.'

'The house would not have gone to Jawed and you anyway,' scowled Aunty Bushra. 'You are forgetting she still has that older brother of hers. He can't even stand a hair on her head falling, and if he finds out about this, I can't imagine how he will react. Silly man, how much I buttered him to keep Samina here with us when he first left. If he'd had his way he would have taken her to Dubai with him years ago.'

'Well don't tell her this?' said Aunty Asma in a hushing sound. 'She thinks Habib didn't care for her and left. She doesn't know we forced him to leave her here. He would have sold the house too by now. Just feel blessed Jawed was her legal parent by law and Habib had no option but to leave her here with us.'

'Samina…'

My eyes opened as soon as his voice approached.

'You okay?' he said as he came and placed a hand on my forehead causing both my Aunties to gasp. But Hassan was never one to care about others and he pulled over a chair. Ignoring him for the moment I roamed my eyes on them two women, whom I once loved with all my being.

'You wake up when your husband arrives,' said Aunty Asma softly, as she stroked a hand over my head. 'And your favourite Aunty has come from Blackpool to see you and has been waiting here for over an hour. Anyway how are you my child?'

'Hassan,' I said taking a deep and painful breath in, knowing full well what I was about to do was the first step in many to show these people what a mother's wrath really was.

'Yes,' he replied taking my hand in his and sending tremors of disgust inside me.

But one step at a time.

Making my voice firmer as my eyes began to leak water against my wishes, I said, 'Can you throw these two women out?'

'What?' he said looking from me to both my Aunt's.

'Get them out!'

'What way is this to behave?' said Aunty Bushra as she raised her hand but stopped it mid-air before smacking me.

'Get out. Get out,' I screamed making Hassan jump on the bed and hold me.

'Just leave,' scowled Hassan patting my head against his chest. 'She's distressed.'

Bushra stared and Asma pulled her by the arm. 'Wait until Jawed hears of this. In fact I think it's time your brother heard of this too.'

'Just go. Just leave me alone, get out of my sight,' I cried as I pushed Hassan off me too. 'You go too. Just go away okay… Don't touch me. Leave me alone…'

'Calm down, please my love calm down…'

Love?

How dare he call me his love? I had to get him out too. Why wasn't anybody helping me to throw him out? I attempted to move. I had to sit up. I had to get him out of my sight.

'What are you doing? You'll hurt yourself,' said Hassan as he debated whether to come near me or not. His eyes were red and wet. But I didn't care of his tears anymore. I didn't care at all.

'What's happening to you?'

'I swear Iqmal go away or I'll fucking kill you,' I said as harshly as I could muster in my distress. 'Why are you even here? My Baby is buried now so you can go back to your life and leave me the hell alone.'

'Sweetheart…'

'Don't call me that. I am nothing to you. Fucking nothing to you.'

The nurses gathered and ignoring the sunken expression on Hassan's pale face, I told them to get him out and to never to allow him in again. I never wanted to see him again.

'Why?' he had asked as he began to leave.

'Because I hate you.'

*****

Five long weeks later, I was ready to go home. Finally I was allowed to walk the streets of London as free as a bird. I had never really flown with my wings spread before and most nights stuck in the hospital, it was all I could dream about. Being on my own. Without anybody. Just me, myself and my loneliness.

But being lonely was good. It was a blessing. Being alone meant you could do what you wanted. You could eat, drink, fart and burb without anybody holding your neck and making a simple task of breathing a nightmare.

Lonely people. They were probably the most contented persons ever.

And those pills. Those anti-depressants. Yeah they went straight in the bin. I wasn't mentally unstable just because I was fighting my Baby was murdered, and I harassed and pushed down the stairs.

They had released Fish boy weeks earlier and he'd already escaped to Pakistan.

My brother had flown over the day after I had learnt how deviant my Aunts were. I knew they were evil before but the revelations had maddened me. And they had maddened Habib too.

The Police had come to see me and I had told them over and over what had occurred during that night. Fish boy had killed my Baby. He had made me touch his manhood and he had pulled at my hair and he had pushed me. The Police didn't do anything though. They simply reported what the doctors had told me many times already.

Uncle and Aunty Bushra had both confirmed Fish boy was merely holding onto me to stop me from falling. I was dizzy and I was swaying because my blood pressure was too high. Uncle Murad had even reported the doctors at Newham General for negligence. Apparently they never should've allowed me to go home. My blood pressure was dangerous and Baby was in trouble.

But no one believed me when I told them Baby was moving inside me before I fell. He wasn't in distress. My Baby was murdered.

And that man hadn't once come to see me and offer his condolences, as normal people would do. Being my guardian, my adoptive father, would have made it his duty to come see how I was faring. At least the once. But like I said, lonely was good.

I was good like this.

The only one I saw was Habib. He was supportive and helped me set my plans into action right away. He got me a lawyer. The house on Ilford Lane. My house. The one my dad had left for me was already sold.

Uncle and his family could go fuck themselves.

Habib told me they weren't happy but did eventually vacate the house and move into the flat above the Cabbie. And Habib had even found a flat for me in Oxford at the university where I would be starting the following week. I had loads of money in my bank account from the sale, and Habib had explained how I needed to stay wise and not overspend.

But because I was a free bird, I would do what I wanted. It was my money. All mine.

I was sorted. Lonely, hollow, but sorted.

Chapter Forty Seven

Goodbye Ilford Lane…

The taxi pulled up outside my house on Ilford Lane and taking small steps, I unloaded my bag and paid the driver, thankful he wasn't one of Uncle's merry men from the Cabbie.

With my plastered hand, I unlocked the door whilst balancing my huge bag in the other. My body was healing. My caesarean didn't pain much anymore. My ankle was completely better, and the bruises and cuts, all gone. The only evidence of my disaster was the plaster on my arm.

And of course the scar from the caesarean section. This would remain forever.

The sun was shining brightly and looking over my shoulder along the never ending line of shops and houses, I felt sick. This whole street was cursed. Dirty, rubbish and cramped. I couldn't wait to get away.

Inside my house, I cringed at the state my doting family had left it in. It ponged of hatred and murder. I quickly made my way to the kitchen and opened the French doors to let some air in. Catching a glimpse of the bricked wall in my garden, rather than looking at it like a helpless bunny, I went over and with mud smeared the word 'fuck' on it. Then I spat at it.

That episode of my life had ruined me proper. It was time for me to find me again.

When I was bored with nothing to do at the hospital, a nurse had once given me a pamphlet to read. In it was a line which I had underlined.

'Having a baby does not cripple a woman.'

And looking at the wall made me realise how true those words were. A baby made a woman stronger. And even if my Kareem wasn't with me anymore, I wouldn't let his mother waste away. I would prove to Baby I was more than a vagabond begging people for their affection and pity. I was a whole universe more. I was his mother, a mother he could be proud of.

*****

The flat in Oxford was ready. I could move in. All I had to do was pick up the keys when I got there and my new life could begin.

I couldn't wait.

However the constant ringing of the doorbell was beginning to annoy me. I had been ignoring it. I'd even put cotton wool in my ears but now I wanted it to stop.

'Open the door before I break in,' he shouted through the letter flap. 'This is my final warning…'

I waved my hands in the air and marched to open the door.

He didn't look happy though. In fact he looked a total mess. And when he glided near me like a hungry feline, I wasn't an old lady willing to stroke his fur and offer him a bowl of semi skimmed milk anymore.

'Keep away from me,' I grimaced before retreating quickly into the living room. He followed of course, but instead of slumping down on the old and battered settee my Aunty had left in place of the nice leather ones, he stood close to me. Staring.

I rolled my eyes and glared at him. In fact I didn't like the way his hair was too long and unkempt. I didn't like how his tee shirt looked un-ironed and kind of tacky. I didn't like the way his face was unshaven, and I didn't like the fact he was looking at me like he had actually *missed me*.

'I've been worried,' he uttered. 'Why did you do that?'

I needed a cold drink. Perhaps I could offer him one too. He looked parched. He had been standing outside my front door under the midday heat for hours. But he grabbed hold of my good wrist and stopped me leaving the room.

'We need to talk,' he said.

'And I need a drink,' I countered into his dull eyes. Prying my wrist free I rushed into the kitchen aware he was following close behind me. Pulling open the refrigerator door, I grabbed a Coke can and held it out to him. He shook his head. I shrugged and pulling the key open, drank straight from it.

'Why did you shut me out when I wanted to be there for you? I haven't slept in days worrying about you. I've been coming to the hospital every day, twice, even three times some days to see you, only to be denied entry into your ward.'

'You didn't have to,' I said with a roll of my eyes. 'And you don't have to worry about me. Why should you anyway?' I said slipping past him and going back inside the living room. I placed my drink on the mantle above the fireplace and began fiddling with the clothing I had ordered online which still needed to be packed.

'What are you doing?' Hassan asked. 'Why are you packing?'

'Why do people pack? Doh, I'm going somewhere.'

He didn't like my sarcasm and snatched my new jacket from my hands and threw it across the room, and came close.

'What do you think…?' As soon as he enveloped me against his chest, I felt a strong urge to breathe in some air. My body struggled. My limbs began to shake. My hands were trembling. My toes were curling. And my eyes began to water.

My heart cried out to me to push him away. To get away from him, before he began to play with it again.

It was still broken for crying out loud.

Somehow I succeeded in pushing him off of me and then I slapped him across his face whilst heaving and glaring at his audacity.

Holding a hand to his cheek, he stared back.

271

'I told you not to touch me,' I said as I wiped at my tears violently. I had vowed I wouldn't cry anymore. I had vowed to be strong. I had vowed to make my Baby proud. Crying over this bully wasn't going to let me achieve any of this.

'I've been dying to see you,' he said as he continued to stare. His eyes were dull. Gone was the mischief. Gone was the smugness. And gone was his shine. 'I can't sleep. I can't eat. I can't go on without you...'

'And I can't believe you,' I said as I tried calming my heart down. I wasn't going to fall for his false promises again. It needn't worry.

'How do I make you believe in me again? How can I make you believe how sorry I am?'

'You can't,' I said and I went to sit down afraid of my knees giving way. 'The damage you've caused is irreplaceable. I've lost too much because of you. I might have forgiven you at some point but...' I rubbed a hand over my empty belly. 'There's one thing I can't forgive you for and I don't think I ever will.'

'You blame me for Kareem's death?'

I rubbed my forehead blinking back my tears.

'I blame me too and every time I close my eyes I can see him. I see his little face. I see his closed eyes and I see him when he was being buried. I see him over and over. I see what I did to him, to you. I see you falling down those stairs screaming my name out crying for help. I see your bruises, your cuts, those machines on you and all the blood. I can't go on Samina. Believe me I can't even look at myself in the mirror without wanting to break the thing to pieces.'

'Like you broke me to pieces?'

'Yes,' he whispered closing his eyes tightly and cupping the back of his head. 'Like I broke you to pieces...'

I didn't know what to say. I could never forgive him for a lot of things but blaming him for Baby's death wasn't something I had planned on doing. However my sorrow was immense. I couldn't sleep either. I couldn't get Baby's face out of my head. I could still smell him. I could still imagine him growing inside of me. If Hassan was suffering, so was I.

'Let me fix your pieces?' said Hassan as he came near and fell to his knees. And he still had enough courage left in him to place his head on my lap. 'Please let me heal you.'

My eyes closed and I tried my best not to keep crying. I remembered I had promised myself I wouldn't. I was free and young and determined.

Hassan would have to deal with his guilt by himself.

'I love you,' he said and I felt the moisture from his eyes as it seeped through my leggings to my thighs.

I had never heard him sound like this. Sincere. So broken. But I couldn't say the same words back to him.

How could I say them so easily?

'I've always loved you but I fought real hard with myself trying to act otherwise. I've killed myself over and over thinking about what I've put you through. Believe me Samina, I've realised how wrong I've been. I was a coward. Look at me, I still am a coward. I can't even look you in the eye whilst saying this. I am so ashamed of what I've done. I am sorry for everything. Believe me my love, had it not been for my father's pressure I would have been a husband to you a long time ago. His ego and his desire to get back at your Uncle stopped me from coming for you earlier. But these are not my excuses. How can they be? When I too was blinded by my hate for Habib and what happened with my sister. I hated that you knew her. I hated that you hid this from me. My God, I did so many wrongs. Please Samina please forgive me…'

He looked up and I had to look away.

'Sweetheart, ease my suffering. Say you forgive me.'

I shook my head and as I closed my eyes I could sense him moving closer to me. I could sense him cupping my face in his palms and I could sense him pressing his lips to my head.

273

'Forgive me.'

I was surprised my body didn't retaliate. Instead my heart began to beat in an unusual pattern and by their own accord my hands pulled him up on the sofa to sit next to me and my head lowered to fit against his chest.

He held me close, as I cried my complaints to him. He held me tightly, as I relived some of the nightmares I'd been through in his absence when I was safeguarding our child on my own. He held me cocooned protectively as I explained what Fish boy had done to me and how he had killed our innocent Baby.

'I don't want to be here anymore,' I said after we had cried all we could. 'I leave for Oxford to start my degree tomorrow.'

'What about us?' he asked.

'Hassan, don't make this difficult. I have to go.' Removing myself from his arms, I got up and stood near the mantel and as I stared at my coke can, my heart ached hearing him cry his regrets.

'Let me come with you,' he begged. 'I'll get a job there and we'll be happy. I promise you, I won't let you down again. I'll support you in anything you want to do.'

'Hassan you've got your whole life ahead of you,' I said trying my best to keep my voice from breaking. 'Don't be childish and go home now. I've forgiven you already so please just go.'

'You can't mean that?' he said as he came and took my plastered hand in his. 'You're my wife Samina. How can we live apart? After everything that's happened to us, we deserve to be together, don't we?'

'We can't be together,' I said in a whisper. And as I looked carefully into his blue eyes, all I could see in them was my own broken reflection. 'I have to fix my pieces by myself Hassan and the only way I can do this is if I go from here. Alone.'

His gaze never faltered from mine as he stared into my broken soul. I watched as tears fell from his eyes.

After a stretched silence, he cupped a side of my face and said, 'You really want to do this? You really want to move away from here, from me?'

'Yes,' I replied.

His eyes closed as he took in a deep breath and he shook his head. My heart wept for everything we had and didn't get to keep.

'Go but take care of my Sweetheart okay because I love her so very much,' he choked with eyes red with water. I wiped at them. He kissed my hand and I did something I thought I wouldn't ever do again, I leaned forward and I kissed him because he was my husband. He was still in my heart. And I promise I had never ever stopped loving him. And I knew there could never be a day where I would stop loving him. Despite every evil and every monster he'd been and done, I had always loved him.

Always and always.

But before he could deepen it, I placed my forehead on his and said, 'I want you to make me a promise Hassan.'

'Anything for you...'

His reply brought an instant smile to my lips. 'Promise me you won't come after me. I'll tell you my address before I go but you can't come in between me and my freedom. Hassan I want to do this on my own. I need the time to be myself without you. Let me prove how strong I am for my Baby's sake. Let me prove to the world I am not what they think I am. Let me live my life for myself for once. Please don't come to Oxford and stand in front of me because I'll fall if you do. I'll fall and I won't be able to get back up. I need you to stay away from me. Promise me you won't come to me. '

'I'll promise if you promise me something first.'

'What?'

'That you won't forget I'm your husband. Promise you'll honour our relationship and stick by our bond. Promise me you'll return to me as my wife. Promise me you'll have forgiven me by then and I'll promise I won't stand in the way of your dreams and I won't show up at

275

your new doorstep. But Samina I'll wait for you to return to Ilford Lane again. Promise me you'll return to me. Promise me this, my Sweetheart.'

'I promise.'

Chapter Forty Eight

Seb was quiet whereas I couldn't be, even if I tried. To me it was by magic we had ended up here in the first place. At the Gardens of Peace. And it was a nature's breeze which had guided me towards the grave. It's no surprise my body was tender, as I stared down at the gravestone belonging to my beloved Baby, for the first time.

I should've come to see him sooner. I hadn't been fair to him, had I?

Seeing the black slab of marble with his name inscribed above Hassan's and mine, was all it had taken for me to break down and yearn for the moments he was growing inside me again.

All around his gravestone were small toys. Teddy bears, cars, and choo choo trains. And despite the season which caused shivers, there were flowers, fresh and fragrant. The place was tranquil, clean and tidy and I never would've imagined Baby's father to have chosen it.

'Daddy's been taking good care of you, hasn't he?' I cried hugging a teddy to my chest. 'Mummy is sorry she didn't come to see you sooner. But it doesn't mean she didn't think of you. Not a moment passed without Mummy missing you my darling.'

'Hun…'

'Let me Seb. Let me tell my Baby how sorry I am for leaving him here alone.'

'He's been in good hands,' said Seb. Taking the teddy from me, he placed it with the others in the gentlest of manners. 'I don't know what to say anymore but I do believe your other half has been repenting.'

I looked up at him. He hadn't put on a coat. His feet were sandaled without socks, and the top of his nose was red. He was too cold. I'd left the flat in a state of madness earlier. It was too painful remembering how my tiny Baby had been taken from me and brought here. I needed to see him straight away, and poor Seb was given no choice but to drive me here, as he was.

'I think you need to go and see Hassan. Enough of this punishing game. Both of you have suffered. End it now. Go see him.'

Giving Baby's resting place one last look of longing, I stood up and took Seb's supporting hand and slowly walked with him to his car.

I was exhausted.

*****

I didn't want Seb doing this but I had no energy to protest anymore. He hadn't driven us home, instead he'd taken the car along a journey which I wasn't sure I was ready for.

'It's that one,' I said pointing to the house I'd once felt was as much mine as it was Hassan's. Still clad in only the thin layer of his lounge wear, Seb left me alone in the car and was knocking at his front door.

I wiped at my tears. A feeling of heaviness was troubling me behind my chest. Seb had driven along Ilford Lane and although I'd urged myself not to, I couldn't help but look at the Cabbie as we passed it.

It was the same. The same signpost. The same windows. The same doors. And the same man, who always sat behind the counter with the same telephone against his ear, was still there.

I swear it was him. I'd seen him. Promise I had. And since then the tears in my eyes wouldn't stop falling because family, no matter how much crap it put you through, it was still family, wasn't it?

That Cabbie and the man inside it, they still meant the world to me. Didn't they?

The hate, the need for vengeance had left my system years back. I was over it. I really was. Eight years, the passage of time, it healed. It certainly did. It made you forget and forgive and I'd done all that. I was a new person. I didn't feel any pity for myself anymore. I was beyond all that.

I was a whole new being with a whole new meaning to my life.

'Sweetheart…?'

Leaving the warmth of Seb's car without debate, I flung my arms around my husband's neck and was relieved when he held all my weight and whispered words which I had waited nearly an entire lifetime to hear from him again.

'I trust you.' Seb's voice held a threat and I became aware he was leaving me here. I didn't argue. Instead I let Hassan take me inside his house.

I wouldn't be able to tell you for how long I was in his embrace because it was the best place I'd been to in a very long time. I swear I could've stayed basking in his familiarity forever. I closed my eyes and felt his lips on my temple, on my cheeks and my nose, coaxing me to stop crying. I could hear his soothing words asking me to relax and I could hear his apologies which he still felt needed to be said.

They didn't. I forgave him years back.

Since our meeting at the hospital and the incident at my flat, and everything else which had happened, I couldn't keep my eyes open for long. I was exhausted and happily allowed my husband to lull me into a much needed sleep.

In the cradle of his arms.

*****

The aroma of chicken and spice being cooked in the house awoke me much later. I felt rested and truth be told, I also felt better. A smile lingered on my face as I switched on the table lamp and looked around Hassan's bedroom. It had completely changed. I liked it. On his bedside table was a photo, and my smile grew larger when I saw myself as a geeky teenager in the image. I giggled remembering when Hassan had taken it. Running a hand over it, my gaze fell on the window which although dressed in heavy grey curtains, still managed to call out to me.

'...Your Aunty will find out you're here.'

The tiny hairs on my arms stood and feeling the need to see Hassan, I tamed some of my unruly hair, pulled at the hem of my cardigan and hurried out of his room. However once inside the living room, the picture in front of me made me regret my choice.

'Samina,' said Madge looking pretty in a traditional pink outfit. 'You're just in time for some great food.'

With my smile faltered, not in any sense able to offer her a greeting back, I stared at Hassan who was holding Omar on his shoulders as the boy looked inside a cupboard choosing something to eat. Seeing me, Hassan manoeuvred his son off his body and sat him down on the worktop.

'It's the doctor from the hospital,' said Omar leaning into Hassan's chest. 'I don't want to go to hospital.'

'She's our special friend,' said Madge as she went and stood close to Hassan to take the child.

I'd seen enough. I turned and left them to play happy families together.

But by the time I was walking down his drive, Hassan had chased after me and grabbed my wrist.

'Your special friend,' I hissed trying to pry my hand free. 'Is that what you do with all your special friends when your wife and kid are out? Do you take them into your bedroom and...?'

'Don't. Don't you dare,' said Hassan as his face turned red and he held a finger over my lips hushing me. 'You're thinking Omar's mine? You think I'm with Madge?'

'It's obvious. Let me go.'

'Let you go,' he said taking his finger off and brushing his hands through his hair. 'So you can go back to the one who calls you Hun, huh?'

My jaw hung low.

'Samina you have a cheek coming back here and assuming a lot about me when you're the one living with another man. I'm your husband for crying out loud,' he said as his forehead creased. 'How can you even think that of me when I've waited for you like a virgin for eight fucking long years?'

I pursed my lips. And a loud honking from a car pulling into his drive made Hassan stop shouting.

'No way mate it cannot be your Samina…'

It was his old friend, Wajid. I recognised his voice before he had even come out of the car.

'Yeah it's her,' said Hassan as he glared at me.

'Long time, no see,' said Wajid as he laughed and shook Hassan's hand. 'I hear you're the doctor you always wanted to be. Congratulations. But Hassan has had a tough time without you. I hope you are staying here for good…'

'Waj your wife and kid are inside my house,' scowled Hassan and I gasped with an open mouth.

'Yeah I owe you, thanks for driving them to the hospital. I couldn't get there in time,' said Wajid as Omar came out of the house and ran into his father's arms.

'Daddy Uncle Hassan got me this.' The boy giggled as he showed his new toy.

'Did you say thank you?' said Wajid kissing the little boy fondly. 'Shouldn't you be in bed?'

I sucked in my lips as Madge came out of the house carrying some plastic bags.

'He was driving me mad saying he wants to see what toy his Uncle Hassan has got him. He's feeling much better now. You are right we should take him home to rest now,' said Madge. 'I hope you enjoy the food Samina. Your husband begged me to cook you a special meal since he can't cook to save his life. But I hope you guys don't mind, we won't be able to join you for dinner. Omar really needs to rest. Hass, I've taken my share,' she said holding up her bags.

'Thanks Madge. You're the best sister in law,' said Hassan still glaring at me. I looked to the floor pinching my lips together until the family had disappeared.

'Come inside.'

Following Hassan into the house, I dropped on his sofa. And when I felt it dip next to me, Hassan put his arm around my shoulder pulling me closer.

Burying my head against his neck I said, 'I've not been unfaithful to you either. I kept all my promises to you. Seb is a friend. He's a gay man whose family disowned him when they found out. Years of abuse from his stepfather and step siblings made him as vulnerable as I. When I first met him at Uni, we just clicked. Maybe because we had so much in common. And Hassan, please don't say anything against him, he's like a brother to me.'

'Shush,' said Hassan kissing my head. 'Everything is all good now.'

'Promise me it is.'

'Sweetheart it's all good, I promise.'

Chapter Forty Nine

I was back at the hospital the following day. Hassan had dropped me off. And I couldn't hide my smile at the thought of how reluctant he'd been about spending the day without me. However the feeling was nice knowing he would come to pick me up after my shift.

I was covering for a colleague in a department I didn't normally work at. Oncology. And I was on the morning rounds with Doctor Deepak, a senior Consultant, as he took me through a ward of seriously ill cancer patients.

I was an observer for the day, taking notes on how the seniors spoke to the terminally ill and gave them updates on their healths despite knowing they were going to get worse than they already were.

Being a doctor could be pretty tough at times.

And now was one of those times. An elderly patient given an estimate of a month's time to live was demanding she be sent home. She wanted to be amongst her cats. But there was no way this was possible. And as I took notes, I managed a silent prayer for her. Because believe me I knew what the longing to return home felt like.

It was the worst kind of cancer.

Before moving onto the next bed, Doctor Deepak informed me the patient we were about to see was on the last stages of lymphoma cancer. She'd recently had a procedure which was to have prolonged her life and given her a better quality of it but unfortunately the operation had adverse effects on her heart. Basically she didn't have long to live.

Taking a quick note of this, I followed Doctor Deepak into the said patient's cubicle. She was asleep and facing away from us. Doctor Deepak greeted the young boy by her bedside and asked if he were her son.

He said, 'Yes.'

I smiled at him as he put his phone down. So many people did that. Hid their phones from us. However as Doctor Deepak busied himself talking with the nurse, I scratched my head wondering why the boy was looking at me strangely. He was cute and innocent looking. Aged maybe twelve or thirteen. His hair was nicely styled with a slight quiff. Actually he reminded me of Habib so bad; I had to look at him again and again.

He stared back, with his face tilted and his lips puckered. I mimicked his expression. My heart started beating irregularly and when he stood up from his chair and said, 'Baji Samina,' I held my head in my hands dropping the file and my notes to the floor.

He couldn't be…

'You've come back home,' he exclaimed as he began to shake his mum up.

Mum?

No way. No bloody way. That was not my Aunty Bushra on that bed. Patient number seven on my list was not her. No. No way. No.

'Doctor Iqmal is anything the matter?' said Doctor Deepak.

The ward sister hurried over and held my arm. 'Are you okay?' she said.

I wasn't okay. And as my baby came and stood inches away from me, I reached out and cupped his sweet little face in my hands.

'Ayaan, my brother…?' I confirmed in case my mind was playing games. I mean Ayaan was five when I'd left. The boy in front of me was almost as tall as me. His face was handsome and like Habib's in so many ways.

'You remember me?' he said as he looked at me.

'Of course I do,' I said pulling him into my embrace. My God, I loved this boy. There hadn't been a day I hadn't yearned for him or his sister.

'Make my Mum better. Make my Mum well again,' he cried into my chest as I refused to let him go. 'Habib bhai said you're a doctor so please make my Mum better.'

'My baby,' I cried in his head as Doctor Deepak brought over a chair and asked me to sit down. I pulled Ayaan onto my lap. I didn't care he was tall and heavy. I didn't care I was on duty and the rest of the patients were looking at me cry over one like them.

I didn't care because this was my family. I wasn't a doctor anymore. I was a daughter and a sister and my family was breaking down.

Again.

*****

Aunty was silent when she woke up. Too quiet. Doctor Deepak had left ages ago and I was off duty, granted on compassionate grounds. I wasn't in any state to work.

I hadn't let Ayaan out of my sight. Even when he wanted some lunch, I'd gone with him and bought him heaps of food. He told me he had recognised me right away because he always looked at my photographs at home. I found his talks adorable.

I wondered why Aunty was silent though. She hadn't yelled. She hadn't reminded me how dirty I was, or told me stay away from her son. She didn't say a thing and I wanted her to. I wanted her to yell at me. Shout. Swear. Just not this.

She looked ghostly and it was frightening. She had all the signs. Her aches, the blood she coughed. All her reports, all her scans, showed the same thing. Cancer cells spread to the point of no return.

'Mum will Dad pick Annie up from school?'

Aunty didn't say anything. However this time she did turn to look at me. My lips quivered and I covered my face behind my hands and cried into them. It was the first time she had looked at me and I wasn't sure what she was thinking.

'Baji don't cry. Mum missed you. So did Dad. They made me and Annie pray for your return for years. I can't believe our prayer has finally been accepted.'

I felt Ayaan pull my hands from my face and he wiped my tears. I felt proud of him, to have empathy at such a young age. I kissed his forehead and the face he pulled made me smile weakly.

'He is right Samina,' said Aunty with a low voice which eventually cracked. Holding a trembling hand over her mouth she cried, 'I have missed you...'

I was by her side immediately. Crying into her bosom. Each limb, each cell of mine racking as she hugged me back, begging me for forgiveness over and over.

'You're my mother,' I cried. 'I can never be upset with you. There's nothing to forgive you for. In fact I should be the one asking for your forgiveness. I committed many wrongs as well. I realise this, and I am sorry I kept away from you all for too long. But Habib knew where I was, he should've told me. He never said a word to me. I would've come back sooner had I known.'

'Beti...'

I pulled away from Aunty when the sound of the simple endearment for a daughter coming from behind made my heart lurch and turn to look at him.

His eyes were narrowed but in a matter of a second a new emotion in them caused the corners of his eyes to crease and his lips to part. I caught a glimpse of Ayaan taking hold of a little girl's hand and whisper something in her ear. Annie. That was my darling Annie.

But Uncle. He was angry at me. He would throw me out again. He would, wouldn't he? I turned my whole body back to Aunty. Too afraid of him.

'Please don't let him throw me out,' I cried helplessly into her tiny body, and when I felt two strong hands grip my shoulders, I hitched a sharp breath and said, 'I'm sorry.'

The hands turned me around.

My forehead was kissed. And my shoulders pulled towards him.

'Meri beti,' said my Uncle. 'Meri jaan...'

And this was when I let it all out. It was as easy as this but it took eight years to finally let it all go.

Final Chapter

Annie was a sweet little madam. And a complete chatter box. It was nearing the end of visiting hours and not one of us had tired of talking. The tears had turned into giggles. Looking beyond Auntie's ailment, there was a peace which had become us. It was like all the stuff which had happened before didn't matter anymore.

This surprised me. The power of forgiveness. The power of family.

Or was it because she was dying I wondered as Annie offered me a bit of her chocolate? Declining her offer, I gazed at Uncle. He was packing a bag of Auntie's dirty clothes to take home to wash. He was also asking her what she needed him to bring the next day. And as she told him where her stuff was kept, I brushed my fingers through Annie's soft hair.

Aunty had apologised to me. As had Uncle. And I had apologised to them.

'I couldn't face you. Not after what Feesh did to you and your unborn baby. Not after I inflicted many injustices to you. I've been a grievous man since I forced you to leave us.'

'It's over now Uncle,' I had told him. 'Let's not repeat the past. It's all behind us now.'

Fish boy. Well he got what he deserved. Seriously he did. Some years back Habib had told me Fish boy had met with a serious car accident which left his entire body paralysed for the rest of his life. This had happened whilst he was in Pakistan, apparently two days before his wedding to some poor girl out there. Though I hadn't laughed or danced about it, I hadn't shed a tear for him either. It was one of those things I suppose. If you did evil, you should expect evil too.

What was wrong with me?

If what went came around, what was I being punished for all the times I'd lost a loved one? Did I ever do any evil to anyone? And Aunty was she being punished for what she put me through? Was this it? Was this her paying for it?

'No,' I thought as my heart ached for having this thought. Shifting Annie to the side of my chair and moving closer to Aunty, I held her hands and buried my head by her side on the bed. If I could, I would take her place. If it was a life God wanted, I'd sacrifice myself for her without a blink of an eye. I didn't want her children being without a mum. I knew what that was like.

'Samina,' said Aunty in a soft whisper. She moved one of her bony hands and stroked my hair with it. 'You've brought your Uncle's smile back today. Look at my bedside, look how my children are glowing with happiness at seeing their sister again. Look at them. They are overjoyed and all I've done is try to take their happiness away by causing you pain. You are my family's happiness Samina. You have returned for a reason, to complete us.'

My tears fell as I looked up. Both Ayaan and Annie were also by my side.

'But before I can die peacefully, I have something on my conscience which only you can ease. My beti do your sinful Aunty one last favour. Take some of my burden away so I can face my Allah with at least one good deed.'

'Don't say that Aunty,' I said. 'Nothing is going to happen to you.'

'Everybody knows I don't have long,' she said as she gazed at her children and back at me again. 'Let me see you settled with the man you've always loved before I die. Let me see you as his bride decked in red, wearing my golden bangles and that necklace your mother left for you…'

I shook my head. What was she asking? What was she saying?

'Be with Hassan. Complete that boy. Go to him with our blessing,' said Aunty and as she cupped my face, she

288

chuckled, reminding me of the times she did play the part of my mother when she'd first come to our house. 'Oh how the boy remained a constant pest in your absence. Despite Jawed's threats, he still managed to befriend our Ayaan. And since my illness, I can only praise him for stepping in as a supporting elder brother to both my children. He has been a complete gem. How could I have pushed him away when every time I saw him, I was reminded of you? I believe even your Uncle has a soft spot for him now.'

Uncle came around the bed, bringing with him his soft laughter. I realised it was the sound I'd missed the most. He pulled me up and said, 'Is this what you want?'

I whispered, 'Yes. I do.'

Uncle kissed my forehead and Aunty sighed as she relaxed back down on her pillow. I could sense Annie hugging me and Ayaan was recording the whole thing on his phone, giving a cute commentary.

'Be strong Bushra,' said Uncle. 'We have a wedding to arrange.'

'I thought she was already Hassan Bhai's wife,' said Annie with a confused frown.

The corners of my lips tilted upwards.

'We can apply for the civil marriage. Legalise it under British law. I can ask the Imam to come and bless my children in front of everybody this time,' said Uncle with a peace shining through his eyes. 'I am going to give my beti's hand in Hassan's with my head held high. I believe he is the perfect groom for my Princess. Call Habib. The sooner we do this the better.'

And when Ayaan said, 'We're going to get 'Amandeep Wedding Services' to arrange it all,' I fell onto my chair. Because I couldn't believe it.

I couldn't believe any of it.

*****

289

Uncle had only needed to ask once and I was at the Cabbie staying over for the night. The flat was huge now. Uncle had converted both properties into one. It was amazing how much it had changed.

I put the phone down having spoken to Habib. He was glad I was home. But I was mad at him for not telling me about Aunty sooner. He didn't want me worrying. How lame an excuse was this? If I'd known the extent of her illness, I would've given everything up to be here with my cousins a long time ago.

'Hassan Bhai is asking why your phone has been busy for an hour?' said Ayaan as he poked his head through the door.

I jumped off the bed. 'How do you even know Hassan?'

'He's my brother in law. Of course I know him. He's asking for you,' said Ayaan as he handed me his phone and ran off.

I bit my lips placing the phone over my ear. Earlier I'd sent him a message telling him not to come to pick me up after my shift. I now imagined, he was vexed.

'Hello.'

'Hi,' I smiled as my stomach fluttered.

'You get home alright?'

'Yes, sorry I ruined our plans for tonight. But Hassan you won't believe what happened. My Uncle and Aunty have…'

'Sweetheart Ayaan's already told me.' Hassan's voice seemed calm. And I was curious as to how he'd become to be somebody so special for my family. 'Meet me.'

'What now?' I asked.

'Yes now.'

'…Where?'

'I'm standing a few doors away from the Cabbie.'

'What here on Ilford Lane?'

'Of course on Ilford Lane.'

Feeling a little naughty but excited at the same time, I said, 'Okay. I'll see you in a minute.'

*****

The late winter evening was drawing to a close and the sky was a mixture of aubergine and silvery fluffs of cloud. I fastened the buttons on my coat feeling a slight breeze caress me.

'Where are you Hassan?' I whispered not seeing him where he said he'd be.

Truth was I was dying to see him. The day had certainly brought a breath of fresh air. My family, my husband, together on Ilford Lane. Maybe this place wasn't cursed after all. Maybe it's where my heart belonged all along.

'Samina…'

I turned to the sound of his voice and saw his tall figure coming out of the grocery store. Feeling a little giddy he was approaching, I glanced up at the sky. The pinks and purples had dispersed and the remaining silver created a peaceful blanket over the horizon. It looked extra special. And as Hassan came closer to me, a majestic glow trailed behind him.

My eyes blinked rapidly and my jaw hung low.

People in love were known for making ridiculous claims. About seeing things. Stupid things. Things beyond any reason. Frankly, crazy things. Like, *the stars being ugly against the sparkle she holds in her eyes.* Or like, *the moon being too dull against the ambience of love in his arms.* Even something as far as, *the beams from the sun being dim compared to the laughter in her voice.* And the worst one, the craziest one would be, *the majestic glow trailing behind him as he neared...*

Was I crazy in love?

Hassan looked beyond beautiful to me. I had never felt like this upon seeing him before. Definitely this night there was a rekindling of something extra in my heart for him.

The moon was hiding and the stars were absent, yet my Hassan's eyes were gleaming. I blinked my own eyes. His lopsided smile teased me and when he stopped inches from me, a magical essence enveloped me.

'I love you…'

As soon as my words flew against his ears, Hassan's eyes twinkled and his lips tilted upwards in the most handsome smile, forcing the moon and the stars to come out early to dance around us.

I had to laugh. Stars. Moon. Magical essences. How crazy was I?

And as Hassan began to stir me in the direction of his house, I knew it was only going to get crazier.

Me and him, we were together forever now.

I swear we were.

Bonus Chapter

Four years later...

According to Seb, 'Doctors didn't get nervous.'

Yeah right, I was as nervous as ever. My stomach was rumbling even though I'd been picking on the food constantly. But it was too late to eat more. The presentation was about to begin. I couldn't possibly get up and waddle down the crowded hall towards the buffet tables. It would've been rude. And where was Hassan? I'd only asked for a glass of water, not for him to fetch the whole of Niagara Falls. He'd been gone for almost an hour.

Seb's out of tune humming made me poke a fingertip to his ribs. Why was I sitting next to him when he had the attention span of a two year old? And why had Ayaan lent his iPod to him in the first place?

Anthony grinned as Seb scowled. Anthony would grin. They were a couple now. And the day meant as much to them, as it did to me.

Annie, on the chair down from Anthony was busy texting away on her mobile phone. Honestly she was hooked on the thing. It annoyed me. With her end of year exams on the way, I'd have to set some firmer rules for her.

Further down the aisle, I couldn't help but smile as I caught Uncle fixing Ayaan's tie for him. Ayaan never wore a tie. He didn't even wear one to his prom despite me fussing for days that he should. But my darling had agreed to wear one today. For me.

In fact everybody was smartly dressed. I wouldn't have it any other way.

Salman stood up. I bet he wanted to swap seats with Annie again. I had purposely made him sit away from

Ayaan. The two of them were a pair of mischievous, trouble makers. My brother glared at his eldest son and I sighed in relief when Salman sat back down without protest.

Maryam was patting her new born daughter asleep over her shoulder. I tilted my head to admire the baby. Baby Zara was three weeks old. Habib was over the moon. Maryam looked exhausted. And I knew the feeling. Believe me I did.

'Baby you okay?' said Habib as he caught me looking.

I frowned when all four of his boys started laughing. They thought it was hilarious their father called me Baby.

'I'm okay,' I replied ignoring my nephews. They were growing up too fast.

Looking behind me, I felt the fluttering in my stomach grow. The guests had filled up nicely. It was amazing they had all come to make this day special. I spotted my mother in law at the back of the hall, where she was probably inspecting the food. And I could also see Baba, my father in law dozing off in his chair. I hoped he didn't start snoring.

Aunty Asma and Uncle Murad couldn't make it though. They never could. It didn't bother me because all my favourite people were here. My old friends, Parveen, Ranjita, and Saira were here with their families too. And you would never believe who Ola had recently married. Yes Darren. The two of them were adorable together. Actually they had only returned from their honeymoon. Ola was glowing.

Speaking of honeymoons, the memory of mine made me shift in my seat. Hassan had flown me to the Maldives. It had been the best time ever, despite me being sick for most of it. Morning sickness was called morning sickness for the wrong reasons because I'd been sick all day, every day.

Hassan had been real cute though and if he'd had his way, I would've spent the whole nine months of my pregnancy then sitting on his lap. However looking to my left, I dropped my shoulders. The seat next to mine was empty.

Pulling the headphones out of his ears, Seb nudged my shoulder and said, 'Smile. It's not every day we get to launch our surgery.'

'I know,' I mumbled.

'Eager much, I've only invested my life savings on this place and all my partner can do is look like its nothing major.'

I chuckled as I nudged him back. 'You know this is a dream come true Seb. Our own Practice. Can you believe it, you and I, General Practitioners at last?'

'Let me remind you I've been a GP for over two years. You're the slow coach who only got her licence last year.'

'Yes, and I have no regrets.' It was true. I had no regrets whatsoever. Delaying my career was insignificant to what I had gained. The love of Hassan, his family and my family. It was priceless. And considering what we had gone through when Aunty Bushra died, we had pulled through quite well.

Her death had been hard. Hard on her kids. Hard on Uncle. And hard on me. But somehow we had made it. I think my falling pregnant straight after my wedding, which Aunty thankfully saw, may have helped, by giving us something exciting to look forward to.

The world worked in wonders. A loved one leaves and another is born. This cycle of life. It never ends. It just keeps on going, doesn't it?

'What's this I see,' said Seb as he flicked away my tear. 'You get emotional too quickly, you hormonal woman.'

I laughed and Seb bobbed his head against mine.

'Thank you for doing this with me,' he said.

'You're my best friend. We'll be good doing this together. I only hope you won't regret moving to Ilford Lane.'

'My heart is here,' he said gesturing to Anthony.

'Sloppy much,' I teased.

'Say's the one who's searching the room for her other half like a lost puppy.'

'Get lost,' I said. 'But he should've been here already. It's about to start.'

'I don't think her highness can wait,' said Seb as he nodded towards the important guest he'd invited. 'We better get up and get the show rolling.'

I felt my heart dip. 'Please a few more minutes. Its important he's here.'

Groaning Seb pulled out his phone and dialled Hassan's number.

'No reply,' he said showing me the missed call.

'Doctor Jones and Doctor Iqmal we should begin,' requested Davina Smith, our important guest from the Medical Council, who'd come to host the event. Seb was so extravagant like that. He had wanted the best bang to launch our surgery, Ilford Lane Medical Centre.

'Of course madam.' Seb turned professional and helped me up from my seat. I followed him to the stage where a seat each was waiting for us. I adjusted my blazer button and cringed when it wouldn't fasten over my belly.

Actually this launch should've happened three months later. But Seb had planned it before I had fallen pregnant. Despite this baby not being in the plan of things, Seb had been supportive and I would go on maternity leave soon.

Davina Smith started her welcome speech and Uncle's smile grew huge. This was as much his dream as mine. And dressed in a black tuxedo, Uncle looked as young and dashing as he had on his wedding day.

My gaze shifted when I heard the familiar voices of my babies. They came running noisily into the room, completely oblivious to the important presentation going on. I gasped as Rani, my daughter fell on her bottom and Raja, my son attempted to pick her up. Tempted to go and see if Rani was okay, I held back when Hassan came into the picture and in one motion swept both the children up in his arms and carried them towards the front row.

'Look there's Mummy,' exclaimed Raja as Hassan sat him down on a chair. But Ayaan was quick to pull him onto his lap and kiss his chubby cheek. 'Yani bhai no. I want to sit on the chair...'

I bit my lips. Davina Smith was looking at him.

Raja and Rani were twins. Why they were named words meaning king and queen in Urdu was all Hassan's doing. Anyway our Raja and Rani were loud, boisterous and sometimes quite untameable, which was why I'd left them at their nursery for the event. I suppose that is where Hassan had disappeared to.

'Mummy, Mummy…' whined Rani pointing at me and whilst Seb waved at her, I shot daggers at Hassan. He never listened to me. This was his problem. He never ever listened.

Hassan smiled sheepishly and when I glared, he winked. But his attention quickly shifted to Rani who was sitting on his knees as she tapped his shoulder.

'I'm going to Mummy,' she said in her high pitched voice. Thankfully Hassan was good with the kids. Maybe because he himself was the biggest kid I knew. He began whispering something in her ear, probably bribing her with treats and toys if she kept quiet. Rani pursed her cute lips earning a kiss from her daddy.

Seb stood. Annie also stood up. Seb had asked her to video the ceremony on her mobile phone but as she took her position, Raja got down from his chair and ran to her.

'I want to play game on your phone. Give me phone.'

Poor Annie pulled Raja onto her hip and gave him her iPod instead whilst she attempted to record whatever Seb was saying. And I should've been paying more attention to him. I was next to talk.

'I won't take too much time. The food smells too good. I'd rather be over there,' said Seb pointing to the food tables, making all the guests laugh. 'On a serious note thank you for coming today, it means a lot to both me and Hun…'

'It's Doctor Iqmal,' grimaced Hassan making our family and friends laugh even louder.

I hid my face behind my hands.

'Let me rephrase that for the benefit of someone,' said Seb hiding his scowl. The two hadn't changed one bit. It annoyed me so much.

And as Seb went on to talk about the facilities which our new surgery would be providing, namely the midwife service and the asthma clinic, I felt someone tug at my knees.

'Mummy…'

Removing my hands from my face, I pulled her on to my lap.

The dimpled smile which appeared on her face gratified me. And looking over her head, I saw Annie was trying hard to stop Raja from running to me too.

'It's okay,' I mimed and Annie let him go. Raja rushed towards me running past Seb, who had stopped mid speech to watch him.

'Peekaboo,' giggled Raja as he lifted his arms for me to hold him too. At the same time Rani held me tighter afraid I may swap child. With their baby sister inside me, I knew holding both at the same time wasn't wise.

'Mummy,' said Raja tapping my knee.

'Hey Raja come and sing a song for us,' said Seb into the microphone as he held out his hand for my son, taking his attention away from climbing up my legs.

'Oh no, Seb no,' I said knowing what Seb was about to make his little Maharaja do.

Without any reluctance, wearing a toothy grin, Raja toddled towards Seb. I gave Davina Smith an apologetic smile. What else could I do? I felt bad for her. I mean she had come here for the launch of a professional health care service, not a pre-school.

'Twinkle twinkle Sebastian's star…'

Yes, Seb was making my son sing the rhyme he'd proudly taught him, all wrong.

'Give my daddy a better car…'

I could kill Seb sometimes.

By now the other children in my family had turned into hysterical hyenas and Habib was having fun filming it all. And Hassan, well his eyes were twinkling even more than the stars my son was singing about.

When Raja had sang his last verse everybody in the crowd stood up and gave him a round of applause. Hassan quickly came over to the front and despite his dislike for the song, he pulled Raja into his arms and kissed him silly.

I hugged onto Rani whilst everyone around us cooed over her brother.

'Mummy Raja sings it wrong,' she said. I watched as the little madam left my embrace and ran to Seb. And as she sang the true version of the nursery rhyme, my heart swelled with pride. I stood up from my seat and to heck with the presentation and Davina Smith, I waddled towards my babies, opened up my arms and giggling like two bells of Heaven, they came running into them.

'My babies always sing beautifully,' I told them over the whistling and cheering.

'This is what our practice is all about,' bellowed Seb's voice from the speakers. 'It's about love and care and most of all, we are family here. This is a family practice, a revolution in care standards for the wellbeing of the residents here. We will strive to give the best care possible, from the very young to the elderly. Because at Ilford Lane Medical Centre, the staff care. They care for everybody.'

My Uncle was the first one to clap. His smile was enormous and he stood tall and proud. I waved at him. He didn't wave back instead he made his way to me. Helping me stand up from where I was crouching down to level with my children, Uncle pulled me into his side and kissed my head.

'My beti, I am the happiest I could ever be today.'

'I couldn't have done it without you Uncle,' I choked. 'Your love and your care when I was a child built a passion inside me for medicine. I had to be a doctor. There was nothing more I wanted.'

'Are you sure about that?' said the voice closest to my heart. Uncle laughed as he moved on to greet Seb, taking both my children with him.

I crossed my arms over my chest. 'Well, I guess there was this one thing or should I say one person I wanted more.'

'Ahan,' grinned Hassan as he leaned close. 'Tell me more…'

'Oh shut up you cheese ball,' I snapped regaining my bearings. 'Why did you bring the twins here? I bet Davina Smith will have a thing or two to report back to the Council about this.'

'You can't deny it was the cutest thing you've seen them do,' said Hassan in defence of our children. 'Way cuter than Seb.'

'Hass…' I said when he pressed a kiss to my chin. 'What are you doing?'

'Congratulating you…'

'Iqmal,' my brother's voice made me move away. And feeling his gaze on the back of my head, I left Hassan to deal with this himself. I had others to meet and thank for coming. And I was hungry again. Seb was right, the food did smell nice.

*****

Whilst Hassan was upstairs putting the twins to bed, I wrapped some of the leftover food from the buffet and piled it on a tray to take over to Uncle's. There were samosas and kebabs, savouries which Ayaan loved. There was also cake, which Annie wouldn't say no to.

I opened the garden door and balancing the tray in my hands, I walked towards the side where a huge wall once stood separating the houses. Now there was no fence or wall. It had come down the day Hassan told me he'd bought the house in which I had once lived in.

However the house was incomplete without my family in it and it had taken much persuasion for Uncle to finally agree to move back in. Conveniently, Hassan and I and occasionally his parents, still lived at his house. Truth be told, I preferred it like this. I enjoyed the privacy, although at times like when Habib's boys had sleepovers, there was no concept of privacy at all.

Habib was settled here now and he worked at the Cabbie again. Life in Dubai wasn't for him anymore. His house was in Seven Kings. We were all close by.

I knocked on the back door and Uncle let me in.

'Sorry I forgot the keys again,' I said as he took the tray from me.

I sat down on the kitchen bench but before my Uncle could say anything I went and planted my backside on the comfy chair instead.

'You put the twins to bed too early,' moaned Uncle as he glanced at the clock on the wall.

'Seven thirty is not an unreasonable time for children their age to sleep. Anyway, have the big kids eaten yet?'

'No. I was about to serve dinner. Join us.'

'Not tonight Uncle.' I wanted dinner with my hubby. 'I'm tired and I better get back to check if their asleep yet.'

I looked up as Annie came into the kitchen.

'They're already asleep. More cake,' she said as her eyes bounced. 'And Hassan bhai just texted saying, 'Send my wife home.''

Uncle shook his head supressing a grin and Annie stuffed a whole éclair into her mouth.

'At least take some rice home then. Its chicken pilau,' said Uncle.

I got up and went over to the pot on the hob. Uncle's food was still the best. And taking a taste, I made myself a plate adding a little extra for Hassan.

'Look how big Baji looks in this pic Annie,' said Ayaan as he too came inside the kitchen.

'Shut up you two,' I scowled slightly embarrassed as they both laughed into the screen on his phone.

'Stop teasing my beti,' chided Uncle adding another heaped spoonful of rice onto the already full plate. 'My beti is giving me another grandchild to play with, she's not fat.'

'Okay,' I said rolling my eyes at the kids. 'I seriously should go before Uncle turns sentimental and my mascara runs.'

Uncle chuckled and I loved that sound.

'Ayaan drop your sister home and come right back. You have revision to do after dinner.'

When Ayaan held the plate for me, I shook my head at how silly this all was. I was pregnant, not disabled.

'I'm walking over there,' I said pointing to the open door across the garden. 'I don't need Ayaan to escort me.'

'It's best to be careful,' replied Uncle placing a jug of water on the dining table. 'Habib's boys have been playing there over the weekend. There are toys everywhere outside. Be a good girl, listen.'

My heart forced me to hold Ayaan's arm despite it being unnecessary and as I walked out of the kitchen with him, the sound of Uncle's prayers reached my ears. I smiled.

'He's getting old,' said Ayaan as he picked at a chicken chunk from my rice.

'That's my Uncle you're talking about. And stop eating my food.'

'Control the appetite,' said Ayaan earning an elbow to his muscled stomach. 'You're going to blow up soon.'

I saw Hassan and I grinned. He was standing by the French doors, waiting.

'I happen to love my Sweetheart feeding my baby,' he said and I grinned even wider.

'See,' I said taking the plate from Ayaan and passing it to Hassan.

'Ayaan, Dad said hurry back,' called Annie from the other end.

'Yeah shoot,' said Hassan pulling me gently to his side.

'I know when I'm not wanted,' grinned Ayaan but he didn't wait for me to tell him otherwise because he was already on his way back.

Closing the door behind us, Hassan turned the knob locking it shut.

'They didn't trouble you too much did they?' I asked.

'They never trouble me,' said Hassan as he placed the plate on the table.

'You hungry?' I said. 'The rice is warm.'

'Oh I'm hungry,' said Hassan as he turned me around and despite my baby bump being in between us, he still managed to snuggle me perfectly against his chest.

'Dinner's ready,' I said smiling at him coyly.

'I'm hungry for my wife, not food.'

I smiled wider. I could smile forever for him.

'Aren't you hungry for husband?' he asked and looking from the tempting plate of Uncle's pilau to the adorable look on his face, my decision was easy.

The food would have to wait because my appetite for Hassan's love was never going to end.

Promise.

Acknowledgement

I would like to say thank to my husband Iqbal and my lovely children Najam, Sameer and Saniya, for persevering with me from the time when Sweethearts of Ilford Lane was only a blurry thought in my head. Look it's a novel now. I finally did it. We did it.

Thank you also to the amazing people at Barking and Dagenham Library Service, for hosting Pen to Print and making it a huge success. Thank you for your guidance and support. Without you Lena Smith, this story would've remained forever hidden as a word document on a faulty USB stick somewhere. You are doing a fabulous job.

Thank you my mentor, my gorgeous friend, Barbara Nadel. Your encouragement and advice will never be forgotten. You are truly an amazing person. And you need to pop over soon!

Thank you Mum and Dad, my brothers, and sister, who have waited patiently (since I was seven), for a book of mine to be released. However this is my debut and the waiting game must continue I'm afraid. Because I still have a load of other stories to tell too…

Shukriya to my glorious, best friends forever, for sticking by me through all of life's ups and downs. You know very well who you are, and I love you both.

Thank you Asad, Afiyah and Zaynah. You were the first people to read Sweethearts... You are rather lucky!

And last but not least, a big thank you from the bottom of my heart goes out to everybody who reads this book. I hope you enjoy it as much as I enjoyed writing it.

On a much serious note, it is also important for you to realise that in all religions, and cultures, there is no room for forced marriage. Forcing adults, teenagers and children into marriage by persuasion, physical abuse or emotional blackmail is not allowed.

Sadly, in our community and across the UK, forced marriages are being conducted behind closed doors in alarming numbers. In most cases, like in this story, the victim is left helpless and under the impression he/she has no other option and unwillingly they do get married. 'The Anti-social behaviour. Crime and Policing Act 2014,' made it a criminal offence to force somebody to marry, yet many find themselves being subjected to this abuse.

If anybody is, or knows somebody who is, being coerced into a forceful bond, do get in touch with the Forced Marriage Unit (FMU) on 020 7008 0151 or through fmu@fco.gov.uk. Or simply call 999. Don't hesitate to do this. Help will be provided. Never ever for once think you are alone. You are not alone.

Stay blessed. X

Farzana Hakim

Follow me on social media for updates on my upcoming novels:

The Silence of a Deep River.
Lady Taliban.
Chief of the Atlantic.

Twitter: @farzanahakim
Facebook: www.facebook.com/farzanahiqbal
Instagram: farzanahakimauthor

Lightning Source UK Ltd.
Milton Keynes UK
UKHW041908280319
340100UK00001B/8/P